TK

Tk

Hayley Aldridge Is Still Here

Also by Elissa R. Sloan

The Unraveling of Cassidy Holmes

Hayley Aldridge
Is Still Here

A Novel

Elissa R. Sloan

wm

WILLIAM MORROW
An Imprint of HarperCollins*Publishers*

HAYLEY ALDRIDGE IS STILL HERE. Copyright © 2023 by Elissa R. Sloan. All rights reserved. Printed in the United States of America. No part of this book may be used or reproduced in any manner whatsoever without written permission except in the case of brief quotations embodied in critical articles and reviews. For information, address HarperCollins Publishers, 195 Broadway, New York, NY 10007.

HarperCollins books may be purchased for educational, business, or sales promotional use. For information, please email the Special Markets Department at SPsales@harpercollins.com.

FIRST EDITION

Designed by Diahann Sturge

Library of Congress Cataloging-in-Publication Data has been applied for.

ISBN 978-0-06-322552-7

23 24 25 26 27   LSC   10 9 8 7 6 5 4 3 2 1

To Alexandra and John

AUTHOR'S NOTE

t^{k}

CHAPTER 1

I wonder what the outside world is like, I think while sitting outside my twelve-bedroom, thirteen-bathroom Spanish-style mansion. After all, there's nothing much wrong with me. I'm fit and healthy, yet stuck in the house with two young women who look unsettlingly like me. And some days, I feel like I'm going to lose it.

I suck on a piece of mango and wish it could be in a daiquiri, but I gave up alcohol years ago. Drinking makes time go by faster, but it also makes you sluggish. What I need now is a sharp mind. No excuses for being kept in this house for any longer than I already have been.

Jessica joins me by the pool, sunglasses perched on her head. I squint up at her. She's the spitting image of her father in the backlight.

"Mom," she says, and I marvel at how my child can speak. She's seventeen now, but will always be my baby.

"Yes?"

"Why don't we go out? Why are we always stuck in the house?"

"We're waiting for your grandfather," I say indifferently. "He and I will discuss it." For the thousandth time.

"I just don't get it."

I wonder, if I knew then what I know now, if I would still make the same decisions, urge my parents to take me to auditions. Gone along for the ride. It's not fair to blame a five-year-old, but that's what I do: put the onus on a younger me, as if I knew better then. Would all this have come to a head like it had now? Or would I be living a free life, unfettered, somewhere else? Something boring and predictable.

"Go get your sister."

Jessica sighs, but leaves and comes back with Jane. I bite another piece of mango, licking my fingers after it's in my mouth. I used to count the calories of fruit; every bite, fifteen calories, until I hit ninety and then I'd stop. Now I can't get enough. My belly is rounded from all the fruit and doughnuts and sugared cereal and potato chips, all the treats I wasn't able to eat when I was younger. It is what it is. I'm having a second-childhood renaissance.

"Mom," Jane whines. She's identical to her twin, but I can tell them apart without any problem. I'm a good mother, no matter what people say. "Why don't we go hiking today? Why are we stuck *here* again?"

"We're waiting," I repeat. "But while we're waiting, should I tell you a story?"

The twins exchange looks. "What kind of story?" Jessica says hesitatingly.

"The story about your mom."

"What kind of story would *you* have that we don't already know?" Jane asks.

"Well, why I'm stuck here."

"We've *seen* the tabloids," Jane says, rolling her eyes.

"That's not the story," I say, slightly horrified that she would have read any of that trash. "That's the screwed-up fairy tale."

Jessica crosses her arms. Jane mirrors her.

I sniff. "I just figured you were old enough now to know."

"Know *what*?"

It doesn't matter which twin said it; I'm lost in my own world again. Remembering Ted and Brandon and Millie and Trey and Anthony and Olive. Where do I start? Do I begin in 2007, when the twins were just two and I was sentenced to this new life? Do I tell them it was only supposed to be temporary, but that it kept getting extended, over and over again, and it's still not over, years later?

"Once upon a time," I say, and the twins groan in unison. "You really don't want to hear this?" I ask them, surprised.

The tablet chimes and I look down at it; there's activity in the front of the house. I watch as a car snakes its way up the driveway and parks. A man gets out: short, bald, hawkish nose. He pulls his pants up over his belly with a snap and moves toward the front door.

"Maybe this can wait until later," I say.

The man has crossed through the kitchen and appears in the back doorway.

"Hi, Dad."

My FATHER HAS no interest in mangoes. Inwardly, I curse, but I smile at him with my winningest grin. It's Tuesday, which means it's social media day. I'm already made up, though I know I've eaten off my lip gloss, and wearing a high-waisted bikini. He's already pulling out his phone and aiming it toward me.

"What today? Maybe a monologue from *Third Time Around*?" I say. He grunts in affirmation. He didn't even say hello when he walked in.

I swipe under my eyes, to make sure my mascara hasn't run, and clear my throat. The twins escaped the moment their grandfather came into the backyard, and I don't blame them.

"Make it a happy one, not a crying one," he instructs.

So I do. I pull out one of the scenes from season eleven—or was it twelve?—where I am telling Ted he'd make a wonderful father. Not to me, of course (I played his kid sister), but to the child he'd conceived with his fiancée, Natasha. I forget the actress's name now; Natasha was just the character's name. I deliver the monologue with a warm smile.

"Good," Dad says, and pockets his phone. "I brought over your mail," he continues, placing it on a deck chair. There's a heap of cards in the pile, from fans who sign #helphayley on the backs of the envelopes. Dad lets me have them because they improve my morale. But it doesn't change the fact that he still controls my life.

"Can the girls and I go hiking today?" I ask.

"No, I don't think so," he answers. He places a Visa on the table. It's another gift card with an allotted amount of money on it for incidentals. Then he gives me a kiss on the forehead and rubs my hair. "Anything else you need, you tell Adam."

"Okay." I'm glum.

Once he's gone—and I watch him snake his way back down the driveway on the tablet—the girls reappear.

"Okay, this *would* be weird if it happened in any other family," Jessica says.

"We talked about it, and we want to know the full story," Jane says.

I lean back in my lounge chair and set one arm across my eyes to keep out the sun. "Here goes nothing."

Church Gazette, June 23, 1991

One of our own is off to Hollywood! Mr. and Mrs. Gerald Aldridge, of Anita, TX, are proud to announce that their daughter Hayley (7) has been cast in a TV show! Everyone in the congregation is urged to keep their eyes peeled for Hayley's debut in *Third Time Around*, coming this fall on CBS!

CHAPTER 2

My life wasn't always controlled. I was raised in a small town smack-dab between Houston and Austin called Anita. We didn't have much growing up, but we did have community. My parents, Gerald and Patricia, were active members in the Presbyterian church, the only one in the town. (There was also a Catholic church and a Methodist church, but no synagogue.) I was on my own until I was four, when your aunt Ashley came along.

My mother said I was born to perform. She claims that I was tap-dancing in her belly even before they knew she was pregnant with me. When I was three, we drove to nearby Columbus so I could start taking dancing lessons. It soon became apparent to me that I could get a lot more attention if I did something well. So I began to excel. I was the best ballet student, the best little singer my preschool teacher ever saw, and I had a lot of time to myself to make up stories and act them out for my exasperated parents.

I think my folks knew I was not going to give up my hamming-up for all the cookies in the world, and they decided to nourish my need to perform. Maybe get it all out of my system before I turned ten.

When I was five and Ashley was one, my mother decided to take me to a talent agency in Houston. This was 1989 and Austin was still a sleepy college town, so my mom picked the busier metropolis. She got dressed in her Sunday best and pressed powder all over her face. Then we drove the ninety minutes to make our appointment.

This was the first time I'd been to the big city and it fascinated me—the skyscrapers especially. Anita's biggest building was the Walmart, and it was only one story. The giant towers boggled my mind. We parked in a parking garage—another first—and entered one of those enormous buildings. It was my first time in an elevator, and I itched to push every single button. But my mother allowed me to press only one, the button that led us to the fourteenth floor, and we were deposited neatly in the waiting room for Mrs. Emma Murray. It held a few other children with their parents.

Mrs. Murray was a dazzling woman. She was tall, taller than my mother, and wore red lipstick. "Let's take a look at you," she said, when it was my turn. I knew I was supposed to impress her. I stood up very straight and smiled with all my teeth.

"She sings, she dances," my mother said. "She can act."

"*How* do you *know* she can act?" Mrs. Murray asked.

"She makes up little plays for us."

"Imaginative, eh?" Mrs. Murray said.

I know that, as a five-year-old, my memory of this event shouldn't be so strong. But that huff of admiration, that *"Imaginative, eh?"* was etched inside my mind from the very moment that it happened. Imaginative! That was me.

The rest of the meeting was a blur, but I know that my mother was pleased. Mrs. Murray added us to her roster, and every so often, I was called forth to audition for something. Juice commercials, mostly. I landed a TV ad for a local toy store and my payment was either one of the toys on set or an actual check. This was the first time my mother and I disagreed on my career: she wanted the check, and I had my eye on a stuffed bunny.

"That's *it!*" she said to me firmly. "I'm the mom and that means you listen to me. We are getting *paid.*"

She took that check to the bank, cashed it, and then bought me the bunny.

"Let this be a lesson," she said. "Always take the money. Now we're both happy."

I DON'T KNOW when the commercials were deemed "not good enough" for my parents or me. All I know is that once we tuned into *Sesame Street* and noticed that my peers were on there—one of the girls I'd auditioned against for Welch's grape juice was a featured player—the commercials I'd been in seemed paltry in comparison.

"Hayley," my mother said, "do you want to be on *Sesame Street?*"

I don't remember my answer.

But what happened next was that my mother and Ashley and I took off for Los Angeles while my father held down the fort in Anita. We booked ourselves in a long-term apartment in Hollywood and began going to every audition that we could find. I was six.

The *Third Time Around* audition I remember very well, and not just because there are clips of the casting video famously floating around on YouTube.

"What's your name?" a voice off-camera says.

"Hayley Aldridge."

"So this is the scene where Amy's mom finds out Amy has flushed her rings down the toilet. And those rings are special to her mom because Amy's dad gave them to her, and Amy's dad is dead. And Amy knows she's done something wrong but she's also a little naughty and doesn't want to be punished. Are you ready, Hayley?"

"Mm-hmm."

"Amy, what have you done?"

My voice immediately wavers. "I didn't mean to do it!"

"Amy, those rings meant a lot to Mommy, you know better than to play in Mommy's jewelry box."

"I know, Mommy. I didn't mean to. I was just playing with them, you know, and pretending to be you. But then they fell in. And I didn't want to put my hand in the toilet, and I was afraid of getting in trouble, and so I flushed the toilet."

"Why would you flush the toilet?"

The quaver in my voice grows even more despondent. "Because! Because if you knew that I'd done it, you would've gotten mad at me."

"Amy, I'm mad at you now. I'm so mad at you. Because now instead of me digging in the plumbing for the rings, they're just gone, and nothing will bring them back."

My voice is small. "Like nothing will bring back Daddy?"

"Like nothing will bring back Daddy," the voice affirms.

My chin shakes and I begin to cry, two perfect streaks down my cheeks. "I miss Daddy," I say.

"And scene. You got it."

After I won the part of Amy, my parents dealt with a new conundrum. They'd already been separated by distance for six months while I'd been auditioning. We didn't have the kind of money where we could fly back and forth between California and Texas every other week to keep the family somewhat intact. I'm sure that the distance put some strain on my parents' marriage. And what could they do now? Should my father upend our lives in Anita for a life in Hollywood, based on the needs and wants of his now seven-year-old?

The answer was no. My dad stayed in Anita, continued his job as a salesman, and wired money to my mother in L.A. while I got started in my role on *Third Time Around*.

It was typical for shows like this to have twins playing a single character of my age, but because I didn't have a lot of screen time at first, just me was fine. The thorny problem of how to stick to regulations for underage actors came into play when Amy's role expanded at my tender age of twelve. But for the first five years of the show—and I realize how impressive that is, that a show lasted longer than five years and wasn't canceled for more than fifteen altogether—it was just me as Amy, with my colleagues Ted-as-Zac and Millie-as-Erica to make up my newfound family.

We looked alike: a trio of siblings with sandy-blond hair, blue eyes, and button noses. Millie had to have her stick-straight hair professionally curled to give it a similar appearance to Ted's and mine, but we looked like we could be genetically linked. Ted was twelve; Millie, ten.

As an icebreaker, the three of us were invited, along with our parents, to Disneyland before we began filming. It was my first time and I was enthralled.

"I want to go on Space Mountain!" Ted yelled, when we were through the entrance.

"I want to go to Haunted Mansion!" Millie countered.

"Space Mountain!"

Ted's father, who had joined his wife, Millie's parents, and my mother, said to me kindly, "And you, Hayley?"

I smiled at Mr. Sumner and said, "I want to meet Goofy."

Ted groaned.

"We'll do all of these," Mr. Sumner said, taking control of the group.

We went to the Haunted Mansion first, but one look at some of the kids coming off the ride and I knew I didn't want to go in there. I hid my face in my mother's bleached jeans, Ashley's legs kicking at my cheek from where she sat perched on my mother's back in a sling. Ted sighed exasperatedly, as a twelve-year-old would when a kid sister is being annoying, and when I peeked out again, he and Millie and a few of the parents were gone.

"We'll just hang out here," Ted's father said kindly, and took my mother and me to a nearby ice cream vendor. It was eleven in the morning, but we still got Popsicles and sat on a bench to eat them. Mom fed a bite to Ashley, who dribbled it down her chin. It seemed like hours later when the group reformed, and off we went to Space Mountain, another trek.

This one seemed fun, but we ran into a block: the height requirement. "Hayley, you're too short," my mother sad, a real note of sadness in her voice. I could tell she was unhappy that we had come to this giant wonderland of a playground and that I wouldn't get on yet another ride.

."Nooo." I could feel a tantrum start to build. I stamped my feet.

Ted sighed, this time a resigned one. "If Hayley can't get on, we don't have to ride," he said, mature beyond his years.

"What! Why?" Millie asked.

"That's very grown-up of you," Millie's mother said to Ted, obviously impressed.

"This *is* a chance to get to know everyone, and how can you do that if you're not even in the same place at the same time?" Ted's father asked, a bit of pride in his voice. He had probably coached his son on the purpose of this trip and Ted had actually listened.

Ted reached out an arm and grabbed a hold of my hand. "Let's find Goofy," he said amiably.

It's funny, what we remember as children. I don't recall the parade we ended up seeing, but we clearly stood to watch it in the photos I have. But the weight of Ted's hand in mine, I will always remember. I'm getting choked up now thinking about his kindness. That was just the type of person Ted was, a lovely and thoughtful person who put others before himself. Just the type of person who would get eaten alive in Hollywood, as we all saw.

We did find Goofy. And it was just as amazing as I thought it would be.

WHEN I LOOK back on photos of that day—which, of course I have photos, sticky-edged prints on glossy paper from my mother's disposable camera—I'm struck with how incredibly young we all were, both in age and naivete. We had no idea what was going to happen to us, good or bad.

We were on the precipice, looking down.

CHAPTER 3

And then it was off to work. But the studio didn't feel like work. Sure, it meant a lot of setting up and resetting and retakes. The lights were hot and sometimes I got hungry, but we had to work through a scene. With three children, there were tantrums that had to be quashed every so often, bribery being one of the solutions: "Hayley, if you finish this scene, you can have a lollipop. A *grape* one. You know how much you love the grape ones, but we don't let you have them because they stain your tongue purple? Well, you can have a *grape* one this time. You're doing great." For the most part, though, the studio felt like playtime. I loved emoting. I loved the camera. I loved seeing my mother's face when we got our first, second, third paychecks from the work I did. Loved hearing the smile in her voice as she called my father in Anita and told him *she* would be wiring money to *him* this time.

When I talked to Daddy on the phone, I could hear his smile too. "Hayley, you're helping this family," he said. "Do you like helping your family?"

I said that I did. My father's face was fuzzy to me in my own memory. I hadn't seen him in a year.

"Think you could help enough that I can buy a new car?" he asked.

I told him I'd try.

"Thanks, honey. Put your mom back on."

The showrunner was a kind person too. His name was Alex Dietrich and he introduced himself to me before he acknowledged my mother, which was a move that I think impressed her very much. After all, *I* was the talent.

"Do you remember me?" Alex asked. "I was at your audition." He was old—at least, what I thought of as old at the time. He had some lines on his face, around his forehead and mouth. He was balding, but now that I think about it, it must have been premature. He was probably in his early forties then. He was tall and lean and wore wire-rimmed glasses, which he adjusted when he crouched down next to me to get on my level.

I nodded.

He stretched out his hand, which was large and with long, tapered fingers. "It's nice to see you again."

Alex shook my hand like we were both adults. I beamed.

He then talked to my mother about various and sundry things, I don't know what. But she left the meeting buzzing, happy that our showrunner was such a great man. "You hear stories about bad directors, mean people," she said to me over her shoulder on the drive back to our apartment. "But Alex seems very nice."

I poked Ashley in the side and watched her squirm. "I guess."

"You should be grateful," my mother reminded me.

"Mm-hmm."

"I swear," she mumbled, turning into the driveway, "six going on sixteen, you are."

"I am seven!" I corrected her.

"Are you? That's right."

We parked. Mom got Ashley out of her car seat and attached her to one hip. We walked into the apartment, where Mom surveyed the worn-out carpet, the beige kitchen, and the linoleum peeling up in one corner. "I hope this pilot gets picked up," she remarked. "We could do with a move."

I don't remember much about the first day of filming, except there was a celebratory sheet cake at craft services and Ted told me it was his birthday while his mouth was full of blue sugar. Millie's mom wouldn't let her have any. There she was, ten years old, unable to eat a slice of cake because it "would go straight to her hips." Brat that I was, I ate my piece in front of Millie as she glared at me, unaware that in a few years' time, her mother's concern for her weight would mirror my own.

I was pleased with my new position as the actress of the family. I was important. People paid attention to me. The work was easy—just a lot of following directions and repeating myself over and over, trying in different ways to be cute. I had boundless energy and the work days were truncated by law, so I didn't burn out.

And I liked my TV family. My on-screen father, Oscar, was really nice. The script often called for my on-screen mother, Tina, to hug me more often than my real mother did. And if I needed something, my real mother was on set, albeit uncomfortably seated in a deck chair with my name on it, Ashley scrambling around on her lap because Mom couldn't—or wouldn't—pay for childcare.

But it seemed I'd made a small enemy in the form of Millie, my on-screen sister. While Ted was friendly to both of us—and I never forgot his kindness at Disneyland—Millie was annoyed with me. We were close in age but not close enough to form a bond. She likely saw me as an annoying kid sister who soaked up all of the attention.

After the show was ordered for a full season, Millie and I understandably saw more of each other. Ten-year-olds are great at passive-aggressive fighting. We were professional when the cameras were rolling, but when we were in between scenes, she would pointedly ignore me. I don't know what it did to my self-esteem, having a person be so hot and cold toward me, flip-flopping within minutes. It was hard to sometimes separate the real versus the performative.

Which brings me to my next thought: that life on set is such a strange reflection of life outside of set. I knew that Oscar and Tina were not my real parents, but I began to wish that they were. I missed my real father, but as long as he was still in Anita, I sought out paternal figures anywhere I could find them. The showrunner, Alex Dietrich, was another one. I remember once I clung to his leg like a koala until my mother admonished me for being too old to do something like that. Everyone was friendly but they were not loving. And that's the difference between a normal childhood and mine.

THESE WERE THE first big roles for me and Millie, and we were sufficiently awed when we arrived at the premiere. Ted, at twelve, had been on an ensemble show before ours and knew the ins and outs of parties like these. "Say hi to everyone. Be nice. Don't forget to eat something. But don't take any escargot if they offer it to you. It's *snails*." He made a face at us and we made one back.

This was a low-key premiere party, for a show that had not made its mark yet, but the venue was still decked out festively: dozens of rounded paper lamps, twinkle lights, waiters in all black offering champagne on little silver trays. There was a photo op at the very start, with the *Third Time Around* family and all of *their* real-life family standing together on the red carpet. Again, there were Ted's and Millie's parents, and also Oscar's and Tina's spouses.

I was dressed in a Laura Ashley dress and my mother wore her burgundy lipstick and teased and curled her hair so it looked like Brooke Shields's. She'd gotten a sitter for Ashley that night, I think, because I don't remember my sister being there. Though Mom didn't tell me to go play, it was implied as soon as we stepped off the red carpet that I was able to roam freely. She accepted a champagne flute and I wandered around, smiling pleasantly at every crew member who said hello and shaking hands when one was offered to me. I was on my best behavior, even though I really wanted to scuttle under table-cloths and poke at people's shoes.

I ate a few things offered to me on trays, careful not to spill on my dress. I posed for pictures. We watched the first episode of the show, which was an hour-long drama. I grew overstimulated by the music and the loud talking. I couldn't find my mother, so instead I did what I wanted to do: walk into the bathroom and curl up into a ball.

But when I walked into the bathroom, I found that I wasn't alone. Ted was there too.

Ted was what a lot of girls would call a "dreamboat." He had long, sandy-blond hair that was parted down the middle and gelled so it fell in two swoops near his bright blue eyes. Though he was a little young to be named a heartthrob in *Bop* magazine, in a few years' time he'd be all over its pages with his charming smile and poet hands.

But at this moment, his eyes were looking a little glassy, his smile lopsided. I noticed the empty champagne flutes on the counter.

"What are you doing?" I asked. But it was obvious. He'd been celebrating in his own way.

"Shh," he said. "Don't tell my dad."

"Why are you in here all alone?" I demanded.

"I'm not alone. I just had my friend Fred here . . ."

I put my hands on my hips, arms akimbo. "I don't see any Fred."

"He went to get more booze," Ted explained.

None of this made any sense. Ted was *twelve*. He was older than me, sure, but not old enough to be a grown-up, and only grown-ups were allowed to drink! That's what my mom had told me. I'd never even had a sip of champagne. And yet here was Ted, slurping down alcohol like he was twenty, disheveled and sloppy. I was confused.

"Can you keep a secret?" Ted asked.

"I guess . . ."

"It's just, sometimes I get really nervous. And jumpy. And this stuff makes me feel better."

"Okay . . ."

"Don't tell my dad," he repeated.

I backed away and out the door. I wanted my mom.

I pushed through velvety hips and wool slacks until I found her. Even though this was an adult soiree and I was supposed to be a big girl, all I wanted was for her to pick me up like I was a baby again. I tugged on her dress. "Mom."

My mother was mid-conversation with Alex Dietrich. It must have been a riveting talk because she didn't acknowledge me until I tugged on her hem again. "*Mom*."

She looked down at me. I hated being a kid, being short and being looked down on.

"Can we go?" I asked.

"We just got here," she said. Which was a lie. We'd been there for at least a few hours.

"My feet hurt," I whined.

To my relief, she picked me up and held me securely from my bottom. "Another half hour. Then we can go."

I spent the rest of the night at her side, her dress firmly enmeshed in one of my small fists, counting the minutes until we could leave.

Top-rated United States television programs of 1991–92: Wikipodia

Rank	Program	Network	Rating
1	60 Minutes	CBS	21.9
2	Roseanne	ABC	19.9
3	Murphy Brown	CBS	18.6
4	Cheers	NBC	17.5
5	Home Improvement	ABC	17.5
6	**Third Time Around**	**CBS**	**17.4**
7	Designing Women	CBS	17.3
8	Full House	ABC	17.0

CHAPTER 4

The show was a smash hit, premiering with huge numbers right out of the gate. Before the first season even finished filming, we were greenlit for a second. And then a third. Before long, I was ten years old and what was considered a "seasoned" actress on a hit TV drama.

My father still lived in Anita, though by this time we were able to fly back and forth. During filming hiatus, my mother and Ashley and I would fly back to Texas and live at "home" with my father for several months; and twice a year he would fly to Los Angeles, stay with us for a week, then return home to get back to his job. I could hear my parents talking in the bedroom of the bungalow we now rented, low murmurings of what was probably them discussing the next step in their lives and our careers. Should Daddy continue to live in Anita when his daughter was in a successful network television show? Should he sell the house and move out here? Should he and the family live off my earnings?

I understood his hesitation. I was ten, and who knew how long the gravy train would run until it ran out.

And so we continued to commute back and forth. Mrs.

Murray fell by the wayside as we continued our lives in Los Angeles. I got a new agent, Mr. Himes. I made new friends at premieres and awards shows. I became a master of the two-cheek kiss, like the French were.

My mother pestered Mr. Himes to let me audition for new roles, to "diversify" my "range." She told him, "A *star* like Hayley should be considering blockbusters. Isn't there anything that we can audition for?"

"Well," Mr. Himes said, "Ned Tucker is casting for his next action thriller with David Reynolds, and needs someone to play David's daughter."

"Okay!" I chirped, excited about any sort of project. The summers in Anita were languid, boring. The town was so small that the most excitement to be found was at Dairy Queen, which got old really fast. I loved the bustling of Los Angeles, loved the energy and the busy streets and the hustle. I loved the cuisine, refining my palate at ten years old. I even loved sitting in traffic in the back seat while my mom cursed under her breath and we inched forward on the 101.

"Don't you need to discuss this with your husband?" Mr. Himes asked.

"I'm sure it'll be fine," my mother answered. "Just let us get our foot in the door."

I was not privy to the conversation between my parents, but the next thing I knew, my mother was coaching me outside the audition room. "Whatever they want, you say yes," she said, hands on my shoulders. In retrospect, it is kind of terrifying that she wanted me to go along with anything that the casting directors wanted, but at the time, I took it to mean that I was supposed to say yes, I could roller-skate, or yes, I could ride a horse. I was game. More roles meant more cameras and more acting and more fun. Soon, I was in a room with the casting crew, being considered for the role of Whitney.

I showed off my acting chops, and killed it, as usual. Then the casting director asked me something I didn't expect.

"Can you lose ten pounds?"

I was flummoxed. Ten pounds? Where would I lose that *from*? I was four and a half feet tall and skinny as Olive in *Popeye*. But whatever a casting director would ask, I was supposed to say yes. So of course, yes, I could lose ten pounds. I hesitated and looked at my mother, who was sitting right outside the door, gazing through the thin rectangular window. She didn't know what was being asked of me. But she gave me a thumbs-up. I said yes.

"Good. We'll let you know."

When I returned to the bungalow, I was in a weird mood. I decided to tell my mom about the ten pounds.

She was preparing a salad for dinner, spinning the lettuce in a contraption that she also used to wring her bras of excess water. What she said surprised me.

"I noticed you gaining a bit of weight over the last few months. You have a problem area like me. I get a poochy tummy. Maybe it's not a bad idea to lose some of it."

I felt sulky. Millie had been ten when she was put on a diet on *Third Time Around* and for some reason, I thought that I'd be immune from such a situation. Now it looked as though I would be joining the ranks of all the women who had to watch their weight to continue working in Hollywood. I hated it. But I also knew that I had to do it.

"WAIT," JESSICA INTERRUPTS. "You were put on a diet at *ten*?"

"Yeah, that's excessive," Jane says. We are sitting around the breakfast table eating dinner now. She spears another piece of roasted carrot.

"You don't understand what it was like back then," I say. "It was 1994. Kate Moss was the reigning queen of the models. Heroin chic was raging. *Everyone* was on a diet. Even ten-year-olds."

"Jeez," Jane says, shaking her head. "I thought it was bad *now*."

"You have no idea," I say.

SO BREAD WAS gone, poof. So were many starches like pasta and pizza. We ate chicken and vegetables, minestrone soup, protein bars, apples. Tuna salad without the mayo. My mother began measuring my Raisin Bran in the morning—only three-fourths of a cup and with skim milk. Anything that was fun to eat, I couldn't have anymore. Sugar was gone. Cookies were gone. McDonald's was a thing of the past. Slowly but surely, a hollow appeared in my belly and my cheekbones began to protrude ever so slightly. By the time I was on set of *The Sky Below* I had lost the required ten pounds.

I was the only child on set—even my stunt double was a very short woman—so I was treated like one of the adults.

Rush, rush, rush. Go here, go there. Hurry up, slow down. And no one said anything about my newfound slimness. I felt cheated. I had given up *pizza* for these ten pounds, and yet no one was going to tell me "good job for losing the weight"?

I rebelled. I scoured the craft services table and chewed my way through granola bars, pudding cups, and doughnuts. At night, after my mother went to sleep, I'd go to the pantry and eat handfuls of dry cereal from the box, even if it was only Raisin Bran and not what I wanted (Cinnamon Toast Crunch). Soon, my wardrobe was getting tight on me and I was called in to have a talk.

"In this production, we respect one another," one of the producers told me. "We respect our work and our time. What does it say to us when you neglect your body enough that Wardrobe has to refit you for outfits?"

Admonished, I hung my head. "That I'm not respecting their time," I mumbled.

"That's right. You were hired with the instruction to lose weight. Did you lose weight?"

I nodded.

"But then what happened?"

I shrugged.

"You stopped watching what you were eating. And now Gisele has to let out your clothes. Does that seem fair?"

I wanted to tell him that I watched every single bite that went into my mouth, but that seemed unnecessary. I said what he expected me to say. "No."

"Okay. I hope you can lose the weight again."

It didn't make sense to me to make Gisele's job twice as hard by forcing her let out my clothes and then tightening them up again, but I didn't know how to say that without getting into trouble, so I didn't.

The Sky Below was an action movie in which I basically acted scared and cried the entire time the camera was on me. You've seen it. Remember? It's sort of like *Taken* except the dad, played by David Reynolds, gets kidnapped by the bad guys and fights his way home. What's that? It sounds like *Taken 2*? Well, everything is a derivative of something else.

I remember the publicity tour for *The Sky Below* was huge. It was going to be an international blockbuster, so we toured the world. It was my first time in places like Australia, Japan, Hong Kong, South Africa. It was my first time to Europe. I was even on Rocky Eastman's late-night TV show in America, as well as on David Letterman's and Jay Leno's.

I remember the questions for the cast were easy, softball-type inquiries. Rocky Eastman asked me if I got along with my costars and what my favorite part of being in the movie was. I answered that the tour was my favorite part.

It was a good experience, I suppose. But this was the beginning of my toxic relationship with my weight and body image. By the time I was back on set for the fourth season of *Third Time Around,* I'd lost the required ten pounds—and then some.

On the first day back, Millie immediately grabbed my arm and encircled my wrist with her fingers. "Gross! You're so skinny! You better not have an eating disorder," she exclaimed. Her fingers overlapped at the knuckle where she'd grabbed me.

"I'm just not eating cake," I said to her with a straight face. She released me with a start. There was another sheet cake to celebrate the start of filming; Ted, claiming that it was his birthday, was the only one of us three who ate a piece. "Ted," I said, "filming always starts on a Monday. It *can't* be your birthday every Monday of every year." He just made a face at me.

Millie was thirteen and newly puffy around her face. I learned later that this was normal for bulimics. Ted was fifteen and still acted like a big brother. Over the years, I had seen Ted drunk at more parties than I cared to remember. He was secretive, but terrible at hiding it. His parents had to have noticed, but his behavior was not curbed.

Alex Dietrich, the showrunner, was surprised when he saw me. I could see it in his eyes. Looking back on photos of the premiere of season four, I can see what he saw in me then: a smiling, happy-go-lucky face, and a body with a waist the size of a large grapefruit. I was extraordinarily lean, but not gaunt.

"Are you all right?" Alex asked me. "Have you been sick?"

"I'm fine," I responded. He gave me a long, quizzical look and patted me on the back, but then went back to his business.

Because that's all it was, right? Business. Alex Dietrich did his due diligence and asked me if I was okay, and I had replied in the affirmative. What else was he going to do? I was still in the realm of slim but healthy. I hadn't done anything extreme. If Alex were to worry about anyone, it should've been for the other two child stars of the show, Millie and Ted, one of whom was getting in deep with an eating disorder; the other, flirting with alcoholism.

SEASON FOUR BUILT upon the stories of seasons one through three. The premise of *Third Time Around* was that Tina-as-Georgette was a single mother of three who had been divorced once and widowed once, who met Oscar-as-Steve, a bachelor, and the shenanigans that ensued when the two families merged. The focus was on everyone, not just the parents, as they navigated whole new relationships with one another. Me-as-Amy was the crybaby, Millie-as-Erica was the comic relief, and Ted-as-Zac was the oldest, who butted heads with his stepfather and supported his kid sisters.

For the first few seasons, Amy did nothing but terrorize her family with her crying. Everything upset her and reminded her of the biological father she had lost. But as she grew, she began to love Steve, and Oscar and I had some great moments on set together as father and daughter bonded.

One of my favorite moments was when Oscar sat me on his knee and we ran lines together. People loved Steve and Amy and what they represented in terms of the new nuclear family. Oscar was always very proper, never made me feel uncomfortable. Sitting on his knee was commonplace; it's where Amy sat on Steve any time they were having a heart-to-heart. Even though I was ten and he was in his thirties, I felt as though he treated me like a grown-up in terms of professionalism and patience.

But now I mourn my lack of a childhood. Having a job at age ten where I had to be on time and courteous and repetitive until I did it *just* right meant that I had responsibilities. I wasn't even a teenager and I was wound up too tight, always worrying about the next line, the next shoot.

When Ted offered me a gulp of his beer the next time we were at a party together, I didn't say no. He looked so relaxed, unlike his usual anxious self; I coveted that for myself.

The taste was foul. Ted laughed at my face. "Hold on," he said, "I'll get you something better." He brought back champagne. I took a cautious sip. It was dry and bitter but not altogether awful.

I could feel my limbs loosening. My knees felt a little weak. When I told Ted, he said, "That's how you know it's working." I nodded and sipped more from my flute.

If there were photos from the rest of that night, they would show me with glassy eyes, half-closed, my arms and legs in perpetual sway. I danced by myself, I danced with Ted. I was easily drunk. It was wonderful.

I'd discovered a new state of being.

CHAPTER 5

I wasn't immediately a lush or anything. But by the time the fourth season finale had wrapped and we were at the after-party, no one blinked twice when I took a champagne flute or two. I took the glasses to a hidden corner where Ted was waiting, and we gleefully gulped down our glasses and laughed.

It was harmless fun. We loosened up a little, and as the music flowed, we got up and danced. "Here," Ted said at one point, when Boyz II Men's "On Bended Knee" started to play, and had me step onto his nice shoes. He held my hands and we shuffled with my feet on his. "I saw my uncle do this with my cousin at a wedding once and always wanted to try it." He chuckled.

When the song was over, I said, "Do you want me to go get more?" and Ted nodded his head.

I threaded my way through the throngs of people and went up to the bar. My little hands reached up for the champagne and someone said, "How adorable, a ten-year-old stealing alcohol," but that didn't stop me from swiping the glasses.

Where was my mother during all of this? I never knew. It was as if she disappeared from view as soon as we stepped foot into the party. She acted like a friend, not a mom, at a college kegger. *I'll find you when it's time to go,* seemed to be the unspoken agreement since that first party, and we adhered to it ever after.

Ted and I drank our champagne together and stared off into the distance, people-watching. There was a point when his drunkenness turned sullen; the boisterousness melted away and left behind a quiet boy. I didn't like it. I liked happy Ted. Not this one that said, "What's even the point, Hayley?"

I was silent.

He slurred, "What's the point of this show, this life? Why do we do it?"

I didn't answer.

"Why won't you say anything?" he whined.

But Ted wanted answers from a ten-year-old girl who just enjoyed being a ham on camera. That's it. That's all I knew and that's all I loved.

ONCE I HAD done *The Sky Below* and signed on for a fifth, sixth, and seventh season of *Third Time Around,* my father decided to drop down to part-time at his job. He would still use Anita as his home base, but would have the flexibility to visit us more often. It seemed that for the first three years of my employment, my mother was a single mother taking care of two kids, rather than a wife who had a husband living fifteen hundred miles away. It was never more apparent than when she would talk to Alex Dietrich. She would be on set with me and I'd come off a take to find her giggling and hanging around

Alex. Her voice would turn saccharine, like when she talked Ashley into going to bed, and she'd smile a lot more when he was around.

"Mom," I said, finally confronting her after seeing it too many times. "What are you doing? Why are you laughing so much?"

She clamped down on her laughter and gave me a smothering hug. "Nothing, baby. Nothing's going on." But I could feel her looking up at her companion; something about the way her chin was sharp on the back of my head. She wasn't giving me her full attention.

It bothered me in a weird way I couldn't quite explain. *I* was supposed to be the center of her attention. I didn't understand why Alex Dietrich was so funny. My *father* was supposed to be the one to make her laugh.

I stomped into Ted's trailer. He was leaning on his counter, sipping from a bottle of water when I barged in, and he sputtered in surprise. He had a guilty expression on his face before he realized it was me. "Oh, Hayley," he said in relief, and took another pull on the bottle before shelving it in a cabinet.

"What's that?" I said suspiciously, aware that he wouldn't act so weird with a real bottle of water.

He scrubbed at his face with one hand. "Ugh, fine. You caught me. It's vodka."

"Why?"

He gave me a look. "Why else?" he said. "Tutoring is boring. I'm spicing it up a little."

I wondered if he got sullen during his tutoring, or if it was boisterous Ted that the tutor saw. If he was anxious all the time, and this was just his usual way of coping.

"Don't tell anybody," he said, his voice rising like it was a question. It was yet another time that Ted asked me to be his confidant and I puffed up in importance.

"Okay," I nodded.

He didn't offer me any, but that was fine. I knew his secret.

Millie popped her head in at that moment and Ted and I turned our heads to look at her. "What are ya doing?" she asked, though it wasn't a pointed question. She seemed bored, curious.

"Just hanging out," Ted said, at the same time I muttered, "Nothing."

It was as if Millie's antennae went up. She noticed something strange about us and needed to know more. But neither of us was budging. She shrugged, holding on to the door frame, and swiveled her way into the trailer. "I learned a new gymnastics trick. Wanna see?"

"Not really," Ted said.

Millie huffed and left the trailer then. She knew she wasn't wanted.

Sometimes I wonder if Millie picked up on Ted's and my connection and wanted a piece of it for herself. She was always inserting herself into our trailers and conversations, and yet we shut her out for the most part. She was probably just lonely on set, the middle child, the comic relief in between her little sister's dramatic moments and her older brother's saccharine ones.

"She's weird," I said to Ted, once she was gone.

"I guess," he said. He was a little unsteady on his feet. Too much to drink.

He wobbled into a chair. "I'll just wait here until it's time for me to get tutored," he said, vowels slightly elongated.

I looked around the trailer. He had a bulletin board adhered to one wall and on it were photos of him at various ages: us at Disneyland, meeting Goofy; us on the first day of filming season two, cake in hand. A picture of his parents, Mr. Sumner with an arm around his wife, a blonde in a tie-dyed shirt, their twin blue eyes glowing like jewels in the direct light of the sun.

"Do you want to run lines?" I asked. We did that a lot, went over our dialogue even though we weren't always in the same scene.

"Okay," he said, grabbing his script off the trailer's little coffee table.

Ted and I knew each other like real siblings. We'd been on set together for four years at this point and we were finely attuned to each other's feelings. I could tell when he was sad, or tired, or drunk. It amazed me that no one else seemed to know the latter, or if they did—they didn't care. Ted continued to churn out great performances, and if anything, was *more* professional on set when he'd had a little bit to drink beforehand. He was more relaxed, so his dialogue seemed to flow easier. And he was more polite, as if to cover up his transgressions.

Why did no one say anything? Years later, I just can't seem to understand. If a ten-year-old can tell when something is up, the *adults* can't be blind to it, can they?

CHAPTER 6

Your grandmother, in her heyday, was an extremely beautiful woman. She's aged kind of badly—lack of sunscreen and excessive plastic surgery will do that to you—but in her youth, she was ethereal. You look at me and see a pretty face, but *she* was something else. You know that adage, "If you want to see what your wife will look like when she's old, just look at her mother"? Casting directors looked at me and then at my mother and knew exactly how I'd age. My mother could've been a model for Calvin Klein if she'd gotten into the job early enough. As it was, she was born somewhere near Anita and lived there all her life; she married someone she went to high school with. She and my father never attended college.

My mother loves to laugh. I think she told me when I was nine that she married my father because he was funny. Indeed, I was always happiest when we were all together. Something about having my father around made me feel like we were whole. He would carry Ashley on his back and extend his hand for me. I'd clutch his first two fingers and he would say, "Hold my hand so I don't get lost!" I thought it was *so* funny that an adult would need my help. It wasn't until I had my own chil-

dren that I realized it was a ploy to make me think that the kid
was in charge.

What possessed a woman to uproot her family from the
town she'd known all her life and pursue a Hollywood career
for her child? Was I that adamant? Was she that bored? Was my
dad that assertive? Were they having problems then and it was
an easy way to gain some space?

Because I don't think my mom was very happy when Dad
visited us in L.A. Despite my happiness at age eleven, she didn't
laugh or smile much when he was around. Not the way she
laughed and smiled around Alex Dietrich. That should've been
my first clue that something was up.

"Patty," my dad once said after he got off the plane and
found us waiting in the terminal—because you could do that
in the nineties, wait at the gate like you were at a bus station.
He tried to embrace my mother but she was stiff, sighing when
he put his arms around her. "You smell so good," he added.
My mother had started wearing perfume, Gap Grass, when
we came into a little more money. Nothing ostentatious, just a
nice, fresh, clean scent. *It's a young person perfume*, she'd said, *but
it makes me* feel *young.*

"How's my little Ashley?" he said, grinning at my sister.
He put her on his shoulders and she squealed with glee. "And
how's my little Hollywood star?"

I smiled at my father and told him with relish, "I got cast
in *Portrait of a Year.*" We were going to film during *Third Time
Around*'s summer hiatus. I'd been waiting to tell him the news
in person. He grinned back at me and looked at my mother

with a new glint in his eye. "Wow, she's really going places!" he said.

LAX has always been a paparazzi cesspool and even at that age, photographers were waiting for me. They snapped pictures of my dad taking my hand and of him guiding my mother with a palm at her waist, walking out the double doors like the perfect family. Dad with his sandy hair and sunglasses, Mom with her beach-blond tresses and perfect toothpaste-smile mouth, Ashley the little tyke on Dad's shoulders, and me leading the way to the new Volvo that one of my paychecks had subsidized, tugging on Dad's arm.

"Soon I'll have to quit my job and move out here," he laughed. "Wouldn't that be nice, Patty, having us all together again, all the time?"

My mother said, "Of course, that would be lovely," but her words fluttered away in the wind. I wondered what she was thinking about.

We drove with the windows down, my father taking over the driver's seat and my mom navigating, and Ashley wriggled her legs in her car seat while I poked my head out the window, mesmerizing myself with the dotted lines skipping in and out of my vision on the road below us. When we finally turned into the driveway of the bungalow where we now lived, my hair was a rat's nest from the wind blowing through it.

That night, I heard my mother submit. I should have been asleep, but the groans of pleasure that roiled through my father could be heard through the thin walls of the bungalow.

PORTRAIT OF A *Year,* which came out in 1996, was a drama.
I played Liz Dayson's daughter, a precocious child who supported her mother emotionally while she "found herself" after a divorce. I beat out Michelle Trachtenberg and Scarlett
Johansson for the role. It was a good experience, very low in
stunt work, and though there were some long days on set I
was only on call for a short while. For several weeks of work,
I was paid three hundred thousand dollars. With that money,
my mother rented a better house than the bungalow, closer to
my work, with a two-year lease.

This was the film that introduced me to my best friend, Olive Green. Olive was a Latina with a beautiful Spanish name
that she once told me, but her manager changed her name so
she would be more "palatable" as an actress. When I met her in
1995, she was my age, with swooping, long black hair and dark
eyes. Olive played my best friend in the movie.

Something strange happened during the promotional tour
for *Portrait of a Year,* though. Olive and I weren't in the same
promo, but she told me later what had transpired. While I was
still lobbing questions about what my favorite part of the movie
was to film, she was being asked about "grown up" things.

"Like what?" I asked curiously.

"They asked me questions like 'Do you fancy your costar?'
and 'Did you wish there was more kissing involved?' Like, that
sort of thing."

"That doesn't even make sense. You have a small part, with
no kissing involved whatsoever. No offense."

"No, like, I know! When I said that *Portrait* was about Liz

Dayson getting her love life back, they all laughed and asked me about my own love life. It was weird, you know?"

"They must think you're, like, old or something," I said.

"Well, look at me." We were on the phone, but I could picture her: those dark eyes could be misconstrued as sensual. Her full lips could be seen as a sign of maturity. And her breasts were growing larger by the day. They were noticeably bigger now than they had been during filming. She probably filled a real bra with cups now, not a training bra.

"If this is what I have to look forward to, I say no thanks to aging." We both laughed.

At the premiere, Olive and I stuck together like fast friends. She was a television actress as well, with a recurring role on the final season of *Full House*, so our television families were invited too. Ted and Millie were there, and the Olsen twins, and I noticed how gorgeous John Stamos was in person.

"He's wearing *leather pants*," I said scandalously to Olive. "To a *premiere*." She giggled at me. We went through the churn of the photo op, showing off the best angles of our bodies and shoes. We were old hands by this point.

Like always, I found Ted after the screening, this time with Olive in tow. He offered both of us beverages and Olive surprised me by downing hers in one gulp. "What?" she said when I looked at her in mild shock. "Like, I've been to a million of these too, you know?"

That's the way she spoke. Like a Valley girl, lots of *like*s and *you know*s.

With champagne sitting happily in our bellies, we did what

all pre-teens do at premiere parties. We played Slide with our hands, clapping once, twice, three times, until we were laughing and out of breath and our fingers were sliding all over the place in our drunkenness. We giggled at our costars, who did nothing funny but walked past us and earned our mirth just the same. We took turns grabbing more drinks from the bar or from the little round trays that were being passed around by waiters.

After a while, Olive and I calmed down and lay back in the now-vacated theater, staring up at the designs on the ceiling. "This is, like, the life, you know?" she said. "Think about it. How much did you get paid for *Portrait*?"

"I don't know that stuff," I said, for the first time a little uncomfortable.

"But your dad bought a car, right?"

My father had bought himself a Porsche. I hadn't seen it, of course; he bought it in Texas. It had to be delivered to Anita on a flatbed truck because there were no dealerships for Porsches in the town.

"Yeah."

"And you're moving to a new house. Like, that's the thing, isn't it? We make a lot. To do *this*." She gestured with her hands. "It's great, you know?"

I agreed silently.

Being a kid in the film industry was difficult, though. Despite the laws that regulated how long we could be on the set, with hard hours truncating our work days, it was near impossible to socialize with someone who wasn't working on the same set as you. Olive and I had days that ended, for the most part, by six P.M., but with parents who took care of other children, we weren't able to see each other due to dinner routines and firm bedtimes. We saw each other at parties, but casual hangouts were few and far between until we were of driving age and could cart ourselves around. The only person I saw with regularity outside of set times was Ted, because he babysat Ashley and me once in a while. (My mother was desperate one day and he was available. Turns out, he really enjoyed hanging out with us.) As it was, I didn't get to see Olive in person very much until we worked together again on *Only Human* in 1998. Until then, we talked on the phone nearly every night, sharing stories about what had happened on set that day, and obsessing about puberty.

At eleven, I was still pancake-flat. Olive and I both had read *Are You There God? It's Me, Margaret* and wondered when we'd start our periods. We weren't boy crazy (yet) but we definitely noticed our attractive male costars. Olive thought that Ted was a hunk, but I could see him only as my older brother. She told me she had a poster of him from *Bop* on her wall.

"Imagine those pillowy-soft lips touching yours," she said, sighing wistfully.

"Ugh."

"And, like, running your hand through his hair, you know . . ."

"And getting stuck with gel? No, thanks. You watch too many movies."

"One day, you'll, like, fall in love with someone," she said darkly.

WHEN I WAS twelve, that moment happened.

For Amy, that is.

Brandon was an eighteen-year-old actor who was playing a fifteen-year-old character. Alex Dietrich told me that Amy and Brandon-as-Thomas would end up together in a few seasons, network willing. Amy was supposed to have a schoolgirl crush on Thomas in the meantime.

In reality, Brandon was a belching man with bad breath. I could smell the everything bagel he had eaten even before he opened his mouth.

"Why does *Amy* get a love interest before Erica does?" Millie whined.

"Erica is aloof and wants to be a feminist," she was told, "so she doesn't get a boyfriend."

Millie made angry eyes at me. Her temper was even shorter nowadays, with her body rebelling against its daily regurgitations. She was often tired, she avoided craft services, and she stayed in her trailer until she was called to the set.

I didn't want it either. I went crying to Ted's trailer, where he was sitting on his loveseat and sipping vodka from a water bottle. He smiled at me lopsidedly and brushed his hand against my face. "What's wrong with Brandon?" he asked.

"I've never been kissed, and I'm going to have to kiss that guy! He'll be my first kiss!"

"Slow down," he said. "When you pace like that, you make *me* nervous. Anyway, the writers aren't going to make Thomas and Amy kiss for a few years yet. And it might not even happen. The network has to okay it."

"But—" Ted and I both knew that a good-looking, albeit oniony-smelling, boy wouldn't just appear out of nowhere to be on a show without an arc already in mind. The network probably already knew—and were on board with—Amy and Thomas getting together in something like season seven. And I was locked in a contract.

"Besides," he continued, "you might get your first kiss before you have to kiss Brandon. That's years away. You might find somebody by then. Have a real boyfriend."

The thought of that slammed into me. "I guess . . ." I said slowly. "But what if it doesn't happen? What if I'm unlovable?"

"That's impossible," Ted said, swiping at my cheek with a thumb. "But if you feel that bad about it, I'll kiss you before Brandon does. Okay?"

"You?" I wrinkled my nose. "You're like my brother."

He sat back, withdrawing his hand from my face. "Right," he acknowledged. He took a sip from his water bottle, the sting of the drink registering on his face as he swallowed. "But it seems like I'd be a better candidate than Brandon."

I thought about it. "Okay." I came to terms with the idea. "If I haven't kissed anybody by the time Amy and Thomas get together on the show, we have a plan."

He nodded at me. "Deal."

CHAPTER 7

Okay, it probably isn't fair to Brandon that I hated him on sight. He was what we'd call "a lovable dick." It wasn't his fault that his favorite bagel came with onion and his breath smelled bad, though he could've popped an Altoid if he were more considerate. But that's just how guys were back then. Though if I catch either of you girls dating a guy who wears tiny basketball shorts with no underwear and his balls hanging out, I'll tan your hides, I don't care that you're almost voting age.

It was 1996 and this raven-haired, blue-eyed guy came on the show and created a ruckus. The female fans of the show went crazy. Not only was there beautiful jailbait in the form of Ted, but Brandon was eighteen and therefore okay to ogle.

With the addition of Brandon, Amy's role expanded that year. (I even got my own hair and makeup team, April and Paul.) No longer was Amy around to just cry on her stepdad, Steve, she was supposed to be lovesick for this new Thomas character. It wasn't a gag; it wasn't like she fawned over him and a studio audience laughed. It was taken seriously, like first loves truly feel. I had no idea what that was supposed to feel like, but I felt the pressure to get it right.

It's strange to pretend to love somebody when you find them unbearable in real life. That's why it's called *acting*, I suppose.

The first time I met Brandon, he sidled up to me and put my shoulder in his armpit, wrapping his arm around me. "Hi there," he said smoothly. "I'm going to be your lover."

"Um, who are you?" I asked.

"I'm Brandon. I play Thomas. The love of your life."

"So, you're *playing* my lover." I extracted myself from his grasp.

"Same difference," he said, swiveling to face me and giving me a huge grin. His teeth were perfect, except for one canine that was slightly crooked. It made him even more beautiful. I hated him for it. In fact, I hated all of him. His introduction to me was gross.

"Amy is twelve," I said. What I didn't say was *I'm twelve. Leave me alone, you weirdo adult man.* "She doesn't know who the love of her life is yet."

"So he'll be her first. She won't know what hit her." He winked. I wanted to throw up.

I was terribly protective of the character of Amy. She was me, and I was her. But she also *wasn't* me, and I also *wasn't* her. It was hard enough dealing with the warm-on-camera, cold-on-set Millie, and to have my on-screen parents treat me with kindness but not love. Now I was going to have to pretend to be in love with someone I couldn't stand. I wanted to be grown-up about it, but just could not muster the energy.

I threw a fit. I went to the head writers and told them I

didn't like the idea of Amy becoming attracted to someone. "She's too young," I argued. "I don't even know what it feels like." All of my crushes had been bestowed on to way-older males from distant TV shows, like John Stamos. *Have mercy.* Uncle Jesse was just too beautiful for this world.

"Amy isn't just about you," I was told. "She's a representative of the full toddler-to-teenage experience. She's growing up, like everyone else on this show, and she discovers love. Just because she's young doesn't mean that her feelings aren't valid. Do you think it's fair to let down some of America's youth because *you* don't have feelings for your costar?"

It was the first time a temper tantrum hadn't worked. I was shocked. They had to talk me down and then I had to beg them to promise not to tell Brandon that I wanted him to get fired. Because that's basically what I was doing, trying to get him off the show. I didn't want it to be awkward.

Our first scene together was our meet-cute. Thomas was a friend of Zac's and was over to play basketball. Zac accidentally pelted Thomas in the face with a bad bounce. Thomas ended up in the house, bleeding from a cut on his lip, and that's where Amy came in. She nursed him with ice and that's where it all began. Her budding love, visible for all to see.

"Isn't this a little . . . cliché?" I said, when I read the script. Ted and I were in his trailer, where we were passing a bottle of his "water" back and forth and running lines together.

"Millie is pissed that Erica doesn't fall in love with Brandon. I think she has a crush," he said, clearly amused.

"Please," I said in a bored voice. "Even Millie has better

taste."

"What's wrong with Brandon?" Ted wanted to know. He asked that a lot during our time together.

"He's just . . ." How did I explain that first meeting without sounding crazy? "Not my type," I finished.

"What's your type?" he asked.

I didn't *have* a type. I was twelve. I didn't know what my type *was* yet. But to appease Ted, I said, "Uncle Jesse."

"Brandon has the same thing going on. Tall. Dark, luscious hair. Nice teeth. *Have mer-say*," he teased.

I was annoyed and left the trailer in a huff.

Someone caught my arm as I reached the bottom steps. "I was looking for you," Brandon said.

"Don't touch me," I said coldly.

"I know we started off on the wrong foot, and I'm sorry," he said. "But I want Thomas to be a crowd pleaser, and to do that, he really needs to win over Amy. Which means I need to win over *you*. Will you please let me try again?"

"Fine," I said stiffly.

"So hi, I'm Brandon. I'm an Aries and I love *The Velveteen Rabbit*. It's my favorite book."

"That book is for little kids."

He rubbed his face. "Okay, I was trying to impress you. I don't read a lot nowadays."

"You could've just said that."

"Please, Hayley. I am dying to do a good job here. I promise never to touch you again, unless the script calls for it. And I'll be on my best behavior. Okay?"

I regarded him warily, but he seemed earnest. "Okay."

We should've shaken hands like adults, but I still didn't want to be touched, so I waved at him instead. He took the hint and left.

The meet-cute was filmed, and I gave it my all. I imbued as much love as I could into the scene, and even Alex Dietrich was impressed with the level of maturity I expressed. He gave me a hug after we finished filming the scene, and in my head, I equated his approval with my parents being happy with me. "Good job, Hayley," he said. "I knew you could do it." He gave me a little kiss on the forehead. I smiled up at him.

My mother no longer sat in on filming days for the full day; she had to take Ashley to and from school. Her days started early, with packing a lunch for Ashley, then driving both of us to the studio, dropping me off, dropping Ashley off, coming back to the studio, observing us for a little while, running errands, picking Ashley up from second grade, and then back to get me when I was done. She missed a lot of things, and asked me how my day was when she came to pick me up. She was beginning to park and wait for me to be deposited in the parking lot—someone on the staff would drive me from the studio in a golf cart—but that day she came in with Ashley in tow, holding her hand. "How did it go today?" she asked Alex Dietrich, and he smiled at me and said, "She was electric. I don't know how you do it, Patty. Raising such a talent."

"She does it on her own, I swear," she said. "I can't take credit for it. She's always been wildly imaginative."

The *imaginative, eh?* sparked in my head again as I remembered Mrs. Murray and I puffed up with pride.

"You're doing amazingly," he said to her, and leaned closer, but stopped himself before he got too close.

"Thank you, Alex. That's so sweet." She smiled at him in a way that I can't describe. It was almost wrong to look at her.

Brandon emerged from the mess of crew and cameras and came over to us. He introduced himself to my mother and shook her hand. "I just wanted to say, you have quite an actress on your hands," he said. "I've never worked with a powerhouse like your daughter. And I know she and I are supposed to be romantically involved in the future, but I will always be careful to listen to what she says."

"Thank you, that's very considerate of you," my mother said. Brandon nodded and smiled at me, all teeth.

"It was great working with you today, Hayley. I think we're going to make real magic on this show." And then, with Alex's and my mother's backs to him, he did something odd. He made a V with his index and middle finger and poked his tongue through it. At the time, I didn't know what this meant, but now I know he was simulating cunnilingus. Just the way he did it, while the adults weren't looking, made me uncomfortable. It *had* to be lewd. Then he disappeared.

My mother said, "What a nice young man." She didn't say, *Alex, should I be concerned that an eighteen-year-old is going to make out with my daughter on television one of these days not so far into the future?* She smiled at me, took my hand with her free one, and guided Ashley and me to the car.

Sometimes, it's boggling what adults don't see.

CHAPTER 8

In 1996, I wrested the titular role of *A Poem for Jeanie* from the rest of the tweens who coveted it. It was the one role I was gunning for, and because it filmed at the same time as *Third Time Around*, I had to ask for special circumstances to be allowed to do both. It was difficult for Alex Dietrich to give his okay; Amy's role had expanded with Brandon's arrival and it was going to make filming tight. But I was adamant.

Mr. Himes, my agent, had given me a stack of scripts to choose from. Filmmakers had taken notice of my past work and were now offering me plum roles at my tender age of twelve. Sure, I still had to audition, but it wasn't as cutthroat as it had been. I was primed and perfect for Jeanie and was the main pick by a mile.

As was becoming a tradition, my mother let me call Mr. Himes to let him know that I was accepting the role of Jeanie. She always let me dial, and when I was patched through to Mr. Himes via his secretary, I would chirp that I was open to taking a role or rejecting it. Then she'd handle the phone and confirm. It was, she said, a way for me to have some control over my career, and to strengthen my bond with my agent.

A Poem for Jeanie was a soft, introspective role about a precocious teen who is in an accident and loses her memory and has to build herself up again. She's joined by her childhood best friend, Gus, who helps Jeanie learn to be herself once more. My costar, Anthony Martens, was a sweet boy; this was his first big role so his ego hadn't gotten inflated yet. Everything he did on set, he did with reckless abandon, not realizing that his impulsive approach to acting was what made him good. In later roles, he would be too in his head, overthinking everything and ruining the vibe of his characters' emotions.

Anthony was one of the few heartthrobs of the late nineties that didn't have blond hair. He had a thick mane of dark brown hair and chocolate-brown eyes. He looked like a model, with chiseled cheekbones and full, pouty lips even at the age of fifteen. In fact, he did get a stint as a model with Abercrombie & Fitch when he was about seventeen. I remember getting that catalog.

Juggling two acting jobs at the same time was hard. There are rules in place so that a minor actor doesn't get taken advantage of. I could work only forty hours a week total, so my weeks were split in half: half *Jeanie*, half *TTA*. My on-set tutor would shuttle between the two sets with me and try to keep my grades up.

Brandon did not like the new arrangement. "How am I supposed to get to know you if I'm talking to your stand-in for half of my scenes?" he griped.

"You don't have to know me," I responded. "Just read the script." I was fine with keeping Brandon at arm's length for as long as we worked together.

Brandon wheedled, "But what if I *want* to get to know you better?" He said it with his eyebrows raised, the insinuation strong. He reached out a hand to lightly touch a tendril of loose hair by my face. I slapped his hand away.

But the scheduling arrangement worked out well with Anthony and me. I learned what kind of person he was without needing a ton of information.

I watched him capture a spider and release it outside the set instead of squashing it.

I watched him as he tried to teach me World War II history during some of our downtime together, his long lashes brushing against his cheeks as he held out the book he was reading: a tome on the Normandy beach landings.

I watched him eat carefully around a mound of cheese, saving it for last, because it was his favorite.

And I realized that Anthony was the opposite of Brandon. Brandon was brute force and gauche manners and good looks. Anthony was good-looking, for sure, but he was kind, sensitive, and thoughtful. I grew a tiny crush.

"Penny for your thoughts?" Anthony asked once, while we were waiting for the electricians to set up the lights. I was in a hospital gown with a mound of gauze wrapped around my head.

"That I've never been in the hospital before," I said.

"Surely you were born in one . . . ?"

"I was actually born right outside of one," I explained. "My parents were rushing there but the closest hospital was an hour away. They didn't make it. I was born in a car."

His eyes grew round. "Wow!" he said. "I've never met any-one who wasn't born in a hospital before."

"There are probably dozens of us," I joked. "Where were you born?"

"In L.A.," he said, jerking his chin as if to indicate the direction of the hospital he was born in. "My parents moved here from Brazil."

"Do you speak Brazilian?" I asked.

He laughed. "You mean Portuguese? No," he said, suddenly morose. "I don't actually speak it, though I can understand it when my parents do."

"This is your first movie, right?" I asked.

"Yeah," he said, his eyelashes fluttering. "I've been wanting to act for a long time. I saw the open call for this role and thought, Why not? My parents let me drop out of school for it, which was way cool of them."

"Way cool," I echoed.

"It helps that it's a Hodges movie," he said. "It's a really good one to have at the start of a résumé."

I nodded. Our director, Ed Hodges, was notorious for being a stickler for perfection. But he was good. Three out of the last seven years, Ed Hodges was nominated for the Best Director Oscar. Quietly, I hoped that this role as Jeanie would be a shoo-in for my own awards.

I talked about Anthony with Ted when I was back on the set at *Third Time Around*. He was content to listen to me chatter on about the guy who intrigued me. "He's smart. So smart, that he helped me with the quadratic formula. When am I actually going to use that in real life, though?"

Ted leaned back on the couch, his delicate hands cupping a bottle of "water." He sipped gently, his Adam's apple bobbing up and down. When had he grown *that*? Ted was becoming a man, too, just like Anthony.

"I don't know if I see the point in tutoring," I continued. "If we're going to act all the time, what do we need to know math for? We'll just hire someone to take care of our finances for us."

"To make sure no one takes advantage of you," Ted said. "To double-check their work."

I sat down on the couch and leaned into him. We both cuddled up on the tweedy material and he passed me the bottle. I took a quick drink and hissed as the liquid burned down my throat. Ted wiped the hair away from my face and we looked at each other. I stared at his mouth and wondered what it would be like to kiss a boy.

"Maybe *he'll* be my first kiss," I said, the thought bubbling out of me unceremoniously. "Maybe I'll beat Brandon to it! And then *you'll* be off the hook," I added.

Ted smiled at me with that quirk of his mouth and said, "Maybe."

But the script for *Jeanie* didn't call for any kisses, and Anthony and I finished the project without having stolen any between scenes. We separated, him to a new script, me back to *TTA*, and didn't see each other until the premiere, where we got drunk together but didn't get close enough to put our mouths on each other.

And so it goes. Anthony faded into the back of my mind, and didn't resurface until we saw each other again several years later.

BEING THIRTEEN IS excruciating. Being thirteen on a television show is even worse.

You're dealing with growth spurts, with sore emerging breasts. With worrying about starting your period, which hasn't come even though your best friend, Olive, has gotten hers, and she tells you with regret that it's terrible, but you want it to start anyway. And you have to do it all with your anxiety hidden, because you're on a show and everything you do is telegraphed to the viewers. I'm just glad that *Third Time Around* wasn't filmed in front of a live studio audience.

And being thirteen on a television show with Brandon was the worst. Gone was the promise that he'd keep his hands to himself. He seemed to enjoy the idea of his nineteen-year-old self corrupting his thirteen-year-old costar. He'd massage my neck when I was standing by the cameras and no one would do anything. I would slap his hand away, but he'd always come back, minutes later, for another rub. And no one said anything to him about his behavior. Even when I complained, nothing would happen. It was like I was alone with my angsty thoughts. Surely, if I was the only one who took issue with what Brandon was doing, it was my own fault for being too sensitive?

I wasn't too sad to lose the role of *Harriet the Spy* to Michelle Trachtenberg. By the time the film premiered, I was knee-deep in self-loathing.

"You should be glad you haven't started your period yet," Olive said to me on the phone. Now that *Full House* had wrapped, she was floating from show to show, doing one-off characters until she found a movie or another long-term project. "One time I didn't realize I had, like, started it and blood soaked through a pair of shorts on set. Wardrobe had to scramble to find another pair for me but they were a different length, you know? So now I look like I changed clothes in the middle of the episode."

I could sense her embarrassment that she tried to exude as bravado.

"It was, like, straight out of Traumarama! in *Seventeen* magazine," she added.

The last big outing I did was the Academy Awards that winter. I wore a blue checkered sundress with butterflies printed all over it, which ended at mid-knee, and a pair of wedges. I looked like I was going to a picnic in the summer, but it was February and my nipples pinched with the cold that year. Ed Hodges was nominated for *Jeanie* but didn't win. I hadn't been nominated. Anthony was shooting in Australia, some new movie about mutants, and didn't attend. But I was there. Feeling miserable and wanting the earth to swallow me whole.

I was at home in Anita for the first time in a while. When I hadn't landed *Harriet*, my mother made the executive decision for me to take a short break from working back-to-back projects and get out of Hollywood for a while. I was secretly glad. No Brandon, no neck massages.

Ashley was nine and had started pestering my parents to

let her join productions too. It bothered me. I liked being the special one in the family. I liked that I'd been able to buy my father a Porsche and rent a better house. I liked providing for my family and being the breadwinner; it made me feel like a grown-up. What would it mean if Ashley became a star, too? Would Daddy not dote on me as his little Hollywood actress anymore?

Things were cautiously better between my parents when we were in Anita that summer. I think we could credit the distance from Alex Dietrich for this change. It was as if he disappeared when we were in Texas and my parents could settle into a routine again.

"Anyway, have you heard this new band, Dial8?" Olive continued.

"Who?"

"Like, Dilate. Because your eyes dilate when you're in love. Anyway, you know, they have a total dreamboat of a singer, Corey B. You should, like, look him up. They're in the latest *YM*."

The next time my mother went to the supermarket, I slipped the newest issue of *YM* in the cart. "Hayley," my mother said exasperatedly. "These teen magazines are a waste of money." Never mind that I had been mentioned in some of them and she had framed a copy of my *Seventeen* cover with the rest of the *TTA* child stars. The photo hung over the mantel in our Anita house.

"Who is paying the bills?" I wanted to ask. But instead, I gave her a winning smile and said, "Please?" At home, I flipped the glossy pages until I found the write-up about Dial8, comprising of Trey, Dylan, Michael, RJ, and Corey. Corey was definitely Olive's type—he looked a lot like Ted, in fact, down to the swooping blond hair—but my eyes were attracted to Trey. Dark-haired, green-eyed, long nose and luscious lips. *Those are kissable lips*, I told myself as I touched the page lightly, reverently.

Trey had grown up in Jackson, Mississippi, to a rough childhood. He'd gotten into dozens of fights and was going down a "dark path," he said, but a middle school choir teacher had given him extra attention and, over time, he learned to channel his emotion into singing. He met the rest of Dial8 at a choir competition in high school and they decided to form a group. Five years later, they were breaking out, on top of the world.

I tuned into the radio immediately, hoping to hear their single. I only had to listen to three songs before "Infinite Zenith" came on. I couldn't tell which voice was Trey's in the medley of singing, but I was convinced I knew him from the very beginning.

That night, I went to sleep with the magazine tucked under my pillow and hoped I'd dream of Trey.

THE NEXT DAY, I asked my father to drive me to Columbus so I could buy Dial8's full album at a Sam Goody there. "You want to buy a CD? Why?" my father asked. "It's plastic trash." I made up the excuse that the music was "research" for a role, which he could never turn down. Anything to make the bottom line fatter. My father and I took the Porsche, ostentatious as it was, and flew down the highway.

I pored over that CD booklet and obsessed over the track listings of the album during the summer. When we went back to L.A. for the seventh season of *Third Time Around,* the CD was the last thing I packed and the first thing I unpacked. It was my most treasured object.

Olive called me the day I got back into town. "Dial8 is touring!" she said instead of a greeting. We both shrieked. I begged my mother to let me buy VIP tickets to their show—the kind of tickets that had meet-and-greets available.

"Hayley, those tickets go for hundreds of dollars," my mother said.

"And I make thousands per episode! *Pleeeease,* Mom! I'll never ask for anything else in my life. I swear it!"

She acquiesced and went to the record store for me, because I was now too recognizable to stand in line for concert tickets on my own. She bought three tickets—one for Olive, one for herself to chaperone, and mine. The total was close to two thousand dollars. Why would I care? It was a drop in the bucket as far as I was concerned. I marked my calendar for October and looked forward to it throughout filming. I even had a little picture of Trey, cut out from the *YM,* in my trailer, tacked to my mirror.

"DIAL8?" JESSICA SAYS. "You mean, those old guys who have a Vegas residency now? They play shows for old people on a nostalgia kick?"

I nod. "The very same."

"Weird."

"Not so weird. Backstreet Boys did it, didn't they?"

"Sometimes I forget how old you are, Mom," Jane says.

It's nighttime and I'm getting ready for bed. I'm not a night owl anymore. The girls will probably stay up past midnight playing video games or surfing the internet, whatever teenagers do.

"We'll talk tomorrow," I say.

"Yeah, you haven't really gotten to the point where you're locked down," Jane says.

"That comes a little later," I say. "But you need the full context of why."

Jane shrugs. "Okay."

"I didn't expect this explanation to take so long," Jessica says with a groan.

"Don't whine," I say. "We'll talk in the morning."

DIVA BEHAVIOR FROM ALDRIDGE

Third Time Around child star, Hayley Aldridge, 13, has been labeled as "difficult" on set. "She's been keeping Brandon Pike, her costar and on-screen love interest, at arm's length the entire time they've been shooting together," a source close to the production informs us. "She yelled at him the other day and held up production because she didn't want to be touched." This adverse reaction to her costar might be bad for the show, but the ratings don't show it: *Third Time Around* is tracking higher than the hugely popular *Touched by an Angel*, which is also on CBS.

CHAPTER 9

Jessica is up early the next morning, but Jane sleeps in. I putter around my giant house doing god knows what. I work out, using the Pilates machine in my exercise room. I eat more mango. I put on some coffee. Not in that order. By the time I'm back on the chaise longue outside in another bikini, Jane is up and she and her sister are sitting on the deck chairs nearby. They both lean forward with elbows on their knees, looking very much like their father.

"What happened next?" Jane asks eagerly.

I look at my daughter. Her brown hair is streaked with natural blond highlights and her eyes are the same color blue as mine. She is beautiful, perfect. To think there are two such specimens in this world makes my heart hurt with love.

"Mom?" Jessica says.

BRANDON HAD THE wherewithal to land another acting job at the same time he was supposed to be Thomas on *Third Time Around*—a plum gig on the new *Superman* movie, not as Clark Kent but as a side character. I never went to see it and therefore never learned who. But that meant that all of *my* schedules got screwy on *TTA*, because Amy and Thomas had so many scenes together, to accommodate his schedule on the movie.

Which was a pain in the ass, but it wasn't the end of the world. Until the day before the Dial8 show.

"Why does this say I'm staying until nine?" I asked one of the head writers.

"Because you're not starting until one in the afternoon" was the response.

"This can't be right. I have tickets to see Dial8 tomorrow."

"Well, you're just going to have to reschedule that, I guess."

"I can't *reschedule*. I have meet-and-greet tickets! I'm supposed to meet Trey Barnes!"

"Listen, Hayley, I know you have a crush on Trey, but—"

"I *don't* have a *crush* on *Trey*," I said emphatically.

"So, then, what's the problem? You run in the same circles. I'm sure you'll meet Trey at some other time, like if you're both hosting some awards show or something."

That comment boiled my blood. "I bought tickets—" I started again.

"Hayley, I can't change the call time for you this late in the game. It's sad but you're going to have to deal with it."

I stomped back to my trailer and wept out of frustration. I hated being Amy at that moment, hated that I was obligated to shoot this stupid show. Hated that I was going to shoot with Brandon *again* the next day and have to deal with his stupid beautiful face. In retrospect, it wasn't the end of the world. But at the time, it sure *felt* like it.

When my mother came to pick me up and I wasn't driven

out in a golf cart to meet her and she didn't see me on set, she found me still sobbing over the injustice of having to live this stupid life. She listened to me rant about missing Dial8 because of my idiotic job. She patted my back.

"You'll meet them some other time. Is it okay if I give my ticket to Olive's mom so that she can take her?"

"Fine," I spat.

The day of the concert, I felt like I was going to my own funeral. I hung out with Olive before my call time, and she gushed about how great the concert was going to be and thanked me again for the tickets. "It sucks you can't go," she said, "like, a lot, but I'll tell you all about it."

I didn't know if I wanted to hear it.

Olive's mom picked her up from my house at twelve thirty and I left for work. I was in a tizzy all day and couldn't get the right energy for the scenes we were going to shoot. More screen time with Brandon-as-Thomas, more serious talks with Oscar-as-Steve. Amy was still sitting on Steve's lap for these talks and I brought it up with Alex Dietrich. "Should she be on his knee nowadays?" I asked. "She's old enough to have a crush on a boy, maybe she should be sitting on a chair now?"

Alex wasn't sure if he wanted to give up the iconic lap-sit. Oscar seemed ambivalent, but said, "No one is too old to sit on Steve's lap! Ted, come here, sit right here," and he patted his knee. Ted looked uncomfortable but sat where he was beckoned, and Oscar jogged his leg so that Ted jiggled up and down on it like a baby. "Soothing, isn't it?" he said.

But I was in a Mood. I wanted nothing to do with the knee

anymore. "Amy is growing up to be an adult. What sort of message does it send to teenagers that it's okay for their stepdad to put them on their knee like that?"

"Whoa, whoa," Oscar said, holding up his hands. "Nothing's like that."

"Hayley, I don't like what you're insinuating here," Alex Dietrich said. "This is a family show."

"And as a member of this family, I think it's weird to sit on Oscar's knee now. No offense, Oscar," I added.

"Some offense taken," Oscar said. "Ted, what do you think?"

Ted looked like he'd rather be in his trailer sipping vodka out of a water bottle than talking about this. "It seems . . . all right to me," he said in a strangled voice.

"What!" I exclaimed.

"We'll revisit this at another date," Alex said. "We've got a long day of production ahead of us. Let's make sure we don't lose track of what we're doing now."

WHEN I TALKED to Olive on Friday, she was over the moon about the concert. "I met Corey B and he is a dream," she cooed. "I got to talk to him and he, like, told me how pretty my name was! We took a picture together and he smells *so* good, like deliciously good, you know? It sucks that you had to work, though."

"Did they play '2 Xtra 4 U'?" I said, naming one of my favorite tracks.

"Yes! You should've been there. Trey danced *so* well."

I was sullen after this conversation and sat in my trailer,

sulking. A PA had to come get me for my scenes with Brandon. I stomped out onto set with my emotions all over my face. Millie took one look at me and grimaced. "It's gonna be a long take today, folks," she said out loud to no one in particular. Her statement did not alleviate my mood. It actually—to no one's surprise—aggravated me more.

"Let's just get this over with," I snapped.

In this scene, I was supposed to be distraught because my stepdad, Steve, was in the hospital. (It was an emergency appendectomy but anything to heighten the tension, right?)

Brandon's line was "Come on, Amy, it'll be okay," with a comforting hand on my arm. But I wasn't having it.

"Did I *say* you could touch me?" I shrieked. "Did I?"

Brandon looked at Alex helplessly. "I'm supposed to put my hand on her shoulder, right?" he said. "It's in the script that I comfort Amy."

Alex nodded. "Hayley, you can't keep telling Brandon not to touch you unless you give him permission. It's in the script. You should know by now that it's going to happen."

"*We* had an *agreement*. He wouldn't touch me unless I said it was okay."

"You can see how this is slowing down production, though, can't you, Hayley? Just because you don't want to be touched today doesn't mean that you can deny your costar permission. It's part of the script."

"So *un*-make it part of the script," I said scathingly.

"Why are you being so difficult?" Brandon said exasperatedly. "Look, I've been tiptoeing around you for the past year hoping that you'd get over this power trip you're on—"

"Power trip? *Me?!*" I scoffed.

"But you're just going to have to deal with me touching you when the story calls for it."

I squeezed my eyes shut and willed the entire production—for Brandon and Alex and Millie, who I knew was lurking around here, too—to fade away. But when I opened my eyes again, there they were, looking disappointed in me. I felt my resolve sag. "Fine." I spit the word like it was poisonous. "Fine, fine. Okay."

Maybe I shouldn't have given in. It was a bad precedent, to allow carte blanche on my body, as I learned later. But when you're thirteen and the older men on the production, including the showrunner, are looking at you like you're being difficult for no reason, you relent.

Nowadays, I don't know if a showrunner would say the same things Alex Dietrich did. If an actress, especially an underage one, was that uncomfortable with a costar touching her, I believe they would rewrite the script or adjust the scene as necessary. But this was 1997. The men dominated the production. I was seen as difficult, and it was apparent that someone leaked my outburst to the media. I started being described as "hard to work with." Which, at my tender teen age, was infuriating. I was already angry most of the time because my hormones were all out of whack, but to be described as "difficult" when I had just been sticking up for myself? It was absolutely maddening.

When I read gossip nowadays, I try to read in between the lines. Is someone actually difficult, or are they young and trying to assert dominance over their own body?

CHAPTER 10

"D oes this look all right?" Olive said to me, turning in a half circle. She was wearing a black, daisy-patterned dress that was made of some sort of silky material and ended at the knee.

"Perfect," I said, assuaging her anxiety.

Olive had been an extra in *Titanic*, but as there had been hundreds, if not thousands, of extras for the biggest blockbuster movie of 1997, she didn't have enough clout to get tickets to the premiere. That's where I came in. A few well-placed phone calls and voilà! There were tickets for Hayley Aldridge, plus one, and my mother got to play chauffeur.

"Okay," Olive said, nodding, and wrapping herself in a black silk scarf like a shawl. "Let's go."

It was a mild winter evening; I was in a silky peach dress with narrow spaghetti straps and wasn't cold at all. My breasts were just coming in, making small points on the front of the dress, much to my embarrassment. I glanced with envy at Olive's chest, which was rounded with B-cups, at the very least.

It was the final week of my thirteenth year and I still hadn't started my period. I was a late bloomer and everybody knew it. Directors passed me over, even though I was long and skinny, because I was no longer cute and child-size; alternatively, I wasn't developed enough to look like a typical teenager, and my self-esteem was taking a hit. The only constant in my life was *Third Time Around*, which had a front-row seat to my development (or lack thereof).

My mother dropped us off half a block away from the theater and we walked quickly in our little two-inch heels to the rolled-out red carpet. We caught sight of Leonardo DiCaprio sauntering down the carpet by himself and squealed together.

"I can't believe he came solo!" Olive breathed to me, as we were held back among the throng of revelers, like we had a chance of miraculously becoming Leo's dates. We pushed our way through and showed our invitations before walking along the red carpet ourselves.

Titanic was a revelation. I loved all of it. The love story, the ill-fated passage, the special effects, the practical effects, the sadness. Gosh, the *sadness*. When the old couple kissed each other goodbye as the water rose in their stateroom, I sobbed. When the third-class mother put her children to sleep, knowing that they had no chance of survival, I sobbed. When the string quartet continued to play on the chaotic deck, I sobbed. And, of course, when Jack floated off into the ether, I sobbed.

Olive and I held sticky hands during the more intense parts and when the movie was over, we looked at each other with tear-stained faces and burst out laughing. "You look ridiculous," she said to me, and I retorted, "Look who's talking."

When I emerged from the restroom, Olive was standing around talking to some people I didn't know. "Hayley, this is Klein and this is Fields." The two boys each held up a hand as she rattled off their names. "And this is Joanne." A redhead with a heart-shaped face smiled at me. "They were on *October Adventure*—remember that movie I was in last year?—with me," she continued. "Anyway, do you want to go to an afterparty with them? Klein can drive."

"I don't know . . ." I hedged, wondering about my mother, who was due to pick us up soon.

"Go call your mom," she said, digging out a quarter from her impossibly tiny purse and handing it to me. I spun on my heel and found a pay phone nearby, and hoped that my mother hadn't left the house yet. But knowing her, she had. She was probably carting Ashley in the Volvo right now, just moments away from showing up at our pickup spot.

No one answered the phone. I bit my lip and wondered what I should do next. I didn't want to look uncool around Olive's friends. After a moment's hesitation, I left a message on the answering machine: "Hi, Mom. I went to an afterparty with Olive and her friends. I'll call you later."

"What'd she say?" Olive asked when I got back to the little huddling group.

"It's fine," I lied. "Let's go."

We weren't invited to any official afterparty—this turned out to be a party at Fields's house, I learned. And it was just us. I felt very awkward, me with my peach silk dress and kitten heels, sitting on the carpet in Fields's room. He and Klein, both of them named Brian so they went by their last names to differentiate, were sixteen. Joanne was fifteen.

"How'd you score an invite to *Titanic*?" Fields wanted to know. He was dark-haired, brown-eyed, his skin dark.

"I'm on *Third Time Around*," I said stiffly. "It's a popular show. I just had to ask my publicist."

"We got in because Klein's dad worked on the movie," Fields said. Klein was fair-haired and pale, with eyes so blue they looked clear in the dark room. Klein nodded.

"And you?" I asked Joanne.

She just shrugged. "I didn't have an invite. I didn't see it. My mom just dropped me off so I could hang out with the Brians."

"You missed out!" Olive said, and proceeded to spoil the movie for her. Joanne looked a little upset. I nudged Olive with my elbow.

"*Anyway*," Klein said, shifting his legs so that he was leaning backward on the bed. He dipped his arm between the wall and the mattress and came up with a bottle of whiskey.

This would be my first time drinking without Ted and I felt a little strange about that. Who would I giggle incessantly with? Whose shoes would I dance on?

"And for the ladies," Fields said, pulling out a baggie from seemingly nowhere, "we have the best." The stuff inside looked like a dehydrated plant. I'd never smoked weed before. I wasn't opposed to it, though. Klein and Fields seemed like nice enough guys, and I was with Olive. She would make sure nothing bad happened to me.

Fields rolled a joint like he'd done it a thousand times, lit it, and took a hit. He passed it along to Olive, who partook and then passed it to me. I put my lips on the wet paper and inhaled. I coughed immediately.

It took a little while for the pot to affect me, maybe—I assumed—because I coughed it out so quickly. But after a while, I started feeling softer around the edges, and I wasn't as anxious about lying to my mother anymore.

We drained the whiskey bottle and someone set it down on the floor, sideways. "Anyone want to play Spin the Bottle?" Joanne asked with a raise of her eyebrows.

Olive was in, but I felt skeptical about the whole thing. "I don't want to," I said, loosened up enough after a few drinks and my singular hit.

Olive rolled her eyes and told the others, "She's holding out for Trey Barnes."

"From Dial8? Really?" Fields asked.

"I met him once, at a Starbucks," Joanne said. "He was actually super nice! I wasn't expecting that from a star like him."

"Of course he's nice," I said hotly. "Trey Barnes is perfect."

"He even gets his own coffee," Klein quipped. I gave him a little glare.

"So Hayley will sit it out," Joanne said. "But the rest of us are in?"

AFTER KLEIN SOBERED up, he drove all of us home. One by one, people left the car, floating away in their cloud of weed perfume. "Got any mints?" I asked Klein when we were the only two left, and he reached into the center console to hand me a tube of Life Savers. "Thanks."

We drove silently. I didn't know what to talk about, so I

didn't say anything. When he pulled up to my house, he killed the engine and looked over at me. It was a weird look. I didn't like it. Before I could unlock the passenger door, he spoke.

"Why are you waiting on Trey Barnes?"

"I told you, he's perfect," I said, my defenses already up.

"You don't even know him. What about someone who's right in front of you?"

"What, so I should kiss *you*? I don't even *know* you."

He leaned over toward me and I scrunched myself back into the seat. I was still wearing my seat belt and it pinned me into place.

"Listen, Hayley—"

"No," I whimpered. My hands scrabbled on the window edge and somehow unlocked the door, but I couldn't open it. He was getting closer with his face, his breath on mine. I hid my chin in my right shoulder. I was pedaling the floor with my feet, trying to get away.

The door yanked open and my mother stood in front of us. "Hayley Dakota Aldridge, you get inside *this instant*," she said menacingly. I was so relieved to see her, even though I could tell that she was furious. As soon as she had materialized, Klein shrank back against his seat like he hadn't just tried to kiss me. I undid my seat belt and dumped myself onto the grass, unceremoniously getting my peach dress wet on the knees from the watered lawn.

"You," she said, addressing Klein. "Who the hell are you?"

"I'm Brian Klein, son of Richard Klein . . ."

"Do I look like I give a rat's ass who your father is? What are you doing with my daughter?"

"I was just giving her a ride home" came the faint answer, as I climbed to my feet and ran into the house. Ashley giggled. "Oooh you're in *trouble*," she sang.

It was only a few minutes later that my mother came inside. "What the hell do you think you're doing, Hayley?" she said to me. "Ashley, to your room. Hayley, you stay right there and explain yourself."

"I wanted to go to this afterparty," I mumbled.

"So you left without telling me? Hayley, you have no idea how worried I was. I sat in the car in front of that theater for an hour, waiting for you. When you and Olive didn't show up, I was convinced someone had kidnapped you. I drove back to the house not knowing what else to do and got your stupid message on the answering machine." She slapped her forehead, like she couldn't believe it. "And now you come home reeking of marijuana and alcohol, kissing some random boy in the front seat of his car? That's it, young lady. You are grounded."

"Grounded?" I squeaked. "Wait, I wasn't kissing *anybody*—"

"Grounded," she repeated. "No phone, no play dates, no premieres, no birthday party, no nothing. You go to work and you do your tutoring and that's it. For a month. Go to your room."

I got up to leave, deflated but ready to change out of the now-damp dress.

"I'm buying a cell phone," Mom said to herself. "You hear that, Hayley? I'm getting a cell phone so that you can call me when you have another harebrained idea like this. Teenagers."

She threw her hands up in the air exasperatedly. "Teenagers!"

CHAPTER 11

My fourteenth birthday came and went, and there was no celebration. It was the worst birthday in my memory. But an even worse thing began to happen at work—Thomas and Amy's relationship started going to the next level. The network began talking about Amy's first kiss as part of February sweeps.

No matter that I was fourteen and Brandon was twenty at this point. As long as it happened under the gaze of a camera, kissing between us was considered strictly professional. Whenever Brandon saw me, he pulled out a canister of Binaca and sprayed the peppermint taste into his mouth, as if to express how excited he was about the kiss. Anything would be better than that onion breath, I guessed.

During the table read, Brandon and I sat across from each other as he munched on an onion bagel with chive cream cheese from craft services. He read his lines casually, in a droning voice, as if he didn't care what happened. I tried my best not to roll my eyes when my line—"I'm obsessed with you"—came out of my mouth.

"Then the kiss happens," narrated Alex Dietrich.

Brandon winked at me. "Can't wait to break you in," he

said.

"Brandon, that's not in the script. Continue with your lines, please." Alex didn't sound amused.

Ted and I exchanged a look over the table. His was a sympathetic glance while mine was a pained "help me" expression.

After the table read, I ducked into Ted's trailer.

"Help," I said.

"What's up?" Ted said, even though he knew well enough what I was going to say.

"You told me you'd be my first kiss when the time came," I said.

"I did say that, huh?" Ted said. "But Hayley, I don't think it's a good idea."

"Why not?" I said plaintively. I could hear the whine in my voice.

Ted's hand touched my chin and raised it gently. We were looking eye to eye. My breath caught in my throat.

"You're fourteen," he said. He smelled like mint and vodka.

"So?"

"I'm nineteen."

"And? You *promised*. We had a deal."

"I just can't, Hayley."

I jerked my head back so his hand fell away. "This isn't fair! You promised me. And now my first kiss is going to be with *Brandon*? It's supposed to be special!"

"You think it'd be special with me?" he argued. "We're just costars. We're just friends."

"Better you than Brandon! That's what you said, wasn't it?"

He put both hands on my shoulders. He leaned over and gave me a soft hug. I could feel his lips move as he murmured into my ear.

"Your first kiss is not going to be the one that you have with Brandon on camera," he said matter-of-factly. "That's just acting. Your first kiss off camera should be with someone you really care about. And that isn't me. I know how you feel about me, Hayley. We're just friends."

He was saying that a lot, *just friends*. Almost regrettably. It made me want to shove him.

Were we just friends? I thought of Ted as more than a friend. More than a brother. He was like someone I knew on a deeper level, but I wouldn't call him a *boyfriend* or anything like that. *Boyfriend* would have cheapened the connection.

I just knew *him*, inside and out. His spiraling anxiety, his jittery presence on set. I *knew* him. Or so I thought.

"Shit," I said. I never swore out loud, but this called for it. "I'm going to have to put my lips on Brandon's mouth. It's going to be disgusting."

"You're a professional actress. You can do it," Ted said.

"Are you sure *you* don't want to break me in?" I said hopefully.

"Break you in? Like a pair of shoes? Come *on*, Hayley."

"It's just . . ." I sidled closer. "I don't know what to do. How to do it. I'll look like a fool on camera."

"I'm sure you'll get a couple of takes and you'll get used to it."

A couple of takes? Doing it more than once with Brandon?

Sick.

"Blech," I said.

"You can do it," Ted said, rubbing my arms in encouragement. "If you need motivation, just think of how much it'll piss off Millie."

I WAS APPREHENSIVE when I stepped on set that day. Alex Dietrich pulled me to the side and said, "We're going to make this as comfortable as possible for you. We've got a closed set today and only essential personnel will be on-site. It'll be small and intimate and hopefully you'll feel only a little awkward doing this in front of us."

"Thanks, Alex," I said, a little bit of relief lifting some of the heaviness from my chest.

Brandon was hanging around the soundstage but didn't approach me. Probably better that way.

April, my makeup artist, brushed one last coat of lip gloss on me before we began. Plum lip gloss. Amy's first-kiss color. I wondered if there would be a rash of buyers for the color once the episode aired. It was a really flattering shade.

I saw Millie standing by the B camera and then she was shooed away. I relaxed a little more. Millie wouldn't be watching my first on-screen kiss. Maybe this wouldn't be as awful as I thought it would.

"First team in position!"

The stand-ins moved off the set and the stars of the show took their places in the house's kitchen. Brandon stood next to me. I've forgotten the lines leading up to this scene, something cheesy probably. We were to exchange our lines and then I—Amy—would say, "I'm obsessed with you."

He would take my head in his hands and look at me seriously, then we'd lean closer and . . .

The sensation of our mouths touching was strange. Wetter than I expected. And that pervasive onion-bagel smell persisted, even underneath the Binaca.

"Cut!"

I wiped my lips on my forearm. Couldn't he have brushed his teeth?

"That was good, but Hayley, you seemed surprised. You should be more tender, if that makes sense. This is the guy you've been crushing on for two years falling for you back. It should make you want to melt in his arms."

"Got it." I scuffed my toe into the fake kitchen's linoleum. More lip gloss application.

"Quiet on set. Rolling!"

Amy said her line. Cue the kiss.

This time, Brandon deepened the kiss while we were filming it. I felt his tongue push past my lips and drag on my front teeth. I gasped in surprise and then his tongue was massaging mine, in my mouth. I broke away.

"Hayley, you acted surprised again!" Alex said.

"I'm sorry, it's just—" I glared at Brandon, who looked at me innocently.

"Let's go again."

We repeated the scene several more times, and Brandon used his tongue in every take. I had to endure. What was I supposed to do? I didn't realize that the tongue was extra. It took something like ten takes for the kiss to look right, for me to stop struggling against the onslaught of slobber that was taking place in my mouth.

I walked into Ted's trailer when the shoot was done, and went straight for the mouthwash sitting on his tiny bathroom sink. He leaned on the doorjamb. "That bad, huh?" he said.

"It was awful." I could barely keep from crying.

"The real thing is much better. I swear."

"If that's what kissing is like, with two tongues flopping around in your mouth—"

"Wait, he *Frenched* you?"

"What's the difference?" I said miserably.

"There's a huge difference! That asshole! He stuck his tongue in your mouth?"

In a small voice I said, "Yeah."

"Damn it," he said. "A first kiss should be sweet and tender and *simple*. A French kiss makes it so much more awkward. That jerk."

"So it wasn't supposed to be that bad?" I said, anger now stewing in me.

"No, Hayley, it wasn't supposed to be that bad."

I flew out of the trailer and knocked on Brandon's door. He opened it. He had his shirt off.

"You—you!" I screeched.

"Me, me?" he said innocently.

"You used your tongue when you shouldn't've!"

He smiled a winning smile at me. "I was just trying to make

it special for you. I knew it was your first."

"You *ruined* my first-kiss experience!"

"Whoa, now."

I began slapping him on his arms and chest in rage. "You defiled me!"

"Hey stop. Security!"

I was crying now. "I can't believe you!"

As security hauled me away, kicking and screaming, still reaching for him, wanting blood, Millie staring open-mouthed from the side of the trailer, he called after me, "You're welcome, sweetheart."

FAMILY FEUD

Things are not copacetic on the set of *Third Time Around*.
Sources tell us that child star Hayley Aldridge, 14, who plays
Amy, had to be physically restrained after a temper tantrum
aimed at Brandon Pike, who plays her love interest, Thomas.
We have a diva on our hands!

CHAPTER 12

The kiss was a sensation. February sweeps brought the highest ratings yet for *Third Time Around*, and both Brandon and I were nominated for Cutest Couple at the Tween Choice Awards that year. Alex Dietrich warned me that the crowd would expect a kiss if Brandon and I won, to which I replied, "Blech," with a flap of my hand.

"You're a shoo-in," Alex said. "Just be prepared."

I asked Ted to be my date. I was *not* going to go to this with only Brandon. No way, no how. Ted suggested we get dinner beforehand. "These awards shows always go for so long, and I'm starving by the end of them," he said. He arranged for a limo to pick us up, drive us to the restaurant, and then take us from there to the Pavilion.

My mother knew and liked Ted, so she didn't give me any shit when the limo arrived. Ted looked very sharp in a navy-blue button-down that brought out the color of his eyes and a pair of crisp jeans. I wore a navy dress with flowy sleeves, to match Ted's shirt, my hair down past my shoulders, and my now-signature kitten heels. Mom watched me get into the limo and told Ted, "Be careful. Precious cargo!"

"We'll tell the driver to be very safe," Ted said, adjusting his cuffs before climbing in after me. We rolled down the window and waved goodbye to her. Ashley stood in the doorway of the house, clutching one arm, and didn't wave back. I could feel her jealousy in that moment.

The mood in the limo was buoyant. Ted served me some champagne in a pretty glass flute and I took tiny sips, careful not to get drunk before the show. He, however, swallowed his glass in two big gulps and poured himself another. I didn't say anything, though. He was older than me and knew his limits. By the time we arrived at the restaurant, he'd downed several glasses and was looking a little bit rumpled. When he saw me eyeing him, he said, "Don't worry. All I need is a little food in me and I'll be good to go."

The restaurant—I can't remember which one we went to now—was gorgeous, but all I recall is how mortified I was that I couldn't eat in front of my date. I ordered a salad and sat there picking at it while he had something substantial, like a steak.

"Why aren't you eating?" he asked me at one point, and I had to make up something on the spot.

"I don't want my stomach to pooch out," I said. It was already kind of bloated, and my lower back hurt for no reason.

Ted surprised me by nodding in agreement. "All those vegetables, all that fiber, they'd definitely bloat me up," he said. "That's why I got the meatloaf." He took another bite and chewed thoughtfully. "Do you want some of mine? Or maybe we can ask the chef to add chicken or something to yours."

"I'm okay. I'm nervous," I said.

"Don't be!" He smiled at me with that lopsided *Bop* heart-throb grin, dropped his fork, and grasped my hand across the table. "It's going to be fun. Thanks for inviting me."

"Ted?" I asked hesitantly, as he scooped up some mashed potatoes. "What is anxiety like?"

He was quiet for a moment and then looked me in the eyes. "You've seen it," he said quietly. "Remember that time I was pacing in my trailer before I had to go out and work with Oscar? It's this . . . spiraling feeling. Like there's a Slinky in your chest and it's coiling tighter and tighter around your heart."

"And the drinking helps?"

"Yeah. It's like putting out a fire, almost. Dampening it. I get a little less careful, a little more carefree. And then I don't feel as weird." He smiled at me. "I got anxiety before picking you up tonight, too, if you want to know the truth."

"What? Why?" I wanted to know.

"Because. This is a big deal for you. I know it's just a silly kid's awards show to some people, but to be nominated for anything—even a best couple award—is a huge accomplishment, Hayley. Remember how you didn't want to do that kiss, and Brandon Frenched you anyway, and you got through it like a damn professional? I'm so proud of you. And I didn't want to fuck it up by taking you to the wrong place or being an embarrassment to you in any way."

"You could never embarrass me," I said truthfully.

He touched the small of my back on our way out of the restaurant and back into the limo, guiding me gently through the throng of paparazzi—called in by another restaurant patron, most likely—who were taking our photo. The flashes made me dizzy. By the time we arrived at the Pavilion, I was in full panic mode and unsure what to do with my hands.

Ted solved that problem by holding my hand as we walked down the red carpet, like a true date. "Hayley! Hayley!" came the cries. "Ted! Are you two an item? When did this happen?"

I dropped his hand immediately and smiled as nonchalantly as I could. "Ted is my date this evening," I said as primly as possible. "But we're not dating."

"Why not?" came the screams.

Why not? I wondered in my head. *He's like my brother and my costar and that's weird, that's why not.* But I didn't say anything in response. I composed my face as carefully as possible, my "Hayley Aldridge is a diva" face, and stood through the photos as best as I could.

"Hayley! Hayley! What's all this about you yelling at Brandon after the on-set kiss? Why did you attack him, Hayley?"

My smile turned into a grimace and Ted ushered me through the maelstrom until we got through the actual doors and into more organized chaos. Ushers brought us to our seats in the auditorium. Brandon was already there, dressed up in a black button-down and white pants, looking like a reverse waiter.

On his arm was Millie.

I was surprised to see her, but didn't say anything. I wanted to know if this was a couple-y thing for them, or if Brandon just asked his costar for moral support, like I had with Ted. But it was certain that Millie thought it was a real date. She clutched Brandon's arm like he was going to run away if she let go.

My distaste toward Brandon had not subsided. I was still angry with him for ruining my first kiss. But we air-kissed on each cheek for the cameras' sake, if any were recording, and we sat down, all four of us in a row facing the stage, like we were at a basketball game together. We knew the value of looking cohesive. Even if the tabloids knew we weren't really friends.

The show was a good one, as far as awards shows go. Geared toward teens and children, the hosts were entertaining and awards were given out swiftly. Acceptance speeches were succinct and the performers got on stage and off fairly quickly. We sat through ninety minutes of self-congratulating chatter, and then the Cutest Couple Award was being announced.

The pain in my back was now excruciating. And then, when I readjusted my legs, I felt a tiny gush. A gush that should not have existed.

"Oh," I said, giving a little gasp. "I think I need to use the restroom."

"Now?" Brandon said. "But they're about to announce Cutest Couple next."

"Now." I said it urgently, and something about my voice made Millie look up with curiosity.

"I'll go with," she offered, and for once, I accepted Millie's presence.

We hustled to the restroom and I enclosed myself in a cubicle, wrenching my dress up before I even had the door locked all the way. Millie stayed outside the stall, with her shoes visible from the space below my door. "What's wrong?" she drawled in a bored voice.

I didn't need Millie's hot-and-cold now. I needed to know what was going on with my underparts. I yanked down my underwear and saw a dark brown stain. My heart froze in my throat.

"I shit myself," I whispered in wonder. But that wasn't right. My stomach wasn't upset. Nothing had happened that made me think I'd done that.

"Are you sure?" Millie said. "Wipe and see."

So I did. And the toilet paper came back bright red with blood.

"I'm bleeding!" I said, panicked.

Millie was quiet on the other side of the door. "Well, do you have a tampon?" she finally asked after a long pause.

"No," I said, tears springing to my eyes. I didn't know what to do.

"Okay, here." She tried to pass me something underneath the door, a little white plastic-wrapped package roughly the shape of a crayon. "I always come prepared."

"What am I supposed to do with this?" I said. "I've never used one before."

Millie sighed. Then, with great detail, she explained how I was supposed to unwrap the tampon and grip it with two fingers like a fat cigarette, thumb on the applicator end, and insert it into myself. "Put a leg up on the toilet seat to make the angle easier," she suggested.

"Who's in there?" a different voice asked, and Millie had the wherewithal to ignore the question. How embarrassing, for my first period to happen during an awards show, and to not know how to insert a tampon either! I didn't want anyone to know that Hayley Aldridge, fourteen, was dealing with her period.

I was sweating, but I was able to do it. I rearranged my dress and stepped out of the cubicle, wiping the sweat off my upper lip with my wrist. I washed my hands. Millie's and my eyes met in the mirror.

"Thanks," I said.

Millie looked uncomfortable. "No problem," she said. "Ready to go back?"

I turned around and looked at my backside in the mirror, trying to spy a stain. Had I caught the bleeding in time? Other girls were looking at me, but they were surprisingly nice. They commiserated with me about starting a period during an awards show. "Bad luck," said Jessica Alba, wiping her hands with a paper towel and smiling with her eyes before leaving.

"Wait. Millie. Look at me. Look. At. Me." I made her look into my eyes. "Are you *sure* there's no mark? I'm not going up on that stage if I have a stain on my butt."

Millie nodded. "You can't see anything," she said.

But when we rushed back to our seats, we found that the show had moved on to Best Musical Act. "You missed it!" Brandon hissed when I was seated again. "I had to go up there by myself like a ninny!"

"I'm sorry," I said, "but it couldn't be helped."

"What, did you get your period or something?" he snarked.

I could feel my face turning warm with embarrassment.

"Really, Hayley? You can't control that shit?"

"If I knew how, I wouldn't have missed our moment!" I hissed back. *Could* it be controlled? From what I could tell, my period arrived without preamble and ruined a perfectly good pair of underwear.

"I can't wait to see what the tabloids say about this," Brandon groaned.

I sat miserably with my shoulders hunched and my mouth in a perpetual frown. If a camera zeroed in on me, I would look as bad as I felt. I could barely even muster the energy to clap when Dial8 won Best Musical Act and Trey Barnes appeared *in person, onstage* to accept the award with his bandmates. Ted put his arm around my shoulder and whispered in my ear, "Are you okay?"

"Fine," I grumbled. My back hurt, I had cramps, and I could feel the phantom drip of blood even though I knew I had a tampon in. I would have to tell Olive about this. Worst first period ever. It might even be worse than her tale of getting it on set.

AFTER THE SHOW, all I wanted to do was go home and curl up in a ball, wearing comfy pajamas. Ted could tell what I was feeling somehow, but he still asked me if I wanted to go to any afterparties. I was about to instruct him to take me home when I caught sight of the Best Musical Act winners sauntering by. "Let's celebrate at Julian's," I could hear one of them say.

Was this it? Was this the way I was going to meet Trey Barnes? I turned to Ted. "Let's go to Julian's," I said.

Julian's was a bar and bistro in Hollywood, on par with the

Ivy in terms of celebrity sightings and hangouts.

"Are you sure? You look like you just want to go home and sleep," Ted said.

I was determined not to let an opportunity like this slip from my fingers again. I'd paid for a meet-and-greet that I had missed; I wanted to actually meet Trey. "I'm sure."

Ted led me to the limo and instructed the driver on where to go. I sat primly in the back, rooting around in the stash of bottles of drinks for some painkillers. "Do you have any Tylenol back here?" I asked.

"No, ma'am," the driver said.

I pouted.

"I have something better," Ted said, and produced a small baggie with some powdery substance in it. "A little bit of this and you won't even notice whatever's ailing you."

I squinted at it. "Is that cocaine?" I asked.

"I thought it would be fun," Ted said, waving the baggie under my nose like he wanted me to smell it. "Are you chicken?"

"Fine, sure," I said, wanting my period pain to leave.

I could tell that Ted was excited to share this journey with me. He painstakingly made two lines of coke on top of a small mirror he had, sifting through the powder while the limo swayed back and forth along the streets of Los Angeles. He rolled up a dollar bill and offered it to me first, but I wanted to watch him to see how to do it. He waited until we were stopped at a light to snort his line. Then I mimicked him.

The first thing that hit me was pain in the back of my throat, which felt like the same burning sensation when you accidentally get water up your nose in the pool. Then numbness. "Wow," I said, blinking rapidly, trying to make sense of what was going on. There was a drip in the back of my throat and I coughed to clear it.

"Right?" Ted said.

I ran my tongue over my teeth, but it was numb too.

My period pain was gone. By the time we rolled up to Julian's, I was feeling immortal. And horny.

When we pushed through the doors of Julian's, I was a woman on a mission. I homed in on Trey Barnes like a missile and walked straight toward him. He was standing at the bar with a few of his bandmates sipping a beer. "I'm Hayley," I said, once I reached him. A slow smile spread over his beautiful face.

"Hi, Hayley," he replied.

I scooted even closer to him and placed my arms around his shoulders. I could hear the rest of Dial8 whoop and holler. "I love you," I murmured into his hair.

"She is *messed up*," someone said. I whipped around to face them.

"I have *priorities*," I said. "My priority is to tell this glorious human that I love him." And then I turned back around and took Trey Barnes's mouth into mine.

This, this was my real first kiss. I could feel it roiling inside me, this kiss that was devastating me inside and out. I touched his tongue with mine, pressing hard because all I could feel was pressure, no sensation, and I wanted the memory of the imprint of his tongue. Then suddenly I was being pulled away, our saliva was parting, and Ted was holding my shoulders.

"Whoa there," I heard him say. "Sorry. She's just a little high."

"I'll say," Trey said. "She must be on some good shit."

Then, Trey turned to the bar and wrote something on a cocktail napkin. "Hayley, page me when you want to talk. I'll call you whenever." He tucked the napkin into my palm. I stared at him in wonder.

"Yes, okay, yes, I will page you," I chirped.

And that is how I met Trey Barnes.

DIVA ALERT

Hayley Aldridge is such a diva that she wouldn't even go on-stage at the Tween Choice Awards to accept the Cutest Couple Award with costar Brandon Pike! Sources say that Aldridge, 14, hates her costar so much that she stood him up during the awards ceremony, for the kiss that took place on *Third Time Around*. Pike was left to pick up the award by himself. Poor Brandon!

CHAPTER 13

By sticking your tongue in his mouth? *That* is how you met Trey Barnes?" Jane says disgustedly.

"Why are you telling us this, Mom?" Jessica asks.

"It's all relevant," I say.

I flick on TMZ. I'd been curious to see what they'd been saying about me. The number of cards and letters with #helphayley on them have been increasing lately and I want to know what's going on in the outside world.

"Wait, how old was Trey when you were fourteen?" Jane asks.

"Twenty-two," I answer.

"So you were disgusted by kissing a twenty-year-old on the show, but fine with kissing a twenty-two-year-old after an awards show, on the same night you started your first period? Am I missing something here?" Jessica questions.

"Also, why are you telling us about your drug use? Shouldn't you be keeping all that stuff a secret from us until we're, like, thirty-five?" Jane continues.

"It's all relevant," I repeat.

TMZ isn't reporting anything about me yet. I bide my time.

I eat more mango, then decide to make a salad, while the volume is turned all the way up on the TV. I place the mango on the salad. It's delicious.

"Do we have to listen to this drivel?" Jane says.

Ah, there it is. "Hayley Aldridge is a shut-in in her own house," the reporter says. "She can't do anything without her dad's permission because of this conservatorship."

"For those of our viewers who don't know what a conservatorship is, can you explain it to them?" another voice says.

"Yeah. So there are conservatorships of the estate, which gives the conservator the right to manage all your financial affairs. And then there's conservatorship of the person. Hayley is under both. It's a legal death. She doesn't have the ability to sign anything, enter into contracts for herself, anything like that."

"Why would her dad keep her under that sort of thing?"

"Well, no one knows why she's been kept under it for so long," comes the answer. "It made sense in 2007. But for it to continue on for this long, it makes zero sense. All I can gather is that her parents are trying to milk money out of her estate. Hayley's supporters are gathered around protesting for her freedom in downtown L.A. today." There's a scene of people with signs that say #helphayley on them, marching around outside a courthouse.

I frown and turn off the television. The girls look at me.

"Is that true?" Jane asks.

"Are Granddad and Grandma really just using you for money?" Jessica wants to know.

"This is why I need your help," I say to my daughters. I can feel my face turn taut with severity.

"I'm in," Jessica says, fingers tapping on the countertop like she's ready to type a manifesto.

"Me too," Jane says.

I WOULDN'T SAY that Trey Barnes and I started dating immediately. He was twenty-two and I was fourteen, for one thing, and my mother would have never allowed it. But that first kiss, heightened by cocaine, lived rent-free in my head for days, weeks, months after it happened. I was already well and truly obsessed—with Dial8, with Trey.

After Ted dropped me off at my house, I crept to my room hiding how high I was, and all I could do was think about Trey. I wondered when would be the best time to page him. If he'd actually answer and call me back. Then I wondered if my mother would interfere with the phone and that stopped me from sending any pages for at least a week.

"Mom, I started my period," I said to her the next morning.

"Good morning to you too," she said, pouring herself a cup of coffee.

"Do we have any Kotex?" I asked.

"Under the sink." She sipped her coffee and looked me over. "Maybe this means you'll grow some boobs. You're flat as a pancake right now."

I hugged my chest and went to the bathroom. All we had were pads. It felt like I was wearing a marshmallow between my legs.

"Mom, I also want a cell phone," I said when I reemerged. "Think about it. You have one. I should have one too. Pay phones are going to become obsolete and then where will I be?"

"You'll be at the studio where there are land lines everywhere," my mother said.

"I still want one," I said. "It's my money. Let me buy one."

She straightened up. I only ever asked for things using "my money" when I was serious about them. "Fine," she said. "We'll go get one after you wrap tomorrow."

That gave me an entire Sunday to dream and to plan my life with Trey Barnes. I sat in my room, ignoring the homework that the on-set tutors had given me, and daydreamed my eventual wedding. I'd wear lilac—so much prettier than white or ivory, I decided. It'd be a fluffy princess dress with a long train and an even longer veil that trailed behind me. We'd get married in a huge church full of friends and well-wishers, and during the reception Trey would sing a custom song he'd written just for me, with the rest of Dial8 singing backup.

It was a full-proof plan. All I needed was to grow up—I could squeeze by in three more years—and then we'd be together forever.

I felt someone watching me. I glanced up from my pillow and saw Ashley, hovering in the doorway. She looked sullen. "So you got your period," she said snidely.

"How'd you know?"

"I heard you and Mom talking about it."

My heart softened toward her just a bit. She must be curious about what it was like. "It sucks," I offered. "I wish it hadn't happened."

"Especially during an awards show," she added.

"Especially that," I agreed.

"Do you really think Mom is going to make you get implants?" she said suddenly.

"What? What makes you say that?"

"I overheard her talking on the phone. She says that if you're not growing them for real soon, she's going to convince you to get them surgically." Ashley sounded smug.

That gave me a whole new thing to think about. "Well, considering she hasn't even told *me* about this plan, I don't think it's serious . . ."

Ashley's face turned even more smug. "You'll see. She'll bring it up soon."

MOM AND I went to get my first cell phone after *TTA* wrapped the next evening. It was a candy-red Nokia, a little brick of my very own. The starstruck Cingular employee asked for a photo with me.

With my own private line now secured, I was able to page Trey Barnes without worrying my mom—or heaven forbid, Ashley—would pick up the phone when I was on it.

At first, I was cautious when paging Trey: once a day, only, and if he called, that was a good day. But when his schedule became apparent—he would never respond before ten A.M., for instance, because he was training at the gym or working with the rest of Dial8; he was never available between five and ten

P.M. because that's when a concert would be happening, but he was always game to talk around three in the afternoon, right when there was a lull in filming on set—I would page with abandon, hoping that he would call me back and we could chat for a little while.

Trey, for his part, never acted like I was annoying him. He seemed to really enjoy talking to me on the phone. He would start off every conversation with "Hey girl," in a soft tone, sounding just like the interlude of one of their songs.

What *did* we talk about? What does a fourteen-year-old discuss with a twenty-two-year-old? I can't remember. But I do recall thinking that Trey "got" me. That we were a good couple. That me paging him *143* at night was romantic, and not at all silly.

We didn't go "out." We didn't hang out in public. But we spoke at least three times a week, if not more.

As ASHLEY HAD predicted, Mom came to talk to me about a boob job. Though she didn't say it in those words. "A surgical procedure to enhance your breasts," she said instead. I thought she was coming into my room to tell me off about how many minutes I'd gone over the cell phone plan talking to Trey, but instead she broached the subject of the boob job.

"Mom, I'm fourteen," I said, defenses already up. "I know this is ridiculous to hear, but I'm going to keep growing."

"I don't know if that's the case," she said. "By the time I was your age, I was already a C cup. I worry about you."

"This isn't fatal," I said, even though in my mind I thought that it kind of was. But the possibility of going under the knife to make myself bustier scared the crap out of me.

"It might as well be fatal to your career," she pointed out. "Your last callback was for what, *Only Human*? And they're not coming in as thickly as they used to. It's because you don't look your age, honey. You're tall, that's for certain, but you're not curvy enough to be fourteen."

I wrapped my arms around my chest self-consciously. It was true, I hadn't gotten many callbacks since my growth spurt. I looked too gangly and tall to play a child anymore, but I had no hips or breasts to speak of yet and so lost out on the teenage roles. I was feeling very sore about losing out on the dual role of twins on *The Parent Trap*, which I'd auditioned for. Lindsay Lohan, who was two years my junior, had scooped up the plum roles. I had to face the fact: I wasn't cute anymore. And my lack of breasts made it so that I wasn't sexy enough to land older characters.

Maybe Mom was right. Maybe I needed to get a boob job.

"Aren't there bras that can fake it?" I asked. "I saw an ad for a water bra . . ."

"Well, yes," Mom said, "but if you get a role where you're supposed to be in a swimsuit or something, it'll be hard to fake."

"Can I think about it?" I asked. "Maybe wait until I'm sixteen? Maybe they'll come in, like wisdom teeth."

"Some wisdom teeth *never* come in," Mom said warningly. "They just sit in your gums and make trouble."

With that in mind, I had to go into work the next day thinking about the betrayal of my body. I could barely keep my attention from wandering during on-set tutoring.

The thing about on-set tutoring: it's never enough. It's just the smallest amount of work to make sure you're getting by, that you can read, do simple math, understand basic history, but if you were like me, you were never going to excel at a subject unless it really interested you. The only reason my vocabulary wasn't shit was because I read magazines in between takes and they introduced me to new jargon like "titillated." Ted was able to drink during his tutoring because it was the bare minimum of attention needed to get through the courses. So when I say that I was having a hard time passing my tutoring because I was distracted by my breast predicament, I mean that it was really on my mind.

I finally dismissed my tutor and paged Trey. He called me back with a soft, "Hey girl."

"Trey," I asked, "would you like me more if I had bigger boobs?"

We had been talking for only a month, and had never gone out in private or public yet, so it was a strange question to ask. A bold one, anyway.

I could tell he was surprised. "Well," he said hesitantly. "I don't know."

"Because my mom wants me to get a boob job."

"How do you feel about that?" No *aren't you a little young* or *why are you asking me?*

"Scared!"

"So tell her that."

"I want to know what *you* think," I said.

"Well, all you need is a handful," Trey said, laughing. "So if you do it, don't go too big, okay?"

OLIVE GREEN AND I reunited on the set of *Only Human* that summer. I played Charlotte, a human girl who meets an extraterrestrial named Pam, played by Olive in a few prosthetics, and teaches her how to act like a person. Conflict arises when Pam is sought after by alien hunters, and the two girls—who are now friends—have to elude them. Think *E.T.* but without the Reese's Pieces or the scary moments. It was an indie film without a big budget and I was overjoyed to be on a movie set again—something different from *TTA*! And with my best friend!

I had the time of my life for the first half of the filming. I was on set with my friend, and we had a blast. We'd giggle through our goofs and spent time in each other's trailers. I wore a push-up bra with so much padding, I increased my breast size from 32AA to 32B. I couldn't help admiring my form in the mirror of my trailer every time I wore the bra. I wore it during fittings, too, though luckily the tailors who worked on *Only Human* stayed mum about my small natural breasts.

The director, John Yelp, seemed to be a kind man—at first. He seemed genuinely excited to meet me during my audition and said he was a huge fan of *Third Time Around*. I wasn't even asked to lose weight for the role, which was a relief, as I was already cutting my calories down to the bare minimum.

My new thing was watermelon. I requested a freshly cut watermelon in my trailer every day and I popped pieces of it like candy every chance I got. I drank watermelon juice instead of regular water and if I got too dizzy, I would eat a hard-boiled egg for protein. Olive was on the Atkins diet instead, and her food made me want to throw up. She ate red meat with nothing else on her plate. We adored each other but had to eat in separate trailers to keep the peace. She claimed the watermelon juice smelled so sugary that it made her feel sick.

One day, John Yelp called me into his office. He was forty-something, with a full head of hair and a lean build. I don't remember what he wanted to talk to me about.

He spoke to me and brushed the front of his pants across my shoulder.

I remember I hastily stood up, understanding that something was definitely wrong. I backed out of the room, and when I reached the doorway, I yanked the doorknob and walked quickly out into the hall, holding back tears. I could hear John Yelp saying, "If you tell anyone—" before the door snapped shut between us.

I knew the rest. If I told anyone, I would reap the destruction of my career, of my livelihood. You didn't live through Hollywood without hearing rumors, every once in a while, about something like that.

I just never thought it would happen to me, and so young. Fourteen.

Of course, I told Olive. She listened in rapt attention and then looked away from me. She had her chin balanced on her hand and she tapped her lips with her fingers. "Remember

Joanne, from *October Adventure*? She told me that that happened to her too. But it wasn't the director. It was the sound guy. He, like, flashed her. Scum." She shook her head. "It hasn't happened to me yet but if it does, I'm gonna tell *everybody*."

Yet somehow, I didn't think she would. She didn't encourage me to say anything. And who would I tell?

I've never told anyone else about this before. I didn't know how to say it. It was not the actual touching. It was the intention. This man in power knew that he could make or break my career and he chose to try to touch me. It was sickening. It *is* sickening, still.

Olive was having such a good time on the production, and somewhere, in my lizard brain, I wondered why *she* hadn't been targeted. She had the bigger breasts, after all. But maybe I exuded some sort of vulnerable vibration. Maybe John Yelp just liked the look of me that day. Maybe it was random and he did it only once and it was to me and he realized his mistake, and that was the end of that. Why speak up about it? His word against mine. Forty-something versus a fourteen-year-old "diva." It wasn't worth it. Even now, I don't know if I would say anything. It was a different world back then. The #MeToo movement was not even on the horizon, and I wasn't ready to be vilified or pitied.

I couldn't have been finished with that production any sooner. On the day of the wrap, I didn't even stay for the party, that's how over it I was. Olive was annoyed. She wanted me to bring Ted.

I saw Ted, my *TTA* costar and babysitter, a lot that summer.

Dad was still in Anita and Mom wanted to "mingle with what Hollywood had to offer." I don't know if my parents were having trouble, but it was the first summer my father didn't come to Los Angeles to be with us, or vice versa.

Like she didn't ask me about coming home drunk from parties, I didn't ask my mother where she went at night. We were two roommates with an understanding. As long as she returned before eleven, we were good.

Who knows where she went, what she did, who she saw.

Ted was twenty at that point, and why he chose to hang out with a fourteen-year-old and her ten-year-old sister is beyond me. He didn't ask for money and he didn't get paid. He could've been out doing God knows what. I think he liked babysitting us because we were easy and the booze was free. My mom didn't check to see how much the liquor bottles held before and after his visits and so didn't seem to care that he and I would sip from them together while she was out. We would hang out like two old friends and shoot the shit. Ted was always careful to drink just enough to get tipsy, but not drunk; then he would drink a lot of water, sober up, and drive home.

One night, Ted and I were drinking together while Ashley watched *The Little Mermaid* with us. "Does Oscar ever do anything . . . weird with you?" he asked.

"Oscar? Our TV dad?" I clarified, feeling mystified. "No."

"Oh."

"Why? Does he do anything weird with *you*?"

Ted shrugged.

"Well, now you *have* to tell me," I said, nosy.

"I just wondered, because he puts you on his knee."

"Not anymore." I'd won that argument, finally.

"Well, he *did*. And when I would sit on his lap, he would . . ." He gestured toward his crotch.

"Omigod!" I exclaimed.

"But"—and Ted sounded ashamed—"I *liked* it." His voice lowered a tiny bit, even though Ashley wasn't paying attention to us. "I think I like . . . men. And women, but also men."

I could barely breathe. Ted was telling me something that I could not believe to be true. My parents had raised me to be a good Christian girl and that meant that homosexuality was a sin. But Ted couldn't be a sinner. His soul could not be damned to hell. In that moment, I made a decision. "Oh," I said, then, curious: "How can you like both?"

"I can't explain it. I just know that I do."

"Okay."

I accepted him. I accepted what he had to say. Ted's friendship with me was more important than my upbringing. I wonder what that has to say about my connection to my parents.

"Don't tell anyone," Ted said.

"I won't," I promised.

He hugged me. It was a comfortable hug.

WHEN WE STARTED back at *Third Time Around* for its eighth season, we had a new hire: the woman who would play Zac's eventual wife on the show, Natasha. I can't remember the actress's name, for the life of me. I want to say it is Sophie.

Over the years, Zac had plenty of girlfriends, usually lasting an arc or a season. This was going to be something different. Sophie started off as a recurring character but then became a permanent cast member on the show.

Amy was still in love with Thomas, so I couldn't get rid of Brandon, even if I wanted to. We had to kiss on camera frequently, and while Brandon didn't use his tongue anymore, it was still so violating that I began to wonder if I should even be on the show at all.

Sorry, girls, I'm feeling sick thinking about it. Give me a minute.

"ALL THAT HAPPENED when you were *fourteen*?" Jane squeaks. I nod, my eyes closed so that I can try to block out the memory. When I reopen my eyes, Jessica is on her phone.

She looks up the actress on IMDb. "Sophia Paige," she says archly, turning her phone around so I can see the actress's face. A little older, a little bit of fillers, but that's her: Zac's fiancée, Natasha.

"You're right," I say. I feel curiously hollow when I look at her photograph. So many feelings had run through me when Sophia first joined the show. Intrigue then ennui, jealousy then dismissal. I couldn't understand my thoughts when I saw her name next to ours on the roster. I think I underestimated how close I'd become to the original cast—Millie excluded—and felt that Sophia was an interloper. I hadn't had the same feelings surrounding Brandon because I'd hated him on sight. With Sophia, I tried to like her, but couldn't.

Is that why I could barely remember her name now? If I met

her on the street today, would we become friends?

Jessica is now idly flicking through Instagram, checking out Sophia's whereabouts these days. "She's not up to much," she says, and Jane looks over her shoulder. "Has kids, bakes cakes, rides bicycles, lives in Vancouver now, it looks like."

"Speaking of Instagram," I say.

Two pairs of blue eyes look up at me quizzically.

"I need you to help me start an account."

CHAPTER 14

The girls immediately know what I mean. They perk up, their eyes serious, and they nod emphatically. They understand that I'm asking them to help me gain a foothold into my freedom, just with this one request.

"What I need is for you to make a new Instagram account for me and to share pictures of me being normal," I say. "I think. I need people to understand that I'm not the person that is on the regular Hayley Aldridge account. That person is a robot, controlled by her parents."

"We'll do it as soon as we get to Dad's," Jane says. The girls aren't usually allowed to have their phones around me, in case I steal one and make calls with it. The powers-that-be like to monitor all of my calls. Adam, my bodyguard, is the keeper of the phone for me.

I soften my gaze at my daughter. "Thank you, baby," I say. "I appreciate your help. Now where was I . . ."

I wish I could tell you girls that my life was smooth sailing from fourteen on, but to be honest, it became more chaotic as I grew older. I was earning $75,000 per episode of *Third Time*

Around at that point and that meant with twenty-four episodes a season, I was pulling in close to two million dollars a year. Add to that any commercials, movie deals, and residuals and I was a very rich young woman.

My parents were over the moon. My father, elated, claimed that if I signed on for the ninth and tenth seasons for $100k an episode, he would quit his job in Anita entirely and move to Los Angeles for good. I don't know why he hadn't already—I think my mother had convinced him that it would be best if we, the children, had roots in Anita. And the constant back-and-forth between California and Texas allowed my mother's relationship with Alex Dietrich to bloom even more.

WHEN *THIRD TIME Around* introduced Natasha, Zac's girl-friend, Sophia and Ted's on-screen relationship galloped off into ratings heaven. The viewers had been aching for Zac to "settle down" and here she was, the perfect, snarky princess ready to put Zac in his place. Sometimes, when Ted and I ran lines together, I wished I were Natasha instead of Amy. Natasha had a wonderful partner in Zac.

Of course, Amy was a bratty little sister toward Natasha, and our scenes together somewhat mimicked how I felt toward Sophia. I didn't *like* her. I don't know why. She was a nice person, but I didn't want to get to know her. I felt like she was an intruder, a third wheel on our bicycle.

"Amy," Natasha finally said to my character, "why don't you go somewhere else?" Natasha and Zac were trying to have a conversation over the dinner table.

This made Amy defensive and Zac supported his little sister. Thus, a little love spat was born. Natasha was on the outs until the next episode, when she and Zac would reconcile.

"And that's a wrap on today!"

I exhaled a sigh of relief and dug my phone out of my bag, finally able to look at it. I sat down on my director's chair while checking my messages; I'd missed a call from Trey when we were on set. I smiled.

Ted looked over my shoulder and saw the missed calls list. "I don't like it," he said. "A twenty-something-year-old shouldn't be calling a teenager."

"I agree," Sophia said, pulling a sweater on over her wardrobe. "Nothing good will come of this."

I waved my hand at them, dismissing their worries. What could happen? Trey was a gentleman. He'd ditched the pager and called me with his new cell phone. We could chat nonstop now, and I could call him whenever I wanted.

"Hey girl," he said when I called him back. "What are you doing?"

"We just wrapped for the day," I said. "What are *you* doing?"

"I'm waiting out in the parking lot. I see your mom. I'll say hi and tell her to go home. We can hang out."

"No rehearsal tonight?" I said, with my heart leaping into my throat.

"Nah, we have a night off."

My mother was displeased. She and Ashley were in the car when I came out into the lot. I leaned into the driver's side window to talk to her. "If I'd known you were going to ditch me, I wouldn't have driven all the way over here," she said. Ashley nodded in agreement in the back seat.

"Ashley, how did the audition go?" I asked.

"Fine," Ashley said. She was trying out for commercials now, just like I had when I was young. I'd had a head start, though.

"I'm not here to be a chauffeur," Mom continued.

"So don't be," I said. "I can hire a driver now, you know? I make enough money."

"Don't tempt me," Mom said. "These car rides are basically the only time I get to see you anymore."

"Whose fault is that?" I asked.

"Next time, *call* before I leave the house," she said. "I gave you that cell phone for a reason. And not just to call Trey Barnes."

Trey had sidled up behind me while we were talking. My mother glanced at him with a suspicious look in her eye. "Be careful with my daughter," she warned.

I could see Trey's reflection in the window that my mother began to roll up. I turned to look at him. He was glorious: those green eyes, that dark hair. He was in an oversize shirt and baggy jeans with a wallet on a chain. I could feel my love for him flowing out of my chest and into the air just at the sight of him. I wanted to put my teeth on him, make sure he was there with me; swallow him. I understood what people meant when they said *love consumes*. All I could think about when I saw Trey was how close I wanted to be with him, and if we could meld into one person. I was well and truly obsessed.

"Hi," I said, as my mother's Volvo peeled out of the spot and took a turn around a corner. "I'm all yours for the evening."

"Let's go shoot some pool," he suggested.

I loved that Trey wanted to take me somewhere, even if it wasn't fancy. We'd eat chicken wings with ranch (well, *he* would). He'd play pool while I watched. He'd probably have a beer or two, sober up, drive me home. We were careful not to show public displays of affection out in the real world—it was allowed only in our soft conversations at night, when he told me I was brilliant and wonderful and that we'd be together forever.

I think the only reason my mother allowed me to go out with Trey is *because* she saw the tabloids talking about us. We'd walk apart from each other, without even linking fingers. I'd have a Starbucks Frappuccino that Trey treated me to, and Trey would be flipping his car keys rhythmically. We never hugged or kissed where anybody could see us. The tabloids didn't know what to make of it. *Friendship?* Between a fourteen-year-old and a twenty-two-year-old? Could it be *possible?*

We were conjectured to be working together on something— Trey with a budding film career, perhaps, or me with a hush-hush recording contract I hadn't announced yet. But we were never discussed as a couple. Even though I knew we were. My mother knew I had a crush on him, but she didn't think it was reciprocated. I think, had she known what we discussed at night under the covers, the sound of Trey jerking off while he spoke to me about our future, coaxing me to touch myself, too, she would have excised him from my life immediately.

Trey knew a private pool hall owned by people he trusted. He gave the bouncer a fifty-dollar bill when he let us in. Technically I wasn't supposed to be there, because they sold alcohol, but no one squealed on us. I didn't like beer anyway.

Trey spoke to me while he lined up a shot. "Do you have any summer projects in progress?"

"Next summer?" I asked. I had just started reading scripts with the intention to audition in the very near future. "Nothing yet, why?"

"Wouldn't it be great if you came on tour with Dial8?" he said, the pool cue flashing as he took his shot. "We're going all around the U.S.A. Forty-four cities, fifty-five dates. Short, I know, but we're cutting a new album next fall and will tour extensively for that one."

"On tour?" I repeated. "With Dial8?" I sounded dumb.

"Yeah, it would be a bro-fest, not gonna lie. Corey B and RJ are bringing their girlfriends and I thought you might want to come with. There won't be a ton of privacy, but we should be able to find some alone time." He smiled. "It'll be fun."

"It *sounds* fun," I said, love welling up in my heart. *Trey wanted me to go on tour with him!* The radio began blaring a Dial8 song at full volume and Trey grimaced.

"This single follows me everywhere," he lamented while eyeing the balls on the table. "Anyway, don't you want to come?"

"I do, but . . ." My mother would never let me go on tour with the guys, I was sure of that much in my life. The cue snapped against the balls.

"Just think about it. Ask your mom."

After pool, Trey drove me home and smiled at me from the
driver's seat. Paparazzi took flashing photos through the windshield so we never kissed goodbye. The memory of his lips on
mine when I kissed him after the awards show was starting to
fade. It would be wonderful to go on tour with Dial8 and be
reminded of his kiss. "Talk to you tonight, beautiful," he said.
"And don't forget about the tour."

CHAPTER 15

*O*nly *Human* came out in spring of 1999. I brought Ted as my date to the premiere and fielded more questions about our relationship. "We're just costars," I said, over and over. "We're good friends."

No matter that we held hands on the way to the premiere. Ted held me protectively against the onslaught of bulb flashes and shouting, hired cameramen.

When we finally shook ourselves off inside the theater, I said, "Thanks."

"I gotta protect my best girl, don't I?" Ted said.

"Your *best* girl, huh? So there are others?" I teased.

"Well, as you know, there's Natasha, and Erica . . ."

"Your sister? Gross." I poked him in the side. He shimmied away from me, laughing. We chased each other down the hallway, bumping into folks from behind. It was immature of us, but we were young, having fun and not caring about what people thought.

That is, until I saw John Yelp. Seeing the director at the premiere made me want to drink. Ted and Olive and I squirreled away to a hidden spot in the shadows and clinked glasses. Ted shook out a baggie and offered it to us. We took turns in the bathroom, snorting coke and rubbing our gums.

The premiere itself is hazy in my mind now. I didn't confront John Yelp, as I considered I would if I had enough courage. I know I was included on a worst-dressed list in some magazine. (I wore an orange muumuu that didn't pair well with my skin tone or my shoes; I vowed publicly to never wear orange again.) *Only Human* was not a big-budget production or a blockbuster, but it had generally good reviews and a modest box office draw.

I was in the throes of teenagerdom and mad as hell. Everything in my life made me angry. My mother, my job, my role as Charlotte with that skeezy director. The only things that were constantly good in my life were Trey and Dial8. I *needed* to go on tour with them in the summer. It became my sole focus: figure out a way to go on tour with Dial8.

And then, one day, my mother gave me a gift.

At fifteen, I was pretty much physically grounded without a professional driver or a driver's license of my own. Ted still babysat for us, even though I told my mother I was old enough to babysit for Ashley on my own. "One more year," she'd say. The good thing about Ted babysitting for us is that he helped me learn how to drive. I had my learner's permit and he was my licensed driver in the passenger seat. We'd cruise around my neighborhood, practice parallel parking on the street, and I sideswiped a mailbox only once. It was Ted's car and I apologized with my heart in my throat, but he laughed and said he had good insurance.

One night, after Ted and I (and Ashley in the back seat) practiced driving while my mother was out, she didn't come home. Ashley asked, "Where is Mom?" and I couldn't answer. I didn't really know. Ted called her cell phone, but it went to voice mail.

"Well," I said, not sure what to do next, "let's watch a scary movie."

Ted's fingers walked through our collection of VHS tapes. "The closest thing we have is *Heathers*," he said.

We watched, the two sisters on the couch sandwiching Ted, each holding one of his palms as Winona Ryder acted up a storm. When the movie was over, Mom still wasn't home and Ted resigned himself to making sure we got to bed at a somewhat reasonable hour. He slept on the couch.

By the next morning, she still hadn't returned. I began to worry, but Ted put out the Raisin Bran for Ashley and me, brow furrowed as he called her cell phone again and again. At nine, I wondered if I'd be late for work—I couldn't leave Ashley alone and I didn't want to bring her to set with me. When our mother walked in the door at ten, she looked a little rumpled but no worse for wear. "Mommy!" Ashley exclaimed, hugging her middle.

"Sorry, girls," she said, her voice full of light and happiness. "I lost track of time."

I examined her face. She had the same look she had had when she'd talked to Alex Dietrich that one time. When it felt wrong to look at her. Something was up.

"You put Ted out," I said in my bossiest voice. "He had to

stay the night and we didn't even have an extra toothbrush for him. He had to sleep on the couch."

The light slowly died in her eyes as Mom realized her mistake. "You're right," she said. "It won't happen again. You didn't call your father, did you?"

"Why would I?" I should've let her think that I had, drawn it out a little bit more. But I didn't realize what power I wielded then. The relief in her voice was palpable.

"No reason," she said. "I wouldn't want him to worry."

"I have to get to set," I said.

"I'll take you," Ted said. "Patty, you can take Ashley to school and I'll bring Hayley to set."

"Thank you, Ted. You aren't late, too, are you?"

"No, I'm not on the call sheet until this afternoon."

But when we arrived on set at *TTA*, the crew wasn't bustling as much as they usually did. "Alex isn't here yet," I was told, and I found that weird. Alex Dietrich was always on time. I went to hair and makeup. Alex came into the trailer twenty minutes later, looking jovial.

"How's Hayley this morning?" he said, and his eyes sparkled. He reached out and held the back of my chair. Our eyes connected in the trailer mirror.

And somehow, I knew. I *knew*. They had been together. Maybe it was the residual perfume, Gap Grass, on his hands. Maybe it was the dual flicker of happiness I saw in both of them, echoes of each other. I knew the smell and *effect* of my mother and it was all over this man.

I looked at him and he looked at me. His eyes lost a little bit of their luster. But his mouth kept smiling and he nodded, as if to say yes to himself. "Okay, see you on set!" he said.

Ted met me in my trailer—unusual for him, we usually met in his—that afternoon during a lull in filming. "Do you want to talk about it?" he asked.

"Talk about what?" I said, feigning ignorance.

"That your mom was with Alex."

How did *he* know?

"It's weird!" I exploded. "She's married. My dad is definitely still in the picture. So what is she doing?"

"I don't know, Hayley, but this is some bad juju." Ted pulled out a tiny canister and sprinkled a minuscule amount of powder onto a miniature spoon. He brought it to his right nostril and snorted. I wondered how long he'd been doing coke on set. I'd been keeping it to premieres and nights out, not days at work.

But there was more to think about. Like my mother and Alex.

"No, I don't think it's bad juju," I said, inspiration coming to me. Knowledge was currency.

"What are you thinking?" he asked, sniffing, noting the look on my face.

"I'll blackmail her."

"For *what*?" he wanted to know.

"To go on tour with Trey."

Ted was shaking his head before I'd even completed the sentence. "I don't think that's a good idea," he said, clearing his throat. "Trey is older than you by a lot. He will probably take advantage of you."

"Are you trying to say that I won't be able to take care of myself?" I challenged. "I'm almost sixteen years old. I know what is up with the world. I'm not a *baby*."

Something about my expression must have left him with no choice but to acquiesce. "Ohhhkay," he said, sighing heavily. "I just worry about you, that's all." He gave me a crooked smile and put the tiny canister in his pocket.

THAT EVENING, I confronted my mother. "Mom," I said, when we were together in the house. "I want to go on tour with Trey this summer."

"Absolutely out of the question," she said. "The answer is no."

"What if I made a bargain with you?" I asked.

"The answer is still no."

"You haven't even listened to my proposition." I smiled at her sweetly. She looked at me with curiosity. "I won't tell Dad that you're sleeping with Alex Dietrich if you let me go."

Her face blanched immediately. As I suspected, her first instinct was denial. "What are you talking about?" she said.

But my mother was no actress. *I* was the actress. "I figured out where you've been going. He smells like your perfume."

Something between my mother and me died, in that moment. She had been in control for so much of my life, and I suddenly had the upper hand. She knew it didn't matter that I couldn't prove it. All I had to do was tell my father about my suspicions and he'd get possessive and come live with us, $100k per episode or not. And that would be the end of her dalliance with my showrunner. Something that, I assumed, gave her much joy. I could see her deliberating over what to say.

Her shoulders sagged slightly. "Okay," she whispered. "You can go, but with restrictions. You have to call me every day, no exceptions. You must sleep in your own bed. You must go on birth control."

"Wait, why do I have to go on birth control if I'm sleeping in my own bed?" I asked.

"Because I know you won't listen to me, and I'd rather you be safe than sorry."

TREY WAS EXCITED when I told him I could go with him. True to her word, my mother took me to the gynecologist and got me started on birth control pills, and made me promise to take one daily. "Call me after you take it," she said. "That way you will remember. And you *will* call me every day."

When I packed for the tour, I chose a slew of amazing designer outfits that I'd been gifted. But when I showed up with two bulging suitcases, Trey took one look at them and said, "Nope."

"Um, 'nope'?"

"This is a *tour bus*, Hayley! There isn't a ton of room. It's full of *people*, not stuff. What do you have in there?"

I began to list off my outfits in order of importance, starting with a pair of leather Dolce & Gabbana pants with embroidery along the legs, when he stopped me. "I don't want to hear about individual outfits. The only correct answer is 'jeans and

T-shirts.' Pull all your shorts out of those monstrosities and stick them in this duffel bag. We'll outfit you with tops."

Which is how I ended up wearing an assortment of Dial8 merchandise every day on the tour, instead of my hot fashion. A personal assistant working for the band had to go into a Victoria's Secret and buy me new underwear because I didn't even get to pack mine.

RJ and Corey B's girlfriends, Amanda and Jennifer, were as casual as I now was. They mostly wore slouchy tops and cut-offs. Jennifer wore cowboy boots unironically, which I found endearing.

We soon fell into a routine: drive all night, make it to the venue by morning, sound check, work out, big "family meal" with everyone, pill, call my mother, concert where I got to stand in the VIP section and hang out with everyone backstage, afterparty, bus, drive all night. If we were staying in the same city for a second date, we bunked in a hotel instead of getting back in the bus. The afterparties went longer on those nights.

I had the chance to meet Pink, Sisqó, and Len, who were all opening numbers for Dial8.

At the first afterparty, on the first L.A. concert date, I wasn't sure if I should do anything besides drink. I was worried that the paparazzi would show up and find me messed up. I was on my best behavior. But when we ventured out to other cities, where the only cameras seemed to be wielded by fans, all bets were off.

"Here," Trey said to me, holding out a rolled dollar bill at the afterparty in Las Vegas. He winked at me. "I want to see you the same way we first met," he whispered.

I grinned and accepted the rolled bill. The drip was immediate and I cleared my throat. Trey was beautiful. The more time passed that night, the more beautiful he became, until I couldn't take it anymore and had to put his face against mine. I sat on his lap as the other members of Dial8 laughed: *Oh, there she is, the Hayley we met at Julian's that one time.* Our mouths touched and I ventured out my tongue to tentatively lick his lips. Gosh, he was a good kisser. The bit of stubble on his chin rubbed against my face and I shivered.

Every night we drank, we smoked, we snorted. I don't know how the guys got enough rest to do what they had to do—put on a concert for twenty thousand people at a time. But they did. They were amazing. The choreography was on point, and I never saw them mess up. All those rehearsals in Los Angeles had honed them into perfect performers of the highest caliber.

What I didn't count on was the fact that a very dedicated group of photographer groupies had followed along on the tour and was taking pictures of the band—on and off the stage. And there I was, all fifteen years of me, blazed out of my mind and straddling Trey Barnes's lap. Those photos were sold to various media outlets, of course.

The tabloids Ate. It. Up.

This was more than just a "diva actress." This was a minor in trouble! This was an actress acting out! This is what the tabloids had been waiting for ever since the first snap of Trey and me walking near each other on a public street without touching. They *knew* there couldn't be a platonic relationship between the two of us! It was impossible. As impossible as a relationship between a fifteen-year-old and a twenty-four-year-old.

TROUBLED ACTRESS HAYLEY ALDRIDGE SPOT-TED WITH BIRTH CONTROL. (This was a photo of me with my pill pack in one hand outside a tour bus. It was my own damn fault for not putting the recognizable pink circle in my purse before stepping outside.)

ALDRIDGE IN DEEP WITH DIAL8'S TREY BARNES. (This was the photo of me on Trey's lap. The shot was from behind, so all you can see is my side profile and a lot of blond hair. Trey is looking at me like I'm a goddess. I actually clipped this one to put in my scrapbook because of the look of adoration on his face.)

WHERE IS HER MOTHER?! (This was an out-of-focus shot of me, eyes half-slitted, mouth slack, as I was mid-blink and mid-speak when the shot was taken. I remember the flash going off as I was stumbling back to the tour bus, and whoever took the picture jumped away.)

I had to assure my mother that I wasn't sleeping with Trey. I said it with a lot of eye-rolling and breath-huffing over the phone, like it was embarrassing to talk to her about it, but I wanted her to know that I wasn't doing anything wrong. Well, besides the drugs. But that was our unspoken agreement. If I was able to do my job, she didn't say anything about the drinking or the drugs.

Sure, Trey and I got hot and heavy. I believed we were wildly in love, after all, and this was the first time we were away from too many prying eyes. I was supposed to bunk with the other girlfriends and sleep on a cot in their two-bed hotel room, but on the nights that the band stayed in the same city for a two-date engagement, Trey and I found ourselves sleeping in the same bed. Why not? We were together, after all.

It was wonderful being with him all night. He would tuck his chin into my shoulder and sleep with his pelvis right up against my back. One arm would encircle my middle. He didn't touch my breasts, though I ached for him to, and he'd snore lightly in my ear. We'd wake up, him with a hard-on that he pressed against one of my butt cheeks, me arching my ass into his hands, and then we'd kiss and kiss and kiss.

One night—I think we were in New York City, which had *three* tour dates planned—Trey and I went farther than we had ever gone before. We were both high on cocaine and I felt like I could fly. He pulled off all my clothes, slowly, reverently, until I was naked on the bed. Then he did the same with his. It was my first time seeing—not feeling—a penis.

I suddenly sobered up with the realization that this was going to happen. "Do you have a condom?" I asked.

"No, but you're on the pill," he said.

I didn't feel like this was right—I was uncomfortable with the idea—but I lay back on the bed and he hovered over me. He didn't ask if it was okay, or if I would like to slow down. I don't think he would've listened even if I had. I know, if I'd had a voice, I would've used it, but my throat was suddenly thick with emotion.

He began kissing me on the neck, slowly moving his lips to mine. I kissed him back distractedly, wondering if I was ready.

I could feel his erection against my upper thigh and I worried about what would happen next. If it would hurt. If I actually wanted *this*.

"Um, Trey," I said, trying to get the words out.

And then he thrust himself inside me. I gasped in pain; there was no easing in, and I wasn't particularly wet. "I'm not sure about this," I said desperately, before he did anything else. I inadvertently pushed against his chest with both hands, my meaning clear: *Get off me.*

But he didn't withdraw. "Come for me," he murmured, thrusting again. I realized I was crying. "Trey—" I gulped.

Trey finally took the hint; I could feel him leaving me, in more ways than one. He coolly and silently put on his clothes as I watched him with my knees drawn up around my chest, hiding my body. Then he walked to the other side of the suite and started watching television.

I got dressed quickly and padded over to where he sat. He didn't look at me. He was zoned into the TV. "Trey?" I said in a small voice. "I'm sorry. I just don't think I'm ready."

"I love you, Hayley. You know that, right?" he said, without looking at me. "I thought we'd have a special moment, but you ruined it."

"I'm sorry," I said again, my voice plaintive and sad.

"Whatever. It's fine."

But it wasn't fine. It wasn't. He barely looked at me for the rest of the dates in New York, and the afterparties took on a desperate tinge as I snorted more, drank more, smoked more, trying to be wild enough to get his attention again. I slept in Amanda and Jennifer's room on my little cot, Trey having barred me from his room after-hours, and I lived with it. I didn't know what else to do.

But the tour dragged on, and it became less and less fun as Trey continued to ignore me. I began to wonder if I should just go home.

CHAPTER 16

J ane and Jessica look at me with wide eyes. "Wow," Jane says.
"Gross," Jessica says at the same time.

"Yeah, gross," I agree.

They don't say what I'm thinking: that I was raped. It took me months in therapy during rehab to work out what had happened. That my entire relationship with Trey Barnes had been a lie. It's why I'm so protective of the girls.

I'd told Olive, of course. After it happened, I found time away from Trey and the rest of Dial8 and called Olive and explained what had occurred. She was unfazed. "Omigod," she said, in lieu of anything better. "What was it like?"

"What do you mean, what was it *like*? It was like a minute and then it was over."

"Sounds like a bad time," she said knowingly.

"What would *you* know," I muttered.

"You're right," she said. "I don't know anything. But it sounds like a bad time." No mention of his or my age. No mention of rape. Just that it was a bad experience, one to regret, but nothing more than that. We just didn't *know* then.

"Sorry," she added, almost as in afterthought. "It's like the worst way to lose your V-card."

AFTER TWO WEEKS of silence from Trey, I knew it was over. I wore the shirt I was wearing the first day of tour—one of my own, not one of the Dial8 ones I was given—a pair of shorts, and some sandals, and got on a plane from Pittsburgh to Los Angeles, nonstop, first class. I felt like crap.

My mother, ever the roommate, did not ask me what went wrong. I didn't tell her either. I said that the tour got repetitive and boring, and that I wanted to come home. She paid for my plane ticket with my earnings and picked me up from the airport with Ashley in tow.

"I got a commercial!" Ashley said in greeting, as I stepped off the tarmac.

"Oh yeah? Good for you," I said, with no inflection in my voice.

"It's for dog food. They want someone to pet puppies while they're being fed. Isn't that the best?" she went on.

"Sounds great."

She chirped about the commercial all the way home, but again I wondered—should Ashley be subjected to this kind of life? Rather than feeling like I was the special one, I felt tarnished, used. It was out of sisterly worry that I considered Ashley's experience in this industry. What if the same thing that happened to me with Trey happened to her? Would I be able to live with myself? What would my *mother* think if she knew what had happened between Trey and me?

The rest of the summer, before the *TTA* filming hiatus

ended and the new season began, was spent with Mom carting Ashley around to all sorts of auditions and callbacks. She was cute, she was a ham, she was Hayley 2.0!

Ashley ended up booking a "friend" role in a blockbuster movie and was thrilled. I was less than enthusiastic. Now Mom's attention span was split between the two of us. She finally asked my father to come live with us in L.A.

I don't know what happened between Alex Dietrich and my mother, or between my father and my mother, for that matter. If anything had changed over the summer while I was away. But there she was, accepting Dad's help, managing our schedules like nothing had happened at all. There was an efficiency about the two of them, and they acted more like partners than lovers.

I never saw them kiss, for example. Not anymore.

But on one thing they were a united front: if I didn't fill out this next year on *TTA*, I would be getting a boob job during the summer hiatus. This season, Amy and Thomas had a lot of love scenes for the show; it was on network television, so no nudity, but the illusion of breasts had to be visible. I was going to be spending more time in my water bra than I had thought.

I was also introduced to the Sock: a padded jockstrap wrapped around Brandon's privates, the rest of him clad in nude underwear, so he didn't inadvertently push against me when we had to hump for the cameras. It was as detestable as you might think. I was still psychologically sore from my experience with Trey Barnes and felt vulnerable pretending to fuck another man under sheets with people watching. Had I known that this is what I was signing up for in 1991, I would have stopped my younger self.

This was the year 2000, and intimacy choreographers were not on set as often as they are now. So while my mother was required to be on set to observe and make sure nothing untoward happened—and it was embarrassing for both of us—nothing was *really* done to ensure that I would be protected from Brandon mishandling me. Which was a challenge.

Especially when Brandon grew tired of wearing the Sock.

I discovered this when I accidentally made contact with his actual penis through his nude underwear, when I slipped under the sheets that we draped over ourselves while filming. He was hovering above me, knees between my legs, when I felt something soft, but not pillowy.

"What's going on! Brandon!" I hissed, when I looked down and saw that the Sock was nowhere in sight.

"Don't worry, babe. I won't get hard. This isn't assault."

I was angry and frightened. I didn't want to feel Brandon rubbing up against me. It was bad enough having to kiss him for the camera, now there was a penis involved too?

"Where is it?" I asked. "Why aren't you wearing it?"

"It squeezes my junk," he explained. "I figured, if I don't get hard, it won't matter anyway."

"Alex!" I shouted.

Brandon placed his hand over my mouth and I bit him. "Ow!" Alex showed up just as my teeth made a connection with Brandon's palm and I was treated to a disappointed look by our showrunner.

"Hayley . . . what did we talk about before? That you can't get mad at Brandon when he touches you as Thomas. It's just part of the script."

"But . . . look! The Sock!" I gestured.

"It's tight on my junk," Brandon said to Alex. "I have a doctor's note. I'm supposed to keep tight things away from my testicles. My girlfriend and I are trying to have a baby."

"I don't want him—it—near me," I exclaimed.

"Brandon, just don't make contact, okay?" Alex said.

"Right," Brandon said.

"Mom!" I shouted, desperate. My mother came scurrying over from the sidelines, where she had been supervising. I gave her a pleading look. "Make him wear it," I whined.

"Hayley . . . if he has a doctor's note . . ." My mother's brow furrowed. "Can't you just be a good sport about this?"

"It'll be fine, Hales," Brandon said. I hated that he had a nickname for me.

As filming progressed, and Brandon grew more passionate as Thomas, there *was* contact. And it rubbed against my thigh. I hated it.

That evening, I went into my trailer and threw a plate against the door. I screamed. I cried. The plate shattered and I left it there, in pieces, on the floor.

WHILE AMY AND Thomas made all sorts of love on the show, Zac and Natasha were getting to know each other and falling in love. I wished I could have had a different storyline, one with more than just boyfriend drama, but the writers fell into a rut that year and the writing was subpar. It was the worst rated season of *Third Time Around* until they added new blood to the writer's room the next year.

I was about to turn sixteen, which meant that I could get my driver's license. I practiced driving with my handlers on the show, clamoring for the driver's seat in the golf cart taking us to and from the lot, and making my costars drive around with me. I drove the Volvo to and from work, with my mother in the passenger seat, and got pretty good at it.

Before I was in line at the DMV to get my driver's license on the day of my birthday, my parents bought me a brand-new VW Beetle (using a portion of my earnings)—light blue, with a plastic daisy on the dashboard. And as soon as I got my driver's license, my parents hauled me to a plastic surgeon to consult with him about my nonexistent breasts.

"Look at her," my father said, gesturing toward my chest. "She isn't built like a sixteen-year-old! She needs to get some breasts so that she can get adult roles."

The doctor nodded absentmindedly. "Hayley, do you agree with that assessment?"

I wasn't sure what to say. "I mean . . ." I stammered. "I know I need to grow. But maybe I just won't and this is what I need to do to get breasts." I laughed awkwardly.

Dr. Young held out a few items for me to touch. "This is saline," he said. "This is silicone. Do you like one better than the other?"

"I guess I like . . . saline," I said, feeling both.

"About what size do you want to be?"

"Umm, a C cup?"

"That seems doable. What day works best for you for the surgery?"

I couldn't believe it was happening that fast.

"We have next Thursday available," he said, "at two thirty."

Which is how I got my implants.

OLIVE WAS INTRIGUED by my surgery. We were on the phone, because I was currently bedridden and sleeping on a wedge pillow as I started to heal, and she asked me all sorts of questions about it. "I don't remember," I said more than once. "I was out."

"Like, it's cool, you know? That surgeries exist for this type of thing. I might need the opposite," she joked. Her breasts were growing larger and larger, without a visible stopping point. "I might need, like, a *reduction*. It's good you went through this first and can tell me all about it."

"It might be different for a reduction," I said, popping the antibiotics I had to take every two hours to keep away infection.

"Just think, Brandon is gonna have something to touch this time around," she said.

"Don't even go there," I warned. "Also, I'm not supposed to get my blood pressure up so don't even joke."

"When can you come out and play?" she said in a mock-sarcastic voice. "I miss my best friend." Now that we had our driver's licenses, we should've been cruising around Hollywood and L.A.

"A few more weeks. Not until I can put my arms above my head," I answered.

"Boo," she said in a deadpan voice. I could hear her cracking her gum.

Olive had grown up to be a total beauty. I'd known she would be, when we first met, but it was uncanny how she looked like a younger version of Salma Hayek. She had perfected Salma's snake dance that she performs in *From Dusk Till Dawn*—the one where she put her foot in Quentin Tarantino's mouth—ready to use at a club if she ever wanted to take off her shoe and seduce a man.

"Maybe we can start with a movie," I said. "Go to the theater."

"And get mobbed?" Olive huffed.

"I'll wear the Wig."

"The Wig" was permanently borrowed from Wardrobe on *Only Human*. It was brown, made with what I thought was real hair, and cut in a flattering bob. I had taken it with me before wrap and never returned it, thinking that maybe no one would notice it was gone. When I placed it on my head, I looked like someone else. My blue eyes took on a glow, my cheekbones were more pronounced, and somehow I looked more lithe. I thought I looked more like a model than an actress—someone *interesting*.

When I was ready to go out, Olive and I ended up going to the dollar theater, where they were playing months-old movies. We watched my old costar Anthony Martens in *The Grief Healer*. I wondered what he was up to now.

His acting was a little wooden; he'd lost some of that spark that he'd had when he was an unknown. "Did you know," Olive said, cracking her gum in the middle of the empty theater, "I was up for the role of Paula?"

"You were not," I said, and she laughed.

"You're right, I wasn't. Were *you*, though?"

I hadn't been. I hadn't even been in the *running* for the role, probably because I didn't look sixteen.

"These better do something for my career," I said, looking pointedly down at my new breasts.

"They really suit you," Olive said. "They look real. May I?"

"Sure. They're still a little hard though."

Olive felt me up. "Can't even tell it's fake," she said.

I felt one of mine and one of hers. "You're right," I said.

Two best friends feeling each other up in a darkened theater. Exactly what girls do.

We looked at each other, our eyes reflecting the light from the screen, and cracked up. "I don't know how I feel about this industry anymore," she admitted, suddenly sober.

The movie was still playing, but I was more intrigued with what she had to say. This was Olive, the same girl who had told me how lucky we were to be doing what we did. "What do you mean?" I asked.

"Every question these days is so vapid. My last presser, people asked me how I feel about being plus-size. I didn't even *know* I was plus-size!"

"Wow," I said.

"And they ask me what I eat, who I'm wearing, who I'm

dating," she continued. "They don't ask me about the project. They don't ask me artistic questions like how I got into character or how I personally felt being the villain, or anything like that. It's just, *looks looks looks.* And I'm getting really damn tired of it."

"I know what you mean," I said. "I did an interview with *TV Guide* last season and the questions were all about sex scenes with Brandon."

"So you know what I mean," she said. "It's not about the art anymore. It's all about the spectacle."

"But we still get paid a lot," I said, thinking about how my raise took me into the six-figures-an-episode territory, and how my father was over the moon excited about it. He spoke of buying a several-million-dollar house in the Hollywood Hills for us, a permanent place to settle down, and a house in Anita that was bigger than our two-bedroom back at home.

"A person who gets paid a lot for their dignity is a whore," Olive said.

CHAPTER 17

When I could finally lift my arms above my head, no club was safe from Olive and me. We went out dancing every night of the week, spilling into cabs at closing hour, our photographs taken by the paparazzi through windshields and not-tinted-enough windows.

Photographers would ring the car doors when we got out of taxis, disorienting us further with strobing lights. They'd shout our names and ask us what we were doing. Sometimes, we'd answer back.

"Where's Ted?" became a familiar refrain, and I would smile and wave, because who knew where Ted was?

There's a famous gif now of me, smiling, answering this question and then turning my head. I imperceptibly force my arms together so that my elbows push my breasts together. In my low-cut V-neck top, my cleavage bobbles in slow-motion. Loop upon loop upon loop. The internet is forever.

ARE THEY REAL?

BOOB JOB FOR HAYLEY? SIXTEEN AND WITH NEW BREASTS.

You'd think I had done porn, the way the tabloids went

crazy.

Because I'd been wearing a water bra for so long on the set of *Only Human* and *Third Time Around*, my growth was noticeable, but it wasn't as though I'd sprung breasts overnight. Denial was not only advisable, it was *probable*. Yes, it was possible that I'd grown these myself. Just look at my mother, who was amply blessed.

I loved Olive and hanging out with her, but Ted had been my drinking buddy ever since I was small, and I wanted to see him before the tenth season of *TTA* started filming. The next time Olive and I went out, I called him.

"You want me to come out?" he asked.

"Pleeeease," I wheedled. "I don't want to just see you at *work*. That's the worst."

"You don't have to ask me twice," he said. "I'm just disappointed it took you this long to ask in the first place."

I hadn't told Ted about my boob job, and to him, it probably seemed like I'd been secluded for half the summer before going wild two weeks from the show picking up again.

"See you at the Serpent Pit?" I said.

"Yeah."

The inside of the bar was dark, lit in small strategic places by different neon signs, and was a good place to hide if you wanted to use drugs. Not that anyone really hid. They surreptitiously sniffed from fingernails and smoked blunts out in the open. The only people who were cautious were those who went into the bathrooms to shoot up.

I would snort coke, but I had not graduated to heroin, and I wasn't sure I wanted to.

Nobody checked IDs in those days. My face was well-known, and I went without the Wig, blond tresses falling into my face as I walked in the door. Olive was already at the bar, brazenly sitting with a glass of whiskey, listening to the band. Dial8 wouldn't be caught dead here, which is why I liked it.

"Hey, bitch," I said to her as I sat down.

"Hey, yourself," she said. There was a structured purse next to her on the bar, and I knew she had left it there to show off. "New bag?" I asked.

"It's a *Birkin*." I could feel her pride.

"What's a Birkin?"

"Only one of the most expensive purses in the world. I got this one for a cheap twenty thou."

"Wow." Almost not worth it, I wanted to say.

I felt a kinship with Olive, that we could speak for just a moment and then not have to talk anymore. A companionable silence fell between us as I got a cranberry vodka—still a childish drink, I know, but I liked the sweet tartness—and paid attention to the music. When the song ended and the band took a break, Olive swiveled on her seat to look at me. But before she said anything, her face broke into a grin as she saw someone behind me.

"Ted," she cooed, and there was Ted, his arms wrapping around my shoulders in a gentle embrace. I could smell his musk, the sort of sweaty scent he got when he hadn't showered in a day or so—it permeated his trailer. It was a familiar smell; it smelled a little bit like I was home.

He pulled up a seat and ordered a beer.

"How *are* you?" Olive continued, a flirty edge to her voice. The two began talking, their conversation arching over me as I listened to them on either side. Ted had not done any film projects over the summer; he'd been practicing guitar in his apartment "like a loser," he said wryly, trying to get good enough to join his friend Fred's band. A distant bell went off in my head. "The same Fred who was at the show's premiere party?" I asked.

"That's the one!" he said. "Have you met him?"

"No, but you've mentioned him before . . ."

Fred knew Ted even before he became a TV star, and was the bassist for Jack and Jellyfish, a rock and roll band. Ted said that their guitarist and main vocalist left to go solo, so Jack and Jellyfish was no more, and Fred was recruiting for a new band. "I probably can't do it because of show constraints," he admitted, "but I want to be good enough to get in, and not just because I'm Fred's oldest friend."

"I'm sure you're great," Olive said. "Why don't you play us something?"

Ted's mouth hung open just slightly. "What, now?" he said. "I don't have any equipment. And there's a band playing tonight already."

"They won't mind," Olive said, and stood up. She disappeared for a minute, then reappeared with a man wearing a fedora. "This is our Ted," she said brightly, and the man clapped Ted on the shoulder.

Ted hurriedly gulped down his beer as he stood up, draining

the glass. "Liquid courage," he said, wiping his chin with the back of his hand.

Fedora, who I assumed to be the manager, gestured for Ted to follow him onstage. Once Ted had a borrowed guitar, he stood on the little dais with the only available light, a weak blue thing that was a poor substitute for a spotlight, illuminating him.

He strummed the guitar with nervous fingers and then spoke into the microphone. "This is an oldie but a goodie," he said, then launched into a rendition of "Smells Like Teen Spirit."

As I watched Ted perform, a kind of pride fell over me. He was a good guy. A sweetheart. Why hadn't I seen it before? I was so proud of him for trying something new, putting himself out there—even though Olive was the one who had to coax him to do it.

When he finished the song, he bashfully bowed. Olive and I clapped loudly and she turned to look at me. "That was *so hot*," she said emphatically. The rest of the bar didn't seem to care about Ted; everyone kept drinking and talking, and there were only a few scattered claps around the room.

Ted returned to us all smiles. Olive threw her arms around him in support. "So good!" she exclaimed.

"That was nerve-racking," he admitted to me over her shoulder. "I'm going to go to the bathroom."

When he came back, he was smiling even wider and his eyes were sparking. I knew what he'd done in the bathroom, rubbing at his nose, body jittery. "I should've done this *before* going up on stage," he joked, clearing his throat.

I wondered, for just a moment, if Ted was having trouble with his life. If maybe he was using drugs too much, had an addiction, *something*. But that thought melted away when Olive grabbed at his hand and said something flirty. Both Ted and I looked down at their intertwined hands. I felt a flash of jealousy before Ted gently removed his palm from hers.

"Let's party," he said.

WORK STARTED BACK up a few weeks later. The first thing Brandon said to me was "Whoa, where did those knockers come from?"

"I grew them, idiot," I replied.

"Bullshit." He winked at me and added, "But I'll never tell."

"Just don't go thinking you can touch them, just because Amy and Thomas are in love," I snapped.

He raised his hands like *okay* and backed away, walking in the opposite direction toward his trailer.

I huffed and stepped into my own trailer, where I took off my top and looked at my breasts in the little bathroom mirror. They looked good—natural. But I knew that people were going to ask questions about them.

And oh, did they. Alex Dietrich took one glance at me and his eyes dropped to my chest. He paused for a moment before he said, "How was your summer, Hayley?"

"Fine, and yours?"

"Good, good. How's your mother?"

"Fine," I said shortly. I guess, with my dad back in town, Alex and my mother didn't get to spend as much time together as before. He was clearly hurting if he was asking me about her. I wondered if he loved her.

The truth was, my mother had also gotten plastic surgery done, refining her nose and pulling back the skin at her temples, at the same time I'd gotten my boobs done. It was her way of mother-daughter bonding. It would not be the last time she went under the knife.

Ted had seen me already, so he didn't mention my breasts, but Millie said, "Oh. My. God. What did you do to yourself?" as soon as she caught sight of me.

"I didn't do anything," I insisted.

"Sure, sure. Okay." She couldn't stop staring. "I guess I need to ask Wardrobe for a special bra for me, then. I can't have my little sister with bigger tatas than me."

I waved her away.

When the first episode of the season premiered, the world went bananas.

HAYLEY'S BREAST AUGMENTATION, claimed a gossip rag. *LOOK AT HER BEFORE/AFTER PHOTOS.*

The tabloids all claimed that I'd had a boob job. There were paparazzi snaps of my chest, blown up and examined from multiple angles. It was disgusting and invasive, but altogether not surprising.

And though I didn't make it a habit to look at any websites about me, that gif of me slapping my elbows together and making my breasts bounce really got everywhere in those days. It was viral before viral was a thing. A gif before gifs were really used. People waited for *minutes* for their dial-up internet to download that gif. I shudder to think what they did with it.

"Did you see this?" Millie asked, waving a tabloid with my cleavage front and center, the next time I stepped onto the set. "This is all they care about now."

"Maybe we'll get more viewers," Oscar said.

"Ew, *Dad*," Millie said. She rolled her eyes. "If this is all they talk about this season, I quit."

But my breasts weren't all that happened that season on *Third Time Around*. New writers came in, infusing new blood into the tired storylines. For the first time in several seasons, Amy and Thomas questioned their relationship and broke up. It was the first time in years that I felt relief going onto set, and I hadn't even realized the weight of my feelings until they were alleviated. No more lovemaking scenes, no more Sock, or lack thereof! I was supposed to act appropriately mopey about Amy's breakup with Thomas, but that was fine. Amy was onto the SATs and college applications.

The main focus was now on Zac and Natasha's relationship, which turned up the heat. Soon, they were the ones making love on the show and requiring closed sets.

Sophia, who played Natasha, came to me one afternoon and asked, "Is he always like . . . that?"

"Like what? Who?"

"Ted. Is he always . . ." She looked around and lowered her voice. "Drunk? He smells like vodka every time we have to do a scene. I never noticed until we had to make out all the time."

A finger of irritation wormed its way into my stomach, but I dismissed it. "Not always," I said defensively. "You must make him want to drink." It was mean of me, and I regret it now, but I was feeling annoyed by Sophia and I didn't know why. I was protective of Ted, my drinking buddy, my best friend on the show.

"Ohhhkay," she said, but she didn't sound okay. "Should I tell Alex?"

"No!" I said. "It's not affecting his work, is it?"

"Well, no . . . but it's *distracting*."

"If you can't act alongside someone who has had a few drinks, you're not a good actress at all. I've been doing this for years." I sounded haughty.

She made a *hmm* noise, and that was the last time we talked about it. I think, if I'd been less caustic, she would've come to me when he was actually high, when things started getting worse and Ted's performances were beginning to deteriorate. But as it was, Ted and I weren't in the same scenes as much anymore, and we didn't share downtime at the same times anymore either. He was in his trailer, presumably drinking or snorting or whatever he did, when I was on camera, and vice versa. And when we went out partying, of course he was going to get trashed. That's just what we *did*.

JANE AND JESSICA are silent when I pause to take a long breath. Then Jessica says, "So what happened to Ted?"

"What do you mean, what happened to Ted?" I ask.

"You never talk about him."

That's true, I realize. I don't talk about Ted. I sigh and run my hands through my hair.

"We'll get to what happened with Ted in a while," I say. "In the meantime, did you make that Instagram account I asked you to?"

"Yep," Jane says. "I'd show you, but . . ." She gestures with her empty hands. Right. She's not allowed to bring her phone to the house. It must be terrible, to be a teenager and not be able to access your phone for days on end. I used to have a phone and I couldn't stop using that thing. It must be a sacrifice for the girls to come visit me. One that I appreciate.

I can't help but feel that being in my house is like living in the nineties again. No internet, no cell phones. When the girls play video games, it's not the newest Xbox game or whatever, but Super Nintendo—a closed system that doesn't require an internet connection. We have Mario Kart 64 and that's as fun as it gets around here. We spend time outdoors when my father says we can, taking hikes around Los Angeles, most notably the hilly areas near my house.

And my house. My house is more technologically advanced than I am. It's wired to detect if someone is coming or going. There are smart locks on the doors that are keyed in via numeral code, so there are no physical keys for me to steal and use if I wanted to. I'm a prisoner in my home, unless Adam, the bodyguard and driver, takes me to whatever set I'm working on at the moment. And even then, I can't hang out with my coworkers after all is said and done, because I'm shuttled right back to the house to convalesce.

It's a lonely existence.

CHAPTER 18

My star exploded seemingly overnight. I hadn't been getting any calls at all, and now I was inundated with them. I was *back*, baby. I was on cloud nine.

The best part of my breast augmentation was getting jobs again: grown-up roles for teenage stars. You know how Jennifer Lawrence was tapped to play a thirty-year-old for that one movie, I forget what it was called, when she was twenty? It was like that.

When I was seventeen, I was cast as a twenty-one-year-old biology student in *Mysterious City*. This blockbuster movie was about a boy who discovers that his murphy bed is a portal to a new dimension, and my character, Denise, is the person he recruits to figure out what is going on in the other dimension.

"These two fall in love," I said, reading the script at my parents' kitchen table. Dad was out of town again, back in Anita, doing God knows what with his business (or pleasure), and Mom was back to acting moony around Alex Dietrich. I wondered if they had some sort of arrangement or if it was all behind Dad's back. "How cliché," I added.

"I think it's sweet," my mother said, downing her coffee.

"When is the screen test?"

"Tomorrow," I answered. A screen test is given to the last few contenders for a role before it is cast; I had a one-in-three shot of nailing it. I knew that the chemistry with my costar would be the way I would win the role.

I can fake chemistry with anybody.

On the day of the screen test, I dressed in a pair of flared jeans, a button-up shirt, and straightened my hair, smoothing it into a ponytail so I looked studious. I tucked a pair of reading glasses into my purse. Gone was any trace of the party girl who had stayed out until three A.M. the previous weekend, and the only jitteriness I felt was from coffee, not coke.

When I laid eyes on Jamie, my character's love interest, the air evaporated from my lungs. He wasn't conventionally gorgeous—long auburn hair, an explosion of freckles, impossibly long eyelashes, and a rail-thin body—but in person, he exuded an amazing energy. I understood why he was the lead in this movie.

The attraction hit me right in the sternum.

There were other people in the room, but I didn't really notice them. They adjusted the camera, said, "Whenever you're ready," and I put on my glasses. Off we went.

"This is against the law of thermodynamics," I said, brow furrowed.

"But it's happening! Can't you see?"

"I see it, I see it!" I affirmed, pushing my glasses up my nose. "But let me do some calculations to figure out what exactly is going on here."

"What was that?" Jamie asked, whirling around quickly, reacting to an unheard noise.

"The government! They're after us!" I said, my fingers moving faster on a fake keyboard, making calculations.

"Denise, I just want to say, if we don't get another chance . . ."
Jamie looked at me wistfully.

"Yes?" I said.

"A sudden rumble, and Denise is pitched forward into Greg's arms," intoned a narrator. I pretended to stumble into Jamie's embrace, and we looked at each other for a long moment, our eyes and lips tantalizingly close.

I didn't have to act. I ached to kiss this person I'd just met. The energy was just that strong.

"And scene."

Jamie let go of me and I brushed off my clothing reluctantly. We stood a short distance apart, and I began to pick at my nails nervously before I realized what I was doing and stopped.

"Thank you, Hayley."

Jamie smiled at me, a rapid grin that showed all his perfect, square teeth. "I have a good feeling," he said, and that was all I needed to hear before I found out that I had gotten it, and that was my summer plans sorted.

I called Olive and told her the good news. "Let's celebrate!" she shouted tinnily on the line, and we both laughed. I invited Ted to come out and play with us at Ivar, a club in Hollywood. Olive had some ecstasy and we each took one while we danced up a storm. I grew hot but didn't want to stop moving. Ted danced up on me and Olive danced up on him, and we writhed

like a three-headed snake. We stumbled out of the club at closing, holding our shoes and walking barefoot on the concrete.
I stepped on a broken bottle and had to go to the emergency
room, amid a swell of paparazzi, to get five stitches on the
bottom of my foot. Then I had to find the energy to go to an
Entertainment Weekly shoot early that day.

The cast had already done interviews with the magazine
about the show's season finale; this was the photo session to
accompany the article. There we were, Tina and Oscar and
Millie and Ted and Natasha and Brandon and me, dressed to
the nines and posing on mopeds in front of a giant backdrop.
I was inexplicably depressed; this was my ecstasy hangover. It
was the last place I wanted to be, but I was required to be there.

And Ted seemed to be feeling the same way. When the
photographer asked him to straighten up, Ted was belligerent.
"Who are you to tell me what to do?" he yelled. Oscar tried
to soothe him, but that just seemed to make matters worse.
"Don't touch me!"

"Hayley, can you try . . . ?" Oscar said, and all eyes turned
to me. It was as if everyone knew about our special bond and
thought that he would listen to me.

"Can we get a minute, please," I said, stepping off my moped and limping across the floor as the room cleared out.

As I approached Ted, his eyes grew glassy with tears. "I'm
sorry," he burbled. "I'm not in the right headspace for this today."

"What's wrong?" I asked. "Is it the anxiety?"

"Nothing. Everything."

"I can't help you if you don't talk to me."

"It's so bad, Hayley. I don't even know how to say it."

"What?" I asked.

He was silent for a long moment, then he reached out and clasped both my hands in his. "Don't judge me, okay?" he said.

"Okay."

"I'm an addict." He coughed, squeezed my hands, and dropped them. He rubbed his palms on his five-thousand-dollar couture pants borrowed from the stylist and then thought better of it, wringing his hands instead.

I resisted the urge to laugh. "You're what?" I said. "If you are, so am I."

"I'm serious, Hayley. I'm already signed up to go to rehab during the hiatus. It's out in Malibu . . ."

"What?" I said, my concern beginning to grow. "You mean you're really an addict? What are you addicted to?"

"I've been soul-searching with Fred," he said, ignoring my question. "He made me realize that I'm sick. I've been off the drugs since last night, but I know I'm overcompensating with the drinking to get me through the day. It shouldn't *be* like this, you know? Having to drink to make it through the day?"

I started to feel sick to my stomach. Ted, my beautiful Ted. Suffering like this. "Well, what do you need *right now*? To get through this shoot?"

"I need a bump, Hayley. Do you have any on you?"

"Yeah." A tiny baggie, left over from the night before, was still in my bag. I hadn't had time to change out purses, what with the shoot so early and my foot needing medical attention early this morning. "But if you take some now, are you gonna be okay?"

Ted sat down heavily on the moped, closing his eyes. He was sweating, a light sheen on his forehead, speckling his hair. "It'll sober me up from the drinking," he insisted. "Then I can make it through the shoot."

"You can't just drink a lot of water and sober up on your own?" I asked.

"That'll take hours. No, a quick bump is all I need."

Luckily, within twenty minutes, we were back on track, Ted and all. But I couldn't stop glancing at him every time we paused in shooting. Ted, my friend Ted. An addict.

My heart grew heavy.

BOY-CRAZY HAYLEY ALDRIDGE SEEN OUT AND ABOUT WITH JAMIE LITTLE

Hayley Aldridge, 17, one of the stars of the ensemble television show *Third Time Around* on CBS, was seen out and about with *Ready Steady* actor Jamie Little, 18. Hayley and Jamie are costarring in the Harry Ninagawa-directed *Mysterious City*, which is filming in Los Angeles and due out next year.

CHAPTER 19

I had always prided myself on being able to turn my party-girl tendencies on and off like a switch. Cocaine was fun, drinking was fun, but they weren't crutches. I didn't *need* them.

What I needed, instead, were *boys*.

Something happened to me after Trey took advantage of me. I had a cute little body with a cute pair of breasts and I began to flaunt them. The attention I received, not only from the press and the tabloids but from other stars as well, could fill a canyon. It didn't matter that I felt both repulsed and flattered by the attention.

Girls, I'm not going to sugarcoat it: When I was seventeen, I got around. A lot.

It may surprise you that I'm telling you this, when you're seventeen yourselves, and I'm stricter with you than my mother was with me. But while I understand that exploring your sexuality and your body with other people is a big part of growing up, it's also an easy way to ruin your self-esteem if you don't do it right.

Case in point: I dated a *lot* of people. I had dates with names that started with every letter of the alphabet. Aidan, Brian,

Charlie, David, Eamon, Francisco . . . I could go on and on. Sometimes women fell into the cracks as well. Daisy, Elizabeth, Felicity. Coke-fueled binges that ended with me in someone's bed several nights of the week. I'd take three days to get over my hangover, eating nothing but peanut-butter toast and lamenting to Olive tearfully that I was getting fat.

I was a selfish lover, and I knew it. When I got mine, I hardly cared about what happened to the others. "Thanks," I'd say, and turn over. Some of the guys groaned and hated me. Some of the girls just accepted it and cuddled my back.

But my biggest conquest of the early summer was Jamie Little. During the first week of shooting *Mysterious City*, we couldn't stop looking at each other. Every time our eyes met, his lip would quirk into a tiny grin, and I couldn't help smiling back. By the time the first week was over, I decided to follow him to his trailer at the end of the day's wrap and shoot my shot.

I tapped on his trailer door, even though he had seen me in his footsteps just moments before, and the door wasn't completely closed. "Come on in," he said, smiling, and reached out an arm to help me climb the steep steps. I took his hand gratefully, and as soon as I was in the trailer, the door swinging shut behind me, I was in his arms, mouth on his, no preamble, just—kissing, kissing. If he was surprised, he didn't show it; we had been dancing around our attraction for the entire week, and I think he expected this as much as I had.

We fumbled along to the tiny couch in his trailer and lay down on it, my back pressed against the tweedy material. Jamie was already ripping off his shirt in between kisses and I was helping him, his knees between my legs, spreading them apart. I still wore my shorts and I wasn't ready to take them off yet, but the skin-on-skin contact of our stomachs made me mew with pleasure.

He scrambled for a condom, which were conveniently in a bowl on a side table next to the couch. And suddenly, I didn't want to say no; I was having too much fun, and besides, my virginity was toast anyway. Might as well start making notches on my belt.

I drove myself home, my legs shaking with excitement so badly that it was difficult to press the accelerator, and took a shower immediately after I got back to avoid any questions about my flattened hair.

We didn't *date*. We went out. Jamie Little wasn't the hottest heartthrob of 2001, but there was enough interest between the two of us that we boosted each other's star. We'd go out to sushi dinners and bowling, like normal folk, and the paparazzi would flock us wherever we went.

I never *loved* Jamie, not the way I had loved Trey. I was just incredibly attracted to him. When I couldn't get enough satisfaction from him, I would go looking elsewhere. It looked like we were exclusively dating, but we had an understanding: each of us could do what we pleased.

I was seventeen; I had a car; I was the breadwinner; I was invincible. My parents tried to rein me in, but I went where I wanted to go, dated who I wanted to date, stayed out until I wanted to come home. I would barely have time to change clothes and shower before I was back on set at *Mysterious City*, and sometimes I would go straight from Jamie's house to my trailer without spending any time with my family at all.

My parents were wary. One day, my mother came to the studio looking for me and gained access to my trailer. She was waiting for me when I came in between setups, waving a tabloid from where she sat on my loveseat. "Do you know that I have to keep tabs on you now from the gossip rags?" she said, in lieu of a greeting.

"Hi to you too," I said, sitting on my countertop and sipping a drip coffee from craft services.

"Do I ever get to meet this Jamie Little?" my mother asked.

"Depends. Do you want to see him with his shirt on or off?"

"Hayley Dakota!"

"I'm *joking*, Mom."

A PA poked their head in after a cursory knock, saying, "You're needed in five, Hayley. And I'm supposed to remind you of the *Entertainment Weekly* interview happening this afternoon at three."

"Okay. Can you get Jamie in here, please?" I said.

The PA nodded hurriedly and ducked back out. I looked at my mother. "There," I said.

"Thank you," she said, mollified. "Have you seen this website?"

"What website?" I asked.

"There's a website—Is Hayley Aldridge Eighteen Yet dot com."

"Oh, that." I waved my hand. "Yeah."

"They're counting down until your legal birthday. It's obscene."

"It's just stupid fan stuff, Mom. No need to worry about it."

She pursed her lips at me. "I'm your mother. It's sick. I'm here to worry."

Jamie chose that moment to saunter into my trailer. My mother stood up to greet him. Outstretching her hand, she said, "It's nice to meet the man who is sleeping with my daughter."

"Mom!" I exclaimed. It was mortifying for her to come out with a line like that. Jamie, however, was cool under pressure. He laughed, shook her hand, and said, "Not a problem." He didn't deny it like I thought he would.

"And when can we expect to see you at our home for a nice meal and to get to know you better?" my mother continued, embarrassing herself and me further.

"I'd be happy to join you one of these weekends," Jamie said. "I'll set it up with Hayley."

"Okay, I have to get to set now, so if you want to leave the trailer . . ." I began ushering them out. My mother swung her bag onto her forearm and huffed. "I'll see you at home, Hayley," she said over her shoulder as she walked away.

Jamie laughed, an easy laugh that showed me he was fine with whatever had just happened. I turned to him. "You really don't have to go to dinner at my house."

He laid a long arm across my shoulders, his fingers playing with the ends of my hair. "It sounds like fun."

I smiled at him, glad he was easy. "Back to the apocalypse,"

I said.

THE REPORTER FROM *Entertainment Weekly* was waiting for me when I got back to my trailer. "I'm sorry we had to do this here," I said, looking around at the small space. I had made my trailer homey, putting up twinkle lights and tapestries so that the room wasn't completely bare and beige, but it was still distinctly a trailer.

"It's fine," the reporter said. "I'm Matt."

"Nice to meet you, Matt." I gestured to the couch and sat down perpendicular to him on my loveseat. I was wearing a pair of cutoffs and a T-shirt, nothing special. I was still wearing my makeup from filming, which was a bit heavy, but I'd rather be with mascara than without. I wondered if I should've gotten dressed up for him—but no. This was only the interview portion of the piece, and the photographer would be booked for later.

"How are you feeling about the last season of *Third Time Around*?" Matt asked, placing a recorder in between us.

"It was interesting. This season was different for Amy, since she explores other things that seventeen-year-olds are interested in: college, her studies, other boys."

"Speaking of boys," Matt said, segueing seamlessly into what I knew he would want to discuss, "how's Jamie Little?"

"He's fine," I said, trying not to say too much, too fast. I liked Jamie, but I didn't want to gush about him in a publication. We hadn't discussed what our relationship was, or if we even *had* a relationship, at all. Dinner plans at my parents' house notwithstanding.

"There are rumors that you are dating others besides just Jamie," Matt said, with his eyebrows raised.

"Rumors are rumors," I said, shrugging. "Isn't this piece supposed to be about *Mysterious City*?"

"It's more of an in-depth piece about you, actually," he said. "The rising star Hayley Aldridge. We're talking to people back in Anita, like your old agent, things like that."

I wanted to say that I'd been working since I was seven, but I bit it back. I knew that audience intrigue and goodwill were the only reasons people were suddenly interested in me after I'd worked for a decade in this business.

"So Hayley," he asked conversationally, "are you a virgin?"

"Excuse me?"

"The readers will want to know if you're a virgin or not."

How is that any of their business? I burned to ask, but I said, "I am. I'm waiting until marriage before I have sex. My parents raised me to be a good Christian girl."

"They'd be happy to know that," he said, marking it down in a little steno pad. "Though I have to say that Jamie Little will be disappointed."

If you only knew.

"I also have to ask," Matt said, his face twisted into a wry smile. I knew what he was going to say even before he said it. "Are your breasts real?"

"One hundred percent," I said.

"Because there are tabloid shots showing before-and-afters . . ."

"I know what's out there. I grew over the summer. Is there anything else you'd like to talk about? *Mysterious City*, perhaps? Or my next project?"

"What's your next project?"

"I've been cast as Linda in the Ed Hodges movie *Tourmaline*. It's still in preproduction but we should start filming soon after *Mysterious City* wraps." My cell phone rang and I looked down at it. Trey Barnes's number. I frowned and silenced the call. "Sorry about that. I thought I had that on mute."

"No problem. So, it'll be your second time working with Hodges, correct?"

"That's right."

"Hodges's movies are notorious Oscar bait. Are you hopeful for a chance to nab an Academy Award?"

"It's too early to speculate, considering we haven't even started shooting yet," I said carefully. "The script is certainly there. And it would be amazing to give a performance worthy of acknowledgment."

"Spoken like a true professional," Matt said, grinning. His eyes flicked over my bare legs and I thought I should've worn jeans. "So let's talk about *Mysterious City* . . ."

Hayley Aldridge extends a tanned thigh across the length of the loveseat. The Von Dutch logo of Aldridge's bright white T-shirt is distorted by her abundant chest and her cutoff jean shorts cling to her hips. Aldridge famously stopped wearing orange after a fashion mishap that put her on a worst-dressed list. "I'm sorry we had to do this here," she says, appraising her trailer on the lot of *Mysterious City*, her newest project, costarring Jamie Little (*Ready Steady*). Her voice has a slight Southern accent that has been coaxed away by years of living in Los Angeles, and probably rigorous speech training. After I assured her that it was fine, that the readers would be interested in hearing what she had to say and not where she said it, Aldridge relaxes into her loveseat and her cutoffs ride up her thighs.

One of the first questions I have to ask is if Aldridge realizes the effect she has on people. She doesn't understand what I mean, and I have to clarify: Does she know that her audience theorizes about her virginity? Aldridge sets the record straight: "My parents raised me to be a good Christian girl," she says. "I am waiting until marriage to have sex."

And what does her costar and beau, Jamie Little, have to say about it? Aldridge doesn't answer.

CHAPTER 20

The powers-that-be wanted Jamie and me to continue "dating" until the premiere of *Mysterious City*—for promotional purposes, I would hazard to say—so we kept each other on speed dial.

I don't want to talk about *Tourmaline*, but I know I have to get it off my chest.

One hundred forty-six days before the website counter would proclaim that I was eighteen, my sister had her first big Hollywood premiere. She had landed the best-friend role in a summer blockbuster, *Shine Street*, and it opened that July.

She was only thirteen, and she was excited. The movie promotion flew her and our mother—her chaperone—around the world. Our mother had gotten veneers for the occasion. Ashley had inherited my father's bad teeth and had to do it in braces, but she didn't seem to mind. "At least the filming was done before I became a metal mouth," she said with a shrug, when asked about it during press events.

Ashley did have a request for me, though: not to come to the L.A. premiere.

"What?" I said, not sure that I'd heard her right. "It sounds like you don't want me to go to the *premiere*."

"Well, if *you* go, it'll overshadow *me*," she said.

"If I *don't* go, it'll look like I don't support you and that I'm a bitch," I responded.

Ashley looked perturbed by that.

"Is that what you want?" I needled her. "For some sibling feud to show up in the tabloids?"

"No . . ."

"All right, then. Let me go to the premiere. I'll be understated, I promise."

I knew exactly how I'd play it. I'd wear a demure dress and I'd skip the red carpet but would show up at the afterparty, pose for some unofficial photos that showed I was there, be supportive.

I had to work on *Tourmaline* the day of the premiere, but I had permission to leave early that day to make it. I had the outfit—a slinky, but not too sexy, black dress with a small train—hanging in my trailer. I would have my makeup artist, April, wipe off my heavy day makeup and put on a softer, glam look.

Let me explain about *Tourmaline*. My part in the movie was small; small enough that I was able to fit in my filming after *Mysterious City* wrapped but before *Third Time Around* started back up again in the fall. I was reunited with Ed Hodges, the director of *A Poem for Jeanie*. I don't know if it was the small scale of the role or my age—seventeen now rather than thirteen—or my party-girl status that made Ed Hodges look at me differently, but he treated me unlike he had when I was playing Jeanie. He was short-tempered, he yelled a lot, he berated me in front of the entire cast and crew. I *have* heard that he was dealing with alcoholism at the time and that might have influenced the way he spoke to me, but it was very different from how he spoke to the rest of the people working on the production.

The evening of the premiere, when I'd taken a verbal thrashing that had nearly put me in tears, I sat in my trailer and took a breath before I started switching gears, getting ready for my sister's event. Why did I subject myself to this torment?

My phone buzzed and I looked down at it: Trey. He'd been calling a lot lately, but I never picked up and never called back. Every time I thought about what had happened in that hotel room, I felt my stomach clench.

There was a knock on my trailer door. "Come in," I called. I expected it to be April, but I was surprised when Ed Hodges lifted himself gruffly up the stairs and sat, without invitation, on the other seat cushion of the little couch that outfits all movie trailers. I tried not to betray my confusion, but I didn't know why he had come. Unless it was to explain himself?

"Hayley, are you fitting in with the cast and crew okay?" Ed Hodges asked.

We were several weeks into filming at this point, and the cast and crew were not the main issue I faced. I nodded, trying not to show my continued confusion on my face.

Hodges stretched his arms out in front of him, twisting his fingers together and knotting them. He was gaining weight in his middle and was graying on top. He was probably fifty at this point in his life and had won four Oscars.

"I'm sure you're wondering why I'm so hard on you," he said amicably.

I shrugged with one shoulder, my eyes turned away from him. I felt like a petulant child. Yes, why was he so hard on me, why didn't he yell at the other cast members?

"You are a talented actress," he said sincerely, unknotting his fingers and placing his hands palm-down on his knees. "But on this production I feel like you haven't been giving me . . . more."

"I'll try harder," I said automatically, because that is what an actress is supposed to say when her director says she's not giving enough.

"Linda is full of *angst*," he continued. "She hates her life, she's a pocket of misery."

I nodded. I remember the next words carefully because they were such a shock to my system.

"So I think you should blow me."

I paused, cocked my head, and tried to hear what Hodges had said one more time. "Ex-excuse me?"

"You've become a beautiful woman," he continued, and his hands, which had been on his lap, slithered their way toward me. He grasped my hands in his, and I was surprised at how dry they felt; whispery, like old leather. "And I think this is what we both need."

"*Excuse* me?" I repeated, not sure what else to say. He was guiding my hands to his zipper, and my eyes flicked down. The grotesque thing was already hard under his pants and I recoiled, taking my hands with the rest of my body. I clenched everything on me, wildly uncomfortable.

"I'll go easier on you," Hodges said. "In front of everyone. I'll be nicer."

Blow him or don't blow him, there would be consequences either way. Could I live with myself if I did? Would he make my life on set a living hell if I didn't?

"I think you should leave," I said, my voice quavering. "Please get out of my trailer."

"It's Hollywood's worst-kept secret that you're the biggest skank around," he snarled. "*Everyone* knows that Jamie Little is just a PR relationship and you're sleeping with half of Tinseltown."

I raised my voice. "Just because I'm sleeping with half of Tinseltown doesn't mean I want to *blow YOU!*"

He stood up, and I was afraid he was going to take me by force. There was no one else around, and I doubted anyone would hear me if I screamed. He took one step back and I felt a modicum of relief. "Fine," he said softly. "So be it." And he left my trailer.

I shook uncontrollably as I hugged myself, waiting until I knew Hodges had left the lot. April never showed, presumably because she was warned off by Hodges before he set foot in my trailer. Ten minutes passed, twenty. Finally I roused myself from my spot on the couch and hurried across the parking lot to my car, and breathed a sigh of relief when I sat in the front seat and locked all the doors.

I drove aimlessly, the dress for the premiere forgotten on a hanger in my trailer. I was in my cutoffs and wearing a pair of thong sandals. The thoughts chewed at my mind: Should I have done it? What were the consequences now? Would he have actually been nicer to me on set, or was he just trying to get what he could? Why did it seem like all directors were predators? Was it the position of power they were in, did it go to their heads? I hadn't realized it as I was driving, but the stoplights and streetlights grew oblong and blurry; I was crying.

The premiere! I'd been so consumed with Hodges, I hadn't considered the time. Could I go like this? I was already late and I was going to skip the red carpet. I could stand in the back, watch the movie. Be there. For my sister.

I parked my Beetle where I could find a space on the street and rummaged through the back seat for a stray blouse. The cutoffs would have to do. I wiped my eyes and tried to unsmear the mascara from my cheeks, checking the rearview mirror in the dark while I did so. Then I hoofed it to the theater, where the fans still stood outside the cordons with signs and pads of paper for autographs.

There wasn't a way in through the back? I craned my neck, but I couldn't see around the crowd. I had to make a decision: walk through them and be recognized, or miss the premiere entirely. I took a deep breath. For my sister.

IN AN INTERVIEW with one paparazzo, named Simon, he had this to say: "We were camped out in front of the Shine Street premiere waiting for Hayley. We knew she would come to a family premiere like this. When she didn't show for the red carpet, we wondered what could have kept her. I almost packed up to leave, and some of the other guys did,

but then the fans parted like the Red Sea and there she was, looking a
mess. Bam! Instant front-page picture. You can make bank on a picture
of Hayley looking bad."

The photos that ran in *In Touch Weekly*'s next issue were
damning. I looked like a homeless woman, in ripped jean
shorts and a blouse that apparently needed to be steam-ironed,
black streaks of mascara in deposits under my eyes where I
hadn't swiped them away. The flashes from the cameras had
surprised me; I thought they'd all packed up by then, but it was
the paparazzi who had stuck around, just in case.

Ashley was livid. "I *told* you not to come!" she shouted at
me, when the photos circulated: in the news, in the tabloids,
online. "Now everyone is talking about *you*, just like I said
they would, and not about me! Or the movie!"

"It says right there, 'Hayley Aldridge's sister, Ashley, stars in
Shine Street,'" I pointed out, but I felt bad for her. I had been
trying to do the right thing and had gotten caught looking
blasted out of my mind. I hadn't been high, but no one knew
that. I *looked* disheveled; it *looked* bad. Should I tell her what
had happened with Hodges? Would it soften her toward me? I
decided to try.

"Listen, Ashley, I'm so sorry. But you should know that right
before this—"

"I don't *care*! I don't care what your excuses are! You think
I don't notice you coming home at random times after midnight? You are off doing god knows what with who knows
who and *you suck*!"

She walked up to her bedroom—a room in the house I had

paid for, with my *Third Time Around* money—and slammed the door. I stood, chewing my lip, hands on my hips. She had gotten the "god knows what" line from our mother, I knew it. I blew my breath out and looked toward the kitchen, where our mother was overseeing our cook prepare dinner. It wasn't worth bringing up with *her*. I knew she had already lost a lot of respect for me, and the feeling was mutual: what she'd done with Alex Dietrich lowered her in my eyes.

Hodges was not easier on me after that, but he didn't solicit me again. In an interview he did with *Rolling Stone* magazine, after he'd won his fifth Best Director Oscar, for *Tourmaline*, he claimed that he had a special way of talking to his actors to get the performances he wanted out of them.

> "I threaten them," he says, voice jubilant. "I tell them awful things. Just like, in *Tourmaline*, I told one of the supporting actors something that probably ruined their day. But wouldn't you know, I got the rise out of that actor. They put on a performance of a lifetime. And you see it in the finished work." He chuckles. "I'm not a monster. But sometimes I act like one to extract the performance I need."

JESSICA STARES AT me. "So he did that to get a rise out of you and make you *angsty* for your performance?"

I shrug. "I assume he did it for one of two reasons: one, to see if he could get a rise out of me. And two, to see if he could get a blow job. No harm, no foul, right?"

Jane is tracing a circle on the concrete by the pool using water. "That's messed up," she says. "Your entire life is so messed up, god."

"What did Olive say when you told her?" Jessica wants to know.

I sigh. "I didn't tell Olive this time."

"Why not?"

"Because. I don't know why. I was just so . . . *surprised*. And disgusted. She was off doing her own thing around that time—her last performance, as it turned out. So I didn't bring it up then. I *did* show her that *Rolling Stone* article, though, when it came out. I told her I recognized that it was *me* Hodges was talking about, and how pissed I was. But in vague terms."

"I thought she was your best friend," Jessica says.

"She was."

"Why haven't we ever met her, if she's your best friend?" Jane asks.

"Because of the restraining order."

"You got a restraining order against your best friend?" Jessica sounds surprised.

I sigh. "No, my parents did. I'll explain it to you soon."

CHAPTER 21

Mysterious City had a lot of CGI and postproduction work, so it wouldn't premiere until 2003. That gave me a whole year of having to pretend that Jamie Little was my boyfriend. In the meantime, I met up with my alphabet of fuck-buddies: Gianni, Hector, Isaac, Kevin, Lance. I often went to the Serpent Pit to pick up guys, now by myself since Olive seemed to be partying it up all around town and Ted was sober. I made new friends—Amanda, who had the best coke; Robyn, who had the best dance moves. But they were shallow friendships, ones that I forged in the club but never brought outside of it, and when I met with a guy I was going to sleep with that night, I would leave Amanda and Robyn there, like Barbies in a dream house.

As a fixture at the Serpent Pit, the paparazzi found me most nights without much trouble. Every new online alert for Hayley Aldridge was about my wild nights out. They caught me walking out the door, my hair disheveled from dancing, sunglasses reflecting their flashes even at one in the morning. The guys I picked up would drive separately to wherever we were going to meet, and the criteria I chose for them weren't just their looks or their game, but whether they lived in a gated community that the paps couldn't breach. And their willingness to sign an NDA.

One night, Amanda and Robyn and I were at the Serpent Pit. We snorted coke and danced in a booth. I was making headway with a guy named Marcos, chatting him up at the bar, when I felt a tap on my shoulder.

I ignored it. Then it came again, more insistent this time. I broke away from my conversation with Marcos and there stood Trey Barnes, looking as beautiful as the day I lost my virginity.

"What do *you* want?" I asked, raising my voice above the music.

"Hi, Hayley," he shouted, and I realized that it was probably the first time he hadn't just called me *girl*. "I just wanted to see how you were. We haven't talked in a while."

"I'm *busy*."

"Listen, I wanted to talk to you," he said, coming closer and lowering his voice. Marcos got off his stool and walked away. I watched him go, feeling a detached sense of regret that *there went a fish off the hook* and turned to face Trey fully, giving him my attention.

"Oh yeah? Gonna apologize?" I raised an eyebrow coolly.

He looked uncomfortable. "What happened . . . it was my bad. But you have to admit, you wanted it."

"How is that an apology?" I shook my head with disgust. "Never mind. Leave me alone, Trey. I'm over it."

But I wasn't over it. I felt the sting of his rejection all over again, and my eyes blurred with angry tears. With the cocaine in my system, I was feeling everything hyper-acutely, and it didn't help that it was *Trey*. Beautiful Trey, my first love.

I gathered my purse and strode out of the bar. Trey followed me. The paparazzi were waiting, a battery of barracudas. They flashed their flashes and called our names. I held one hand in front of my eyes, shielding them from the worst of the flashes, but was still blinded, and walked off a curb. Groaning, I heaved myself into a sitting position and looked at my skinned knee.

Trey was there immediately, sitting on the curb next to me, one palm flat on my thigh. I sighed.

There we were, damn near in the street, cameramen flocked all around us, ringing us in a cacophony of flashes, and I looked at him. And I hated him. The coke riled up something in me; I felt invincible. And as I gathered myself to my feet, I began shouting, pointing, gesticulating wildly, reaming Trey for his insensitivity and awfulness. He stood there, mouth agape, as if unable to believe that his sweet Hayley had stood up for herself, finally. "Look at you," I screamed. "Acting like you didn't *break my heart.* Acting like you didn't *use me.* Like nothing happened between us on tour. When you know good and well that *something* did happen, and it was fucked up, and you were in the wrong! You insensitive, brutal, piece of shit! Don't"—he started to talk, and I shushed him with a finger jab to the chest—"don't even try to explain yourself."

"Hayley," he hastened to say. "I *loved* you."

"Funny way of showing it," I retorted. "You ghost me, you ignore me. I'm over it. I'm over *you.* I never should've gotten involved with you. I hope you eat shit and die."

What ran in the tabloids the next day were jubilant head-lines about how I'd lost it:

HAYLEY LOSES HER MIND, YELLS AT TREY!

MENTAL DISORDER? HAYLEY ALDRIDGE SCREAMS IN THE NIGHT.

DRUGGED-OUT HAYLEY YELLS AT EX-LOVER IN PARKING LOT.

The accompanying pictures were also awful, to say the least.

But I was still able to keep my personal and my professional life somewhat separated. We started shooting *Third Time Around* again, and I was on set without a single complaint lodged against me for unbecoming conduct. I like to think I was able to keep it together.

REHAB HAD BEEN good for Ted. He'd been gone the entire summer to a spot in Malibu and when he'd returned, I visited him at his new home in Calabasas. I brought a bottle of sparkling grape juice. He accepted it graciously, but we didn't pop it; we sat on his back porch drinking still water and discussing anything but his recovery. As an act of solidarity, I didn't even get high before going to his house.

"How's Olive?" he asked me then, and I had to grimace and say I didn't know. Olive had exploded at that time, doing the promo she was supposed to do for her latest project, *The Goddess Report,* and partying it up around town to an excessive amount. Some said she'd suffered a mental breakdown, but I didn't think so. Olive was rock-solid; annoyed, perhaps, or angry, but not broken down. "She's nonstop," I offered. "I can't keep track of her. But she will have to come up for air sooner or later."

He nodded, evidently having kept up with Olive's antics in the tabloids as I had. She was almost outshining me in the rags these days.

"More importantly, how are *you*?" I asked. He looked fitter, leaner. I wondered if he had traded one habit for another, and made exercise his focus.

"Ready for filming," Ted said. "Did you know that I saw what's in store for us this season, and Zac and Natasha are going to get engaged? Maybe they'll even get pregnant. Not sure what order it'll be in."

"That'll be great for sweeps," I mused.

"Imagine me, as a dad." He chuckled. I looked at him and the strange thing was, I *could*: strong, sweet, dependable Ted.

What I said instead was "It's just pretend, Ted," and he nodded sagely, like I'd said the most obvious thing in the world. I regret that now. I should've told him how much I'd looked up to him. How he would make a great father to someone, someday. And not just as a line of dialogue from a TV show.

The countdown clock ticked down to my eighteenth birthday. One hundred twenty-one days before that happened, we started filming season eleven. There was a welcome-back sheet cake sitting at craft services the first day back, and again, Ted claimed it was his birthday. He was twenty-two that year; he ate half a piece and then threw the rest away. Millie wolfed down some cake and made a beeline for her trailer. I looked at a square of cake, but didn't touch it.

My new thing was zucchini. Spiralized and steamed, I ate it like noodles with a teaspoon of extra virgin olive oil and some salt. I was extremely thin but didn't see it; all I could sense were the little knobs and dips of spots on my skin sticking out and in, and I wanted to smooth them out, make them two-dimensional. It was hard.

To promote the eleventh season of *Third Time Around*, I was invited to New York to host *Saturday Night Live*. You've seen the reruns, haven't you? Where they poke fun at the birthday countdown clock, and Horatio Sanz acts like a creeper waiting for me to turn legal?

It was a good experience, all told. But it made me realize just how widespread this countdown clock was, and I felt vulnerable and weird about it. That gif of me-at-sixteen with my arms bumping my breasts together was still floating around the internet, and I'd always known that the Web was full of the worst of humanity, but I hadn't actually realized that the rest of the world accessed it and was *influenced* by it. Case in point: until the *SNL* writers suggested the sketch, I'd assumed that the only people who had seen the countdown were the perverts on the Web. Olive was a few months older than I was and had already turned eighteen; the first thing the paps did when she went out for her birthday was take upskirt shots when she was climbing out of her car. Online tabloids plastered these images everywhere, and yet *she* was blamed for it, like she had known that photographers were going to be lying on the ground next to her vehicle when she emerged in a skirt, sans panties. I took note of what had happened and filed it away for later: if I really wanted to get attention, I should forgo underwear.

What you girls have to understand is that the internet was young in those days. The World Wide Web hadn't become widespread until somewhere in the late nineties, so in the early 2000s it was like the Wild West. Decency laws didn't exist. So a print tabloid wouldn't share a photo of a naked upskirt shot, but the internet certainly would. It was vulgar. But it came with the territory of being famous, unfortunately.

I was (almost) as eager to turn eighteen as the fans were for me to; it meant that I would have access to my money. My parents had been squirreling it away for years, and I had barely touched any of it. I had huge plans, including buying my own house. Olive convinced me to buy a twelve-million-dollar mansion in Hidden Hills. It came with eight bedrooms, eleven bathrooms, a home theater and spa, and its own wet bar. I was tickled by the idea of having a bar in my home even though I wasn't twenty-one yet.

My parents tried to talk me out of it. "The taxes on that property alone—" they said. "You won't be on *Third Time Around* forever, and you'll want to save."

"It's my money and I'll spend it how I want," I said.

My mother sounded nervous when she said, "It's just— Well, Hayley, our mortgage isn't cheap, and your father and I think it best if we . . . well, if *we* handle your money and you get an allowance. A big one. Bigger than what you've been given before. Because you haven't been taught anything about handling money and we're afraid you're going to—"

"Chill out, Mom." I cut her off. "I'll still pay for your stuff.

You'll get to keep your lifestyle just fine. But I'm going to handle my own money. And that means buying this house."

On December 16, the world celebrated the aging of Hayley Aldridge—and so did I. I signed the title on my new pad and sat in its empty living room, relishing the space. Away from my parents, away from my sister, away from everybody!

But soon the room felt empty, and I knew I needed to throw a party, get some life into the house. Everybody was invited, no drug was left out of the rotation, and booze flowed freely.

I hired a professional DJ to curate the playlist and paid for a company to stage the house with three dozen couches of different styles and sizes, so that people all had a place to sit if they wanted to. I wore a long, slinky gown with a thigh-high slit and had my hair done up like Marilyn Monroe's.

When Olive stepped across the threshold of my kitchen, looking absolutely fabulous, I shrieked and hugged her. "Where have you been?" I shouted. "Wait, I can answer that for you. You've been everywhere! Don't you need a break? How are you not dead?"

"I'm very much alive," she said wryly, spinning in a circle to show me her outfit: a flowy high-low dress with a deep V neck that showed off her sternum and breasts. "I'm leaving the profession," she continued, without preamble. "I'm done."

I clutched at my chest reflexively, as if holding on to my heart. "But Olive!" I gasped theatrically. "What will you do?"

"I dunno. All I know is that I'm finished with this dumb industry that chews up girls and spits them out. I'm tired of discussing what designer I'm wearing when I'd rather be talking about my process to get into character. If they want a dumb bitch, they'll get a dumb bitch."

"What do you mean? It's not like they're gonna ask you anything if you're not working," I pointed out.

"Nah, I'm still gonna be around. Somehow. I can't just *leave* the *spotlight*. Just keep inviting me to parties, okay?"

"Where are you living these days? You should come live with me!" I gestured with an arm, spinning it overhead to show her the grandiose living area. "I have plenty of rooms! And you can invite people over for parties all the time!"

"That'd be great!" she shrieked, and she hugged me again. We jumped up and down together, yay-ing, and separated, giggling. It would be great, having Olive as a roommate. And if it wasn't, the house was huge—I could ignore her if I wanted space.

That settled, we both took a Jell-O shot and laughed some more. I began mingling with the rest of the party attendees, and spotted Ted looking slightly anxious by the banister.

"*Ted*," I shouted. "I see you, Ted! You didn't have to come!" I was touched to see him there. I knew how hard it must have been for him to be at a party where so much was freely available.

"Thanks for including sparkling water in your lineup," he said in response, raising a bottle of Perrier. I whooped, a little drunk, and hugged him around the neck.

"You're my favorite," I said, my voice slightly slurred. He disentangled my arms from his shoulders and grasped my wrists, looking at me with a slight bend in his neck. It was as if we were the only two people in the house, for a moment. His mouth was close to mine. I imagined kissing him, just for a split second, and remembered it was *Ted*. I shook my head, the spell broken.

The front door opened and more people poured in. They looked around at the expansive main entrance and took it all in: the underage teens drinking, the plastic baggies that were being passed from hand to hand, the people making out on various couches. I greeted them with an enthusiastic "Hello!" and each of them by name, like a good hostess. When I turned around, Ted was holding a red Solo cup and taking a tentative sip. "Ted!" I said, running toward him.

"It's fine. It's just one drink," he assured me. "I can handle myself."

I didn't know what Ted's rehabilitation looked like, if this was something he was allowed to do. I'd never been through rehab myself. So I shrugged and did a shot with him, hoping for the best. Maybe he'd learned control.

I'm sad to say that that was the party where Ted began using again. He drank a little, toked a little. Nothing too egregious, but it was the slippery slope unto which he slid. I think it was worse, him being cautious at first instead of going hard. All I know is, he was back to smelling like vodka while we filmed, but he was also back to Capable Ted, one who worked diligently and didn't trip over his lines. The drinking made him more fluid in his acting again. I think that's why he did it, to be honest. I still feel guilty about my party. But I have to remember, if it wasn't *that* party, it would've been another where

Ted's addictions came up again.

True to his conjecture, Zac and Natasha got engaged on the show after Natasha found out she was pregnant. There was a highly rated episode we filmed where I gave a teary speech about how Zac would be an excellent father. That episode was in the running for the Emmys that year, and when I was up for an award, that was the clip they used to introduce me:

"Zac, I know this isn't what you expected, becoming a father so early. But if there is anything I know for sure, it's that you have always been there for me. For the last eighteen years of my life, you've been there for me when Mom hasn't, Dad hasn't, Steve hasn't, and Erica hasn't. You're my constant, my North Star. I know Natasha can count on you to be the best father I've ever seen. Better than Steve, even. I know you think you aren't ready, but you are. You *are*, Zac. Look at me. You *are ready*. And this baby is going to be the luckiest baby in all the world."

Ted genuinely teared up when I said those words to him, and I knew he was taking them to heart.

Cut!

I patted his shoulders after the camera stopped filming, and Ted gave me a hug. "Thank you," he said, and the scent of vodka stirred in my hair. "I know it was just a line, but it meant a lot to me."

"You're welcome," I said, squeezing him back.

"Let's celebrate at the Serpent Pit," he said.

"Are you sure?"

"Yeah, I'm itching to get out."

I regret the invitation. I blame myself for what happened. I know it's not entirely my fault, but I started it. I got the ball rolling downhill.

CHAPTER 22

Olive moved in a few days after the party. She suggested that I hire an interior decorator whose fees were deep in the six-figure range to outfit the house "in true Hayley fashion." I didn't even know who I *was* yet, but she had me convinced. The decorator racked up bills in the millions, as I bought couture couches, expensive artwork, and Swarovski crystal everything. I was hyper when we were spending the money, but after the bill came, all I could do was sit in an over-decorated room and wonder what I'd done.

But I willed myself not to care. I was stretching my muscles! I was exploring my newfound wealth! I was eighteen, had been working since I was seven, and was suddenly able to reap the benefits of my success. And I did reckless things with my money. I bought a pair of golden sunglasses and then decided to buy a custom-painted gold Bentley to match.

Olive and I went partying every night, even on nights before *TTA* shoots. One such night, we got into Joseph's, one of the hottest clubs of the time, and a famous chanteuse sent over daiquiris as a gesture of goodwill. Olive and I sipped them to get a buzz on before we started dancing. She leaned close to me. "Okay, spill," she said. "Like, what's going on with Ted?"

"What do you mean?" I asked, playing with my straw.

"I mean, have you fucked him yet or not?"

I had a brief moment where I imagined his sapphire-blue eyes above me and felt warm inside. "No . . . " I said.

She took the hesitation as encouragement. "But you *want* to."

"Maybe. But he's been my 'older brother' for so long. Isn't that weird?"

"He's a babe! And not really your brother. You're warped if you think so. He's been crushing on you for, like, ages." She sighed. "Wish it could be me, you know?"

I chewed on my straw. "He's been looking really good since he came back from rehab," I giggled. "He's been working out."

Olive drained her glass and gestured to her purse. "You want?" she asked.

"Hmm, should I?" I wondered out loud. "I have work tomorrow."

"Come on," she wheedled, and I laughed.

We went to the bathroom and railed some lines. Flying high, we ordered VIP service and slaked our thirst with Cristal. When it came time to sign the check, Olive pushed the tab toward me and I put my card down. I never looked at the totals anymore, after one particular night that was fourteen thousand dollars. I could afford it. Why should I care?

We danced and danced and danced. When we got tired, we took another hit in the bathroom, jazzed up, and danced some more.

I paid for all of our adventures, of course. Olive was currently watching her bank account since she wasn't working, and it wasn't fun to have a partner-in-crime who was conscientious about her money. I flung bills around like they were confetti and tucked receipts into my purses; I owned so many handbags that I switched them out at every outing. I never cleaned them out and let the papers languish in the dark, flung on the floor of my walk-in closet.

When I did see my parents, which was at the end of each month as I wrote them a check for the next four weeks of their living expenses, they looked around at my house disapprovingly. It had become a den of partygoers and squatters, Olive's friends (now mine) who preferred my couches to their own bedrooms, and our company to the silence at their homes. At any given point in the day there were five to eight people in the house, drinking my bottled water, sleeping on my sofas. And along with that, they were smoking out of bongs and snorting coke—that I kept in good supply, so the fun times would never stop—each of them always in danger of falling apart when no one was watching.

"What will your summer project be?" my father asked this time, gripping the check I gave him with an iron paw. As if worried I would snatch it back after writing it.

I waved my hand, the pen swirling in the air. "*Mysterious City* comes out this year, and I don't feel like doing anything besides that promo. It's a summer blockbuster, you know?"

"Hayley, you're using up a lot of your money just existing in this house," he said, looking around at the languid pair of couch surfers who were high and staring at the ceiling in my enormous living room. "You should probably sign up for a new project to keep the funds coming in."

"I'm good; thanks anyway," I said. "How's Ashley?"

"Not well, not well. She crashed and burned at a recent audition and is sure she didn't get the part."

"That's too bad," I said vaguely, though inside I was glad to hear the news. Ashley had dipped her toe into the dramatics-filled world of movie stardom with *Shine Street*, which had been a good experience, thank goodness, but if it were up to me, she would be a normal teenager. Of course, two heads are better than one, and my parents were probably angling for a way to get dual income streams from their progeny.

I wouldn't put it past them.

Dad left with the check and a backward glance at the couple on the couch, who hadn't moved.

It was around this time of my life I started having trouble sleeping, and Olive suggested her "good friend" Dr. Alicia Johnson to prescribe me some sleeping pills. Dr. Johnson was a psychiatrist who didn't mind being trotted out to write scripts for needy celebrities who would rather stay under the radar. Hayley Aldridge going to a psychiatrist for sleep meds would be a great scoop, but Dr. Johnson was an iron vault. She palmed off some Klonopin with the warning that they were addictive, so "don't take one every day—just as needed." I got a thirty-day supply and tried to ration them.

THIRD TIME AROUND was becoming a chore. The writing

wasn't fresh anymore—though that didn't stop the show from being a critical darling. Brandon and I were still required to canoodle—Amy and Thomas were back together again, and likely endgame—but it was mostly alluded to and thus we didn't do it on-camera. Brandon was off doing a movie adaptation of Jane Austen's *Persuasion* and his part on *TTA* was reduced considerably, much to my relief. My character of Amy became withered and tired, as I struggled to make it to my call times, sometimes even showing up residually drunk from the night before.

Instead, most of the story revolved around Zac and Natasha, and their impending nuptials and baby. Sophia walked around the set in a maternity suit, the padding of which had to be adjusted every week so that she seemed to be gaining weight at the same time as the "baby" grew. The due date coincided with the wedding episode, of course. Nothing like sweeps to have your bride going into labor prematurely and actually getting married in the hospital room.

I was glad my part had been shrunk to that of cheerleader and confidant for Ted-as-Zac. It meant that I didn't have to be on set as often, and my call times were later. I wonder now if Alex Dietrich had accommodated my partying ways by reducing my screen time, and that my smaller role was because I was hungover every filming day. It was as if he knew the show would get canceled soon, and was winding down every storyline.

Ted and I would sit in his trailer, waiting for a PA to come knocking to grab one of us. We were back to drinking vodka out of water bottles, and I didn't say anything when he shared the first one with me. It was unspoken, that his regression was a private thing, and I wouldn't nag him or question it. I thought I was supporting him by drinking in solidarity. Maybe I enabled him instead.

We played a lot of card games together in his trailer, waiting. Silly games that were easy to navigate while a little tipsy, like Go Fish and Gin Rummy. Today he was playing Solitaire and I was looking over his shoulder, pointing out where the next card should go, even though it was obvious.

"The four of spades can go *there*," I said, my finger touching a five of hearts.

"Yes, thanks, I saw that already," he said good-naturedly, and placed the card there.

"And then that three of diamonds can go on top of the four of spades!"

He laughed and handed me the card. Our fingers brushed. "You do it, then."

"I hope we find the ace of spades soon," I said, eyes narrowing at the pile of cards. "I bet it's buried under one of the piles though."

He was silent for a minute, and then tossed the cards down. "Hayley, why are we on this show?"

It wasn't the first time he had gotten all broody on me and I knew it wasn't the last. "Because it pays us money," I said.

"Money isn't everything."

"What is, then?"

"I don't know. Happiness, maybe?"

"Money can buy happiness."

"The saying is the opposite, actually."

"That's bullshit," I said matter-of-factly. "Money may not buy you soul-shining, smile-all-the-time, good-mood-happiness, but it is better than the alternative of having no money at all. Tell me, did you worry about being able to eat today? Or where you'd fall asleep? Are you worried about where to find a place to crash because you don't have a home?"

"No . . ." he said, looking at me now with a frown on his face.

"Exactly. Some of the kids who come stay at my house, they have nothing. They're Olive's friends but they're becoming mine too. And they tell me how they got kicked out of their parents' houses and they have no money and they can't find a job or whatever. And it is *heartbreaking*. I like having money so I can give them what they need."

"I didn't realize you were such a good person," he said jokingly, but his frown was still in place.

"There's a lot you don't know about me," I said.

"Even after working on this set together for eleven years?" he asked. "And going out clubbing with you a few times?"

"Even then. I mean, did *you* know, up until I told you, that I had Los Angeles refugees in my house?"

"No . . ."

"All right, then." I took a swig from the water bottle, and it stung a little as it went down.

He was still looking at me as he took the proffered bottle from my hand and capped it without taking a sip. "I'd like to get to know you better," he said simply, interlacing his fingers and leaning on his elbows.

"What's there to know, though?" I mused aloud. "Just read a *YM* magazine and you'll find out everything. My favorite color, blue. My favorite movie, *The Little Mermaid*. Don't laugh—I still love it even after all these years."

"Your favorite costar?" he said, raising an eyebrow.

I gave him a little shove. "You know it's you," I said good-naturedly. "Always has been. Ever since you skipped going on that ride with me at Disneyland and went to find Goofy."

"I didn't think you'd remember that," he said.

"I don't remember Goofy," I admitted, "but I'll always remember that you were so nice."

We gazed at each other for a long moment, and he smiled. My eyes trailed toward his lips, and when I realized I was staring, I flicked my eyes up to see that he was looking at my mouth too.

What we were doing?

"And then," I said in a rush, feeling embarrassed, "many seasons later, we're still here and making a ton of money."

"If the money is so good, why don't you want Ashley to do this job?" he asked. It was not a challenge, but he raised a good point. I quirked an eyebrow.

"How do you know that I don't want Ashley in the industry?"

"Because. I notice things. And while you act like you're a supportive big sister, I can tell that you don't want her doing this."

I sighed and kicked back onto the tweedy couch. The vodka was in my head, making it hard to think. But he had me. "Jealousy," I offered.

"I dunno. I don't buy that."

I thought back to John Yelp, whose crotch grazed me; *"If you tell anyone—"* And then Ed Hodges, whose blow job comment was still fresh in my mind. I thought about Brandon and his reluctance to use the Sock when we were filming intimate scenes. And I decided to tell Ted about all of that.

"It's just," I finished, "I don't want Ashley to have to deal with that sort of bullshit. The money is good, but . . ."

"Then why do you keep doing it?"

I shrugged with one shoulder. "Contracts." And the fact that I was already so experienced, the damage wouldn't mean anything more to me. Ashley was still a fresh flower.

Ted grasped my hand. It was warm and soft. "I'm sorry you had to go through all that," he said. "If I'd known Brandon was that terrible, I would've encouraged you to go to Alex."

"It's okay," I said, feeling a warm tickle in my stomach. "But that doesn't explain why *you* stick around. If you hate it so much, why have you been here for eleven seasons?"

He was silent. "I don't know," he said slowly. "I've been thinking about it a lot—for years—but I've never come up with a reason. It's a good enough job, I guess. I don't get manhandled like you do. And I meet cool people and do cool things, mostly. Like you." He smiled at me.

I batted my eyelashes theatrically. "I do declare," I said in a Southern accent.

"You should speak that way more often," he said. "I know you're from Texas. It's pretty."

"A Southern accent is *pretty*? Now I *know* you were dropped on your head as a baby."

"Ha ha," he enunciated, but he swept his hair out of his face and smiled genuinely.

"Do you ever think about leaving the industry?" I asked.

"All the time," he said seriously. "But then who would look out for you?"

There was a ripple in the pit of my stomach. What it was, I couldn't tell you. But I said, "I can look after myself."

He wrapped me in a hug then. "I just worry about you, is all," he said, speaking into my hair.

"Don't worry about me; I'm strong." The thing I didn't add: *Worry about yourself. I worry about you too.*

CHAPTER 23

I sauntered onto set a few days later. I was still a little drunk from the night before and felt good, swishing around. The onset of a hangover hadn't started yet, and I was still riding a high.

Ted intercepted me on my way to hair and makeup, pushing me into his trailer. "Hey!" I protested, but I stumbled up the steps anyway and sat on his tweedy couch. "What's the deal!"

"Alex is on the warpath," he whispered, his eye flickering with light through the blinds as he looked for our showrunner. "He is pissed you're late."

"All the more reason for me to go to hair and makeup right now," I said, standing up and dusting off my jeans.

"Hayley, you don't think you're—well, *overdoing* it lately?" he asked.

"Look who's talking," I retorted.

"I know, I know," Ted said, his gaze on the water bottle on his countertop. "But you're showing up drunk, and Alex has noticed. He's going to call you in for a talk."

I pursed my lips. "He can do what he wants. Everyone knows I'm one of the biggest stars of this show. He can't fire me."

"But he *can*. He's already started writing you out. Can't you see?" Ted was pleading. "I love seeing you on the set all the time, Hayley. I don't want you to get fired."

I straightened up. "If I get fired, we'll see each other in other ways," I said. But my toes were curling in my shoes. I was suddenly terrified. I loved being on the set of *Third Time Around*. It wasn't until I was faced with the alternative that I realized I owed most of my fame to the show. Sure, I'd done a bunch of movies, but this is where I'd made my *name*. I would hate to get unceremoniously dumped.

Ted noticed that I was starting to tear up and came closer, touched my shoulder. "It's okay, Hayley. Just tone it down a bit. There's only a season or so left after this one wraps, I'm sure of it."

"But I don't want it to end at all!" I mewed. "I love this show so much. I love everyone on it—well, excluding Millie and Brandon, but still."

"Does that mean you love *me*?" he asked, both hands on my shoulders now.

"You know I do," I said, the remaining alcohol in my body making me extra truthful.

He gave me a hug then, and I breathed him in. That musky smell on his many-times-worn sweatshirt, and under that: clean boy. I would always love Ted.

We parted, and we couldn't seem to make eye contact after that. I cleared my throat. "Okay, I'm going to hair and makeup," I said.

"Okay. Be careful when you see Alex."

I nodded, unable to speak. I disappeared from his trailer and tried to remember what Olive had said. Ted had a crush, *on me*? I wondered if it was true.

TED AND I spent more and more time in his trailer, despite not having many scenes together on the show anymore. He was always with Sophia, and I was relegated to Brandon. We talked and sipped his vodka and inched ever closer to each other, not knowing what it meant when we found ourselves staring inadvertently into each other's eyes.

Finally, one day, Ted broke the ice.

We were lying on the trailer's sofa, him with his socked feet near my armpits, and my socked feet on his chest. We were languishing, half-asleep, watching the dailies on his little television set. There he was, kissing Sophia passionately, sure to be nominated for a Cutest Couple Tween Choice Award. He sat up suddenly, setting his feet on the floor of the trailer, and switched off the TV. He seemed anxious, wringing his hands, and that made me pay attention. He wanted to say something and was gathering his courage to do so.

"When I kiss Sophia on the show, I don't feel anything," he said finally. "But when I'm around you, I do."

I sat up too. "Um, what are you trying to say?"

"I'm saying, I have feelings for you, Hayley. And I think you have feelings back." He reached out tentatively and felt a ringlet of my hair. My heart gave a jolt. I could feel my palms sweating.

We weren't high, but I *was*.

"What do you think?" he asked, his eyes on mine.

I gave him a little smile. Encouragement.

"Can I kiss you?" he murmured.

I nodded.

He slid over, so our thighs were touching side by side. The fingers that were touching that ringlet of hair let go, leaving it to bob in the air. His hand caressed my cheek. I could feel my eyes closing in pleasure as he cupped the back of my head and leaned in to me. Our noses brushed. His lips glided over mine, capturing my mouth with a slight gasp.

It was a sweet kiss, no tongue.

Well, that wouldn't do. In typical Hayley fashion, I took control of the kiss, deepening it. My tongue forced his lips open and he took a deep breath in through his nostrils. I nibbled on his lower lip. He gave a little squeak that made us both laugh into each other's mouths.

We were still sitting there, in his trailer, the most unromantic place in the world, and as we pulled apart to take a couple of breaths, we leaned our foreheads together and looked at our intertwined hands. "What do you think Millie would say?" I joked.

"Millie can eat shit," he replied, and we giggled some more.

My usual MO with guys was to lay them, and quick, but for some reason I didn't want to do that with Ted. Wonderful Ted, gentle Ted. I wanted to savor every moment with him, I wanted to breathe his breath and explore his body with my hands. I didn't want to just *fuck*—I realized that I wanted us to take our time and ease into this slowly. We'd been friends for so long.

Evidently, he was thinking the same way, because he said, "I don't want to just fuck you, Hayley. Okay?"

"Okay." I nodded.

"I want to take you on a real date. And if the paps catch us, so be it. We'd be on a real date, after all."

"After years of them hounding us about dating, they're finally going to get the real thing," I said, giggling.

He grinned his Teen Heartthrob grin with the dimple and kissed me gently on the cheek. "Tomorrow?"

"Tomorrow sounds good," I said shyly.

"I know we have work tomorrow, but I want to pick you up at your house, like a real date. Does seven work?"

I smiled at him and nodded. Wined and dined like a proper lady. I could get used to this.

I WAS IN a good mood all that night, and wondered if I should call Ted to let him know how excited I was about our date, but I refrained. Olive asked me why I had a shit-eating grin on my face, and I had to break it to her that I was going on a date with Ted.

"Ted, *Ted, my* Ted?" she said, mock horrified.

"I know you've had a crush on him forever, but he asked me out and . . ." I grimaced at her, but it was really a grin with all my teeth. "Don't hate me?"

"I can't hate you! You're my best friend! Though I *am* jealous." She sidled next to me at the kitchen island and sat on a barstool. "Though once you have sex, you *have* to tell me all about it."

I threw an orange from the fruit bowl at her, and she ducked, laughing.

My good mood didn't evaporate in the night; it was even more potent the next morning as I stepped onto the set. I looked around for Ted as I got coffee at craft services, hoping to exchange a wink and a smile, but I didn't see him.

There was a small group huddled near the doughnuts and they all looked at me. Finally, one of their delegation walked over tentatively. Millie.

"Hayley," Millie said. "Did you hear the news?"

"What?" I poured the slightest dash of cream into my coffee to cool it down.

"Ted's dead."

CHAPTER 24

I stared at her blankly, uncomprehending. "What do you mean?" I asked simply.

"Ted's passed away."

"You mean, for a role?"

She was shaking her head. "No, Hayley. This isn't a movie. This is real life."

Oh my god.

I continued to stare at her, trying to let the words soak in. But they would not. There seemed to be an impermeable shield on my brain that wouldn't allow the words to become real.

"What?" I said dumbly.

She took me by the shoulders, hugging me, and I was letting my arms dangle from their sockets, not hugging back. Coffee spilled from my cup onto my shoes. Why was she hugging me? Ted was just fine.

"What?" I repeated. But there was a note of hysteria in my voice now, as it seemed the news *had* begun to settle in. "Omigod, omigod . . ."

This can't be real.

"You're lying, right?" I said, pushing away from the embrace. "This is just a joke. A hoax."

"No, Hayley. It's for real." There was a sadness in her voice that made me take notice.

"How? *How?*"

"They think it was an overdose."

"*What?*" But he'd been clean for months . . . At least, that's what I had *thought*. I realized then that I didn't know for sure how clean Ted had been. After all, he and I had been drinking vodka in his trailer just the day before, in full rejection of his rehabilitation. Though we didn't call it that at the time.

Though it should seem obvious, we didn't film that day. Normally, a TV set is bustle-bustle-bustle, go-go-go, no matter what tragedies occur. When the space shuttle *Columbia* disintegrated earlier that year, we heard about it, had a moment of silence, and moved on. We were always on a timetable. But Ted's death had us at a standstill. He was a third of the episode—but not only that, he was *family*.

We sat huddled in our directors' chairs on the set, sipping coffee and wondering what to do next. Some of us sobbed. I could feel a trickle of tears leaking from under my eyelids without ever stopping, and my nose ran so much I was wiping it with the sleeve of my sweatshirt instead of searching for any tissues.

Somehow, the rumors trickled too: That he was found with a balloon, a spoon, and a syringe. That the needle was still in his arm. That it was probably an accident.

I had no idea that he had graduated to heroin. I could just imagine the scenario: Ted was excited about our date. Then his telltale anxiety began to gnaw at him and he began to second-guess what would happen. He got the heroin and shot up, just to feel good again. It had been so long that his tolerance had dropped and his body gave out.

Not everything is about you, I told myself, and wondered if maybe Ted had decided, on a whim, to use just this once. Or maybe he was a habitual user and no one knew, and he just misjudged. Because the possibility of him being suicidal was out of the question. *We had a date. We had a DATE.*

The tears streaked down my cheeks harder and faster, and Millie was on my arm, crying, too, and everyone in the room was weeping, including Alex Dietrich, who was not trying to organize us but let us mourn quietly, in our own little ways.

I shook Millie off me and stood up. I couldn't be there any longer.

"Hayley . . . " Alex called after me. "You're not in any state to drive right now!"

But I got in my Bentley and, wiping my face with both sleeves of my sweatshirt, I started to the Hidden Hills house, where Olive would be, and the rest of the crew, and we could blitz our brains until we could forget this entire thing occurred.

I DON'T KNOW what happened. One moment I was in the Bentley, driving home, and the next, I was lying down, my eyes felt too large for their sockets, and I heard a noise like a wailing whale—but it was me, moaning. Something was rubbing me hard on the sternum. It hurt.

"She's coming 'round," said a voice I didn't recognize. "Hayley, can you hear me?"

I slotted my eyes open. There was an unfamiliar person with a uniform shirt bending over me. There was something over my nose and mouth—an oxygen mask?

"What did you *do*? What did you *do*?" I heard from far away. It sounded like my mother's voice.

Thoughts swam up from behind my eyelids, out of the blackness of my brain. I suddenly remembered *why* I had been out of control the night before. Ted. I'd come home and gotten drunk with Olive. Then I'd taken a Klonopin. Maybe I'd taken three. My eyes filled with tears. "Is Ted really dead?" I sobbed. But the words didn't come out of my mouth. There was a disconnect between my brain and my lips and all that I could hear was a low groan.

The tears continued to trickle from the corners of my eyes. My mother was in the room, which gave me a flicker of irritation. This was my sanctuary. Why was she there?

I tried to raise my arm but found it was strapped down. I struggled a little. I wasn't in my bed, but I was prone. Somehow, I was moving, the lights from my hallway trailing slowly above my head. It took me too long to realize that I was on a stretcher.

The EMTs wordlessly rolled the stretcher into the ambulance and I stopped struggling, wondering what shitshow was going to unfold in the tabloids this time. *This isn't happening.* I turned my head just in time to see my parents at the edge of the ambulance doors. They were blurry.

My mother stood by my father, crying, while Ashley hovered somewhere in the background. The ambulance doors slammed shut.

SUICIDE WATCH FOR HAYLEY ALDRIDGE
COMMITTED! HAYLEY ALDRIDGE 5150'd
ALDRIDGE-GATE: HAYLEY IN MENTAL HOSPITAL
HAYLEY ALDRIDGE HOSPITALIZED FOR OVERDOSE

If you're just waking up to the news, this is what you missed. Hayley Aldridge was carted off to UCLA Medical Center early this morning after being involuntarily hospitalized on a 5150: that is, a 72-hour psychiatric hold. Sources say she was so drugged up last night that her parents were worried she would overdose like her costar Ted Sumner, who tragically passed the day before. She allegedly went willingly. Her ambulance was escorted by 20 police cars, 6 cops on motorcycles, and over 100 paparazzi.

Comments

1994baybee: 20 police cars? 100 paps? Even during a medical crisis, Hayley is such a diva.

purplehaze415: this sitch needs a good nickname. aldridge-gate is so boring. how about hostage aldridgration?

ohyesshedid: too long

1994baybee: hostage hayleyation?

---

cucumbermelon: she's gone crazy

---

turquoise-tetrahedron: full-on loco

---

pineapplover825: listen to all of you, you're so mean. leave hayley alone!!

CHAPTER 25

After several days at UCLA Medical Center, where my stomach was pumped and I was evaluated for mental illness, I was transferred to a new place, a brick one-story building in Van Nuys. There was so much paperwork, and a technician kept asking me questions. What did you drink? What did you take? Are you suicidal? Do you smoke pot? Do you do cocaine? Have you done heroin? (Yes; yes; not that I know of.)

Finally, the technician was satisfied with all of my answers and did a physical examination, which was basically checking to see if I had anything that could be considered hazardous, and took a blood sample.

After my intake forms were processed and my shoelaces were confiscated, it was three in the afternoon. I went straight into group therapy. It was unnerving, being in a room with ten other people, not knowing anything about them, and struggling to understand what was happening.

"We have a new addition to the group today," said the counselor, Debra.

"No shit," said one of the group, and I shifted in my seat.

"Isn't she . . . ?"

"We'll meet our newest as we go around," Debra said. The group started their introductions.

The first was a girl with mousy brown hair. "Hi, I'm Hazel and I'm an addict," she said.

I looked at her and wondered if I could utter the same words. I didn't think I was an addict. I still didn't believe I had a problem. I was sitting there in the clothes I'd been wearing since the day before, my hair in limp ringlets, feeling defiant. When my turn rolled around, I said simply, "I'm Hayley."

"We know who you are," said the mousy girl, Hazel.

"Hazel," Debra admonished. Then to me, "Why are you here, Hayley?"

"I don't know."

Debra didn't push. She just moved on to the next person, and I didn't contribute to the rest of the conversation.

After group was dinner, and then an hour of recreational time. I spent it watching television, which was tuned to a cartoon channel. No gossip rags, no TMZ.

I was introduced to my roommate, Sara, who had taken too many benzos one day, too, and had a rampant eating disorder. And yet I didn't see myself reflected in her. She had marks up and down her arms that looked like they'd hurt, but she didn't bother to cover them.

Then, when it was barely dark out, we were locked in our rooms. If this were a normal night, I would be getting ready to go out with Olive. We'd be at the Serpent Pit. I'd have my hands on some coke and all would be well.

"Try to get some rest," Sara said.

"I won't bother you for long," I promised. "I'll be out of here soon."

She looked at me with a knowing flick of the eyes; then she settled on her own bed.

My bed had restraints, but nobody snapped me in. I stared at the blank walls and turned in a circle; this was like a jail cell, with an aluminum toilet in one corner. I lay down and tried to turn my brain off, but instead I thought of Ted again and started to cry. How was it that I was thinking about *Ted*, of all people, when right now I was stuck *here*? I didn't know how long I was going to be in there and I worried what would happen when I was supposed to do promo for *Mysterious City*. Surely, I would be out in three days.

Then I wondered how *Third Time Around* would work around my and Ted's absences. Didn't these people know that I had an obligation to my job? That I needed to be free to work?

At the same time, I felt a relief I hadn't felt in a long time: that I was going to be taken care of, and that my fate was in someone else's hands for once.

First things first: I had to talk to a psychiatrist, *not* Dr. Johnson, about my life. I was asked a number of questions, all aimed at making sure that I was diagnosed with *something* that would contribute to my brash behavior. Was I abnormally upbeat or wired? Did I have trouble sleeping? Did I have increased energy? Did I have racing thoughts? And on the flipside, did I feel sad, empty, or hopeless? Did I feel fatigue or loss of energy? Did I feel worthless or full of guilt?

Within days, I was noted as having bipolar disorder and prescribed medication to ease my symptoms. To this day, I don't know if I am actually bipolar. I do understand that my behavior fit the bill, and the medication chilled me out, but I'm unsure if I really do have it. Didn't a *number* of starlets go out clubbing and take drugs and cry over their dead costars and feel guilty for perhaps encouraging them to ignore their sobriety? And are *all* of those starlets bipolar? It's hard to believe. And wasn't I in mourning? If I ever get out of this situation, I'm going to get a new psychiatrist and have them test me again.

My 5150 was just the beginning; I was admitted for thirty days. I had to follow a strict schedule while in the mental hospital: wake up early, line up for pills (I was tapered off Klonopin slowly, and given Lamictal), have breakfast, go to group therapy. The other patients were confused when they saw me, whispering, "Isn't that the actress from *A Poem for Jeanie?*" until the administrators told them to treat me like everybody else. Then came recreational activities, lunch, more group therapy, and a mandated ten o'clock bedtime.

The first week I was there, all I could think about was what the tabloids were saying about me. There was no way to get that information inside the facility and I was craving to use the internet. But soon I was caught up in all the therapy, and I looked inward. My parents and I had family therapy, I had group therapy with the rest of the patients, and I started feeling better about myself.

I wasn't the only person in the world who had the same problems as I did. People were fighting their demons every day. It took me a little while to realize that if I was open and honest,

I would get more out of the situation than if I stayed quiet and sullen. So I made an effort.

I don't want to dwell on my time in the mental hospital. It was not a good time for me. But I realized some things.

I didn't need alcohol.

I didn't need cocaine.

I almost believed I was better.

"IF YOU WERE in rehab and got better, why are you on a conservatorship?" Jane wants to know.

I purse my lips. "I'll get to that," I say.

"Let's take some photos of you doing mundane things," Jessica says, changing the subject.

So we take the rest of the day off from storytelling, and dive into the pool. I change into an orange shirt, a color I never wear—not since that *Only Human* premiere with the orange muumuu that got me on a worst-dressed list—so the viewers who see the Instagram account know that these photos weren't taken for the "official" account. The girls brought their shared digital camera this time, and they take pictures of me hanging off the side of the pool wall and splashing. A photo of me drinking a homemade smoothie out of a water glass. A photo of me reading a book while on my messy sofa, strewn with half a dozen throw blankets. No Adam. It's nice, being myself and having the girls see me. Really *see* me as me.

They promise that they'll upload them to TheRealHayleyA Instagram account when they have a chance, when they're back with their father and have access to their phones. They leave that evening at seven on the dot, and I won't see them again for half a week.

When they come back, though, they're just as eager to hear about my life story as before. So I continue.

AFTER A MONTH in the facility, I was released. I felt like a new woman, and I was excited to live my life with a clean bill of health. I had been sober for thirty days and I sensed that I was strong enough to make it to thirty-one and thirty-two and thirty-three, and on and on.

I never once thought that Ted had felt the same, and look at what had happened to him.

Third Time Around had wrapped for the season while I was gone and was in editing, to be screened in the fall. It was now early summer, and I had promo for *Mysterious City* to deal with. It was a huge blockbuster and the promotional tour would take us all around the world.

I met up with Jamie Little, and things were the same as before—almost. Now, when we were out somewhere and someone offered me a drink, I turned it down. Jamie didn't do any drugs in front of me as an act of solidarity, which I thought was very sweet. And we didn't go out anymore; we didn't sleep together. Our PR relationship was very much just for show.

But the questions! Olive hadn't been kidding when she said that it was a desert out there. I could tell that the reporters were itching to bring up my overdose, my breakdown, my hiatus, the stint in the mental hospital. The publicity team for *Mysterious City* specifically said that the reporters couldn't ask those questions, so they made do with others: How are you feeling these days, Hayley? How did the movie affect you, Hayley? They walked on eggshells.

I was invited back on Rocky Eastman's late-night TV show. I had been a regular on his show when it came to movie promos, having been on it since my first role in *The Sky Below*. This time, however, Rocky acted cagey around me. It was as if he didn't know what to say—even though there were topics we were supposed to discuss.

"What's wrong, Rocky?" I asked, finally, and the studio audience hushed.

"I just keep thinking about your friend and costar, Ted Sumner," he said, and the audience was so quiet, I could hear my arrested breathing. I considered walking off then and there.

"What about him?" I said, my voice choked.

"How sad it is, and how needless a death from drug abuse can be . . ."

I swallowed, and made the split-second decision to undo my lapel mic and exit the stage. Rocky watched me go, his mouth dropped open.

Didn't Rocky know that Ted's untimely death was also a topic that shouldn't be broached?

Despite the interview questions focusing elsewhere, the tabloids continued to blare such headlines as *HAYLEY AL-DRIDGE CANDIDS, HAYLEY ALDRIDGE LOOKING A MESS, HAYLEY ALDRIDGE WALKING POST,* and they shared photos of me doing the most mundane things: walking to and from interviews, sitting on panels, eating a spinach salad. They conjectured whether I was drunk or using, and these rags posted *every day*. There was money in me just being me, but I didn't see a cent of it.

I was getting pretty peeved about the constant exposure. I didn't want to be reminded that I'd had a problem. I wanted to enjoy my fragile sobriety in peace.

And evidently, so did the publicity staff of *Mysterious City*. "Hayley," I was told by Harry Ninagawa, the director himself, one day in New York, "your personal problems are overshadowing the promotion of the movie. We think it's best if you stepped back for a bit."

"You want me to *leave*?" I asked, hackles rising. We were just outside the boardroom of the Bowery Hotel, finishing our promo spot there, and he had caught me before I made my way to the ballroom for mocktails with the rest of the crew. At the time, I had gotten into sparkling lime water with a twist of orange. I'd drink several of them thirstily while looking at everyone else's vodka tonics.

Ninagawa evidently had taken this upon himself so that no one else would get blamed. "You've done a beautiful job with the filming," he said. "But I think it best if you go back to Los Angeles."

"What about my relationship with Jamie? I cultivated that for over a *year* for publicity for this movie!"

"I don't know anything about that." He looked flummoxed. "But thank you?"

Of course the director didn't know the goings-on of his two stars, their manufactured romance meant for tabloids. He probably thought it was genuine. Or didn't care one way or the other.

"You can come to the premiere in L.A.," he said. I wanted to bite back with *Oh, okay, THANK YOU.*

I felt knocked sideways. I had been doing so well! I hadn't touched a single drop; I had been clean for fifty-two days! It wasn't my fault that the tabloids wanted to write about me, was it? I hadn't given them any fodder for them to use, and I was *still* front-page news.

"I'll book a ticket to L.A., then," I said stiffly, and Ninagawa patted me lightly on the back.

As soon as I touched down and made my way to the Hidden Hills house, I was greeted by Olive and all of her friends doing coke in my living room. "Oops," she said, covering up the lines with a cupped hand.

"I told you I was coming back." I was irritated. It was one thing to avoid cocaine on the road, it was another to have to avoid it in my own house.

"I thought it was tomorrow," Olive said guiltily. Then, ever the hostess, she asked, "I'd ask if you want some . . ."

I was tired, I was crabby, I was feeling down because I'd been kicked off the promo tour. But I stayed strong. "I'm good."

"Okay." She snorted a line in front of me and I watched enviously. I wanted to feel the burn in the back of my throat. I wanted to feel invincible again. What was waiting for me in my bedroom? Nothing, except boring sleep, and waking up tomorrow with the same depressing story of being in the tabloids for no reason at all.

"On second thought," I said.

Olive turned toward me with a light in her eyes. She'd missed her buddy. "Are you sure?" she asked, but she was already handing over the straw, and I was already leaning in toward the coffee table with my neck bent.

The first line felt like chlorinated pool water hitting the back of my throat. I sputtered a little, remembering what it was like. I did another line really quickly. Before long, I was flying high. But something was different. I was babbling, talking about things that didn't exist. Olive was so concerned, she tried to make me sleep it off, but when I started to cry and wail, she called 911.

Within the hour, I was back at rehab.

CHAPTER 26

The girls and I are sitting at the kitchen island while I fix us some fruit salad. I'm dicing kiwis to put in the big glass bowl when Jane says, "So you went back to rehab."

"That's right. This time, when I stepped into the Van Nuys building, I was coked out of my mind. They had to restrain me to a bed while I detoxed. It was gnarly."

When I walked into Group, I saw Sara, my old roommate, and a flash of what I interpreted as pity reflected across her face.

Dr. Goodman, my psychiatrist, was there the next day, and we had two meetings a day to discuss my issues. I tried, I really did. I knew that I was a mess.

I dice some bananas into the bowl and then squeeze lemon juice over the entire thing to keep the fruit from oxidating. I mix it all up with my hands so there's an even distribution of different fruits in each spoonful.

"I don't want to get into the whole time I was in rehab," I say. "It's long, and tiring, and frankly, a little boring. But I learned a lot about myself—again. I learned that honesty was the best policy with myself, and I also learned that I couldn't go back to the life I had led before.

"I talked to my doctors and they helped me realize that I had a bad relationship with men. Which is why, when I met your father, I initially didn't want anything to do with him. I thought that, because he was attractive to me, I was going down the wrong path again. Like I did with Trey Barnes."

The twins place their heads in their hands in an identical fashion, which cracks me up. They're always doing inadvertent sibling-like things that remind me how similar they are, even though nowadays they have very different personalities.

"Finally, Dad shows up," Jessica says. She rolls her eyes. "We kinda know this story though."

"You know *part* of the story."

"How he chased you down in the middle of the street asking for a date? Sure, sure." Jane giggles.

"That is very much just one tiny slice of it," I say. "So where was I . . . oh yes. I was in rehab for three months and a day. I worked really hard while I was in there. And while I was there—"

"Yeah?" Jessica says.

I frown. "Your grandparents cleared out my house. Of people, I mean. They thought that the partiers were not conducive to my well-being. They were probably right, but I was still pissed about it when I found out."

"What about Olive?" Jessica wants to know.

"Olive was kicked out for a few months, but I invited her back when I got out of rehab—*on the condition* that she not bring any drugs into the house. She was allowed to go out and party if she wanted to, but I didn't want that stuff under my roof. I know, I sound like such a mom right now. But it's the only way I knew I could stay clean. I wanted to stay friends with Olive, my best friend, but I didn't know how else I could do it if she was still using. And I couldn't ask her to *stop*. She had to come to that conclusion on her own." I shake my head. "She never did. That I know of, anyway."

"So you were in rehab for three months," Jane says slowly. "And when you got out, you were clean and sober and went back home. And Olive came back to the house, even though Grandma and Grandpa obviously didn't approve."

"So when did you meet Dad?" Jessica asks.

"Well, that was about five months after I got sober . . ."

Seventeen Magazine, November 2003 issue

MEET ANTHONY MARTENS, this month's heartthrob!

Age: 21

Eye color: brown

Profession: actor

Zodiac sign: Leo

Biggest guilty pleasure: just-out-of-the-oven blueberry muffins with a pat of butter on top! My trainer would kill me if he knew how often I indulge.

Favorite person: his mother

Favorite project he's worked on: *The Grief Healer*

Current crush: Hayley Aldridge. "We worked together on *A Poem for Jeanie* and there was this spark . . . I'd love to take her out now that we're older."

I REMET ANTHONY, my costar from *A Poem for Jeanie*, at the Golden Globes when I was twenty. It was January 2004, and I shouldn't have been at the Globes in the first place; I had missed so much filming of *Third Time Around* with my first stint in rehab that I was barely in the season. But the producers were gracious and invited me anyway, and I went because it was something to do.

I was five months sober and very careful about how I conducted myself. I didn't want any reason for a tabloid to write about me. Though they did anyway: *HAYLEY ALDRIDGE SLIPS UP; HAYLEY IN TROUBLE?* Any time I held a glass in my hand, it was conjectured to be alcohol, even though all I drank now was water. Not even the bubbly kind with fruit in it; just plain, still water.

I had been chaste the entire time too. Jamie Little and I barely spoke to each other now that *Mysterious City* was out and we didn't have to have a publicity relationship. I was trying really hard to be good by myself. To rely on just me, and not use men and sex as a coping mechanism for my insecurities anymore. And I dutifully took my Lamictal, thinking that if I stopped, it would ruin whatever balance I had in my life thus far.

Which is why it was *highly* inconvenient when Anthony Martens walked up to me and smiled his megawatt smile, and I felt it all the way down into my knees.

I remembered the kind boy who released spiders, whose

voice rasped as he described World War II history to me, and I wondered what kind of man he had become.

"Aldridge," he said, his voice now warm honey. "It's so good to see you again."

"Hi, Martens." I smiled back at him. "How are you?"

"Better now that I've seen you," he said.

I laughed. "*Smooth*."

"A guy's gotta try."

He really *was* a good-looking guy—that square jawline, those dark brown eyes. I felt a pull toward him, but admonished myself: No, let's not do that now, Hayley. I smiled at him, but didn't engage further, and he gave me a nod before schmoozing with other guests.

The Golden Globes were tedious, as always; people *think* that awards ceremonies are fun and games but it's four hours of sitting around, hoping to use the restroom at any opportunity. Without the added bonus of getting tipsy, I felt every hour, especially in my hipbones as I sat on an uncomfortable seat waiting for a chance to get up during commercial breaks to talk to anyone who would approach me.

When the evening was at its merciful end, I got into my ride and leaned against the back seat in relief. My feet hurt, my hips ached, and I was dehydrated. My driver, who had started to pull out onto Wilshire, suddenly stopped. "There's a crazy man in the middle of the street," he said to me over his shoulder.

"What's that, Rodney?" I asked, and glanced through the windshield.

There stood Anthony Martens, his bow tie undone and suit

jacket unbuttoned, looking wild in the headlights. He was standing in the middle of Wilshire Boulevard, and I zipped the sunroof open to ask him what the hell he was doing.

"I'm asking you out, Hayley Aldridge," he yelled breathlessly, still standing in front of my car. There was a backlog of other limousines and drivers behind us, all starting to honk like we were in the middle of a Manhattan traffic jam.

"I . . ." I didn't know what to say.

"I'm not moving until you say yes," he said, and I could see the determination in the set of his jaw.

A prominent HBO actress was on the sidewalk and she yelled at me, "Go on, honey, just do it."

"Come on, Hayley," Anthony pleaded. "One date."

The roar of honks and yells behind us grew louder, more frenzied. Paparazzi were photographing the encounter, and I felt the pressure of all those eyes on the back of my blond head. "All right," I yelled. "I'll go out with you. Now will you please move?"

There was a smattering of applause from onlookers on the sidewalk, though I wasn't sure if that was because of my answer or, the more pragmatic reason, Anthony finally moved away from the middle of the street. He was grinning wide as Rodney accelerated slowly, and I could see Anthony jumping in elation as we passed by him. I leaned back against the leather again and smiled. It wasn't what I had been expecting from the night, but it was nice to be wanted.

"Huh," says Jessica. "That's kind of manipulative, actually."

"Oh, shut up," says Jane. "It's romantic."

"Not really. She *had* to say yes. I mean, in front of all those people? Right, Mom?"

I smile at them, but there's no warmth behind it. Yes, it had been manipulative of Anthony to ask me out that way. And yes, it seemed romantic at the time.

Jessica continues, "It's like that part in *The Notebook* when Ryan Gosling threatens to let go of the Ferris wheel if Rachel McAdams doesn't agree to go out with him."

Jane rolls her eyes. "Yes, because stopping a car is the same as plummeting to your death if a girl rejects you." A pause. "But I see what you're saying. 'Stopping a car.' Ugh."

"Same era," I say, "2004."

"Okay, so what happened next?" Jessica asks.

FOR OUR FIRST date, Anthony took me to a nice restaurant. It was not a paparazzi trap, like the Ivy, which was appreciated—I didn't want our first date to be some kind of media circus.

"Have you perused the wine list?" the waiter asked, and I smiled awkwardly and said, "Water is fine."

"Sir?" the waiter asked Anthony, and he murmured, "Water's great."

The waiter filled our glasses. Anthony said, "Is there any way to get a special menu without any alcohol?"

"Yes, sir," the waiter said, and disappeared.

"You didn't have to do that," I said. "If you want wine, go for it."

"I like water," Anthony said, smiling at me. I smiled back.

I wondered how much of my wackiness I should show Anthony so soon. My newest thing was shrimp. All I ate those days were cocktail shrimp and seaweed salads. It was infinitely more filling than just watermelon or zucchini, but it had the tendency to upset my stomach.

The first items came out: aged beef and caviar, sweet corn and truffle cream. I nibbled on everything, not committing to eating a full portion of anything.

"So," I said, lightly dabbing the napkin across my face, hoping not to smear my lipstick, "um, how have you been since *A Poem for Jeanie*?" I didn't know what else to ask. I felt extremely awkward on that date. It was a far cry from my usual excursions with other guys, where small talk wasn't warranted or even expected.

"I've been doing really well," Anthony responded. "I've had steady work, which is always a good thing in this business. As you would know"—he gestured with his fork—"being on that show for so long. *Not* that I think it's bad to be on a show for a long time! I love that job security. I've been hopping from movie to movie and it's been a *task* to keep the calendar full."

"It's been nice," I said, "having the show to fall back on. I enjoy movies, but *Third Time Around* is like family." The painful reminder of Ted stabbed at my heart, and I blinked at Anthony slowly, trying to minimize my pain. I hoped he wouldn't bring up Ted and his death. But of course, he did.

"I'm so sorry about your costar," he said, like the topic wasn't eating me alive inside. Would Ted have taken me to Mélisse? Would we have eaten black cod in tomato sauce together, eyes grinning over our spoons?

"Thank you," I said, for lack of a better response. Anthony's hand found mine on the tabletop and clasped it gently. I expected to feel raw about it, but his touch was soft and soothing. I appreciated the gesture.

We ate our way through two more courses, until I was as full as I'd ever been in my life. Anthony drove me back to my Hidden Hills house and idled in my long driveway. I sat in the passenger seat, hesitating, wondering if I wanted to ask him in, but ultimately, I realized he wasn't waiting for that. He was waiting for a kiss.

"I had a nice time tonight." I spoke to my hands. I was feeling shy all of the sudden, which was such a difference for me, I was surprised at myself.

"I did too. Thanks for letting me take you out. I know I asked you in a way that was hard to say no."

My head snapped up as he made that declaration. So he *knew* it'd been a manipulative thing to do, and yet he'd still done it? "I forgive you," I said archly. And I leaned in imperceptibly.

He chuckled and placed his hand at the nape of my neck, drawing me closer. Our lips met.

It was a soft kiss, one full of promise. When I left the car and walked up to my door, smiling, I wondered what would come next.

CHAPTER 27

Once the paparazzi caught on, the press was on it. Anthony and I were prime tabloid fodder. This time, my mental illness wasn't in the headlines, and I enjoyed myself—as much as I could when I was discussed, anyway.

We went on several more dates, each culminating in a few kisses at the end of the night. He never asked to come in, and I wondered when I should ask if he'd like to. Dating Anthony was easy, in that he didn't force me to do anything I didn't want to do. We ate at nice restaurants, we were each other's plus-ones at premieres, and the most frustrating thing about him was that we *didn't* have sex, something I was sorely missing. I could've gone out to the Serpent Pit and gotten laid easily, but something about Anthony told me that I shouldn't, that he was special and should be treated monogamously.

And there was something about him—I could see just how amazing of a father he would be, just in the way that he treated me. It was like a switch flipped inside me and I ached to have his children. I'd never felt that way before, but I *knew* he would be a good father. *We* may have fallen out, but I've never doubted his love for you two.

We'd been dating for several weeks at this point, and I asked him if he wanted to come inside. Now girls, this is your father, so I won't go into detail, because I know you'll hate it, but he was a very attentive lover. I felt like I could bask after our first lovemaking session, like a turtle sunning on a rock. I felt gloriously alive; I didn't even miss drugs at that moment, because it was that good without it.

Anthony was good for me, and good *to* me. It was the first time I felt secure in a relationship. So when he asked me to marry him, three months into dating, I hesitated for only a moment.

"So soon?" I asked, unsure if what I felt was genuine or not. It could've been the three-carat bubble-gum-pink diamond ring he held out to me swaying my decision, but what do I know?

"All I know is, you've always been the woman for me," Anthony said. "You bewitched me when I first met you all those years ago, and you're just as amazing now as I thought then."

"But I was a kid then . . . and I have baggage now . . ." I hesitated.

"Hayley," he said, and his dark brown eyes were shining with happiness. "Just say yes."

"Okay. Yes," I said, and then I whooped and cried, because *I was getting married!*

My parents did not like it. When I announced it to them over the phone, there was a long silence, and then my father said, "Are you sure? You've only known this man for a couple of months."

"I've known him for eight years, Dad," I corrected him. "We met on *Jeanie*."

"But you haven't talked to him for those eight years. This isn't, like, *Ted* or anything," my mother said, speakerphone making her sound far away.

My stomach froze. Why did she need to bring up Ted, of all people, on my engagement night? "No, but Ted is not here," I said through gritted teeth. "That's not fair."

"I'd just feel better, you know, if we *knew* this man a little more," my mother said. "And not just what we've read about in the tabloids. Every Starbucks run you two do, I read about, but I don't know anything about him. Where did he grow up? Where did he go to school?"

"What does that matter? What matters is that he loves me, and I love him, and we're getting married!" I snapped my hot-pink Motorola Razr closed, which was very satisfying.

"That could've gone better," I said to Anthony, who was nuzzling one of my calves. We were in bed, lounging, not postcoital but just hanging out, which I loved. I loved that we could have amazing sex but also that we could chill out and enjoy each other's company. It was what made him so special.

I brooded. I decided that I didn't want my parents at my wedding. They were naysayers and full of bad energy.

"Baby," I said, "what sort of wedding do you want?"

Anthony grinned at me through half-slitted eyes. "Whatever kind *you* want."

"So if I wanted to have a tiny wedding, just you and me and the priest or whatever, you'd do it?"

"Sure. As long as you showed up in a wedding dress. Or, any dress, I guess," and he started massaging one of my feet.

"I guess Olive would have to come," I mused. "She'd kill me if she wasn't there."

"And I'd want my brother Frankie," he added.

"Maybe a wedding on the beach," I said. "Well, *a* beach. Something small and private."

"We could go to Mexico," he suggested. "Or someplace in the Caribbean."

"I want to go to a place I've never been before. With you." I smiled.

ENGAGED! CHECK OUT HAYLEY ALDRIDGE'S RING!

Hayley Aldridge is engaged to whirlwind beau Anthony Martens. The actress was snapped showing off her ring as she walked to Starbucks. Sources state that she's wearing a three-carat pink diamond from Moussaieff that was specially made for the couple. The price of the ring? Somewhere in the neighborhood of ten million dollars.

Comments

Lucyducy913: OMG that ring I am obsessed

---

barre-none: That ring is so tacky. I can't believe Anthony Martens has ten million to blow on a hideous ring like that. When was he last relevant?

---

burritogirl: oh my god hayley is so lucky, anthony is so fine

---

lunarocket973: I'm so glad she didn't end up with Brandon. He's aged like curdled milk.

---

pinkhair34: barre-none, he was JUST in a blockbuster movie, like ??? i don't understand how you could ask about his relevance when he is literally like RIGHT THERE

---

cockatoowhereareu: I give it 6 months

It was decided: a wedding in Turks and Caicos, with Olive as our witness and Frankie as our officiant. April and Paul, my makeup and hair artists, would join us, but no one else. Getting married in a different country was full of headaches that we didn't need, but it was so secretive, nothing else mattered. And it was going to happen in two weeks. We figured: Why wait?

The set, when I returned to *Third Time Around* for the middle of the fourteenth season, was full of well wishes for Anthony and me. Someone had purchased giant letter balloons that spelled out *Congratulations Hayley* in gold. There was cake at craft services, and I was touched that the crew signed a card for me.

"When is the big day?" Alex Dietrich asked, and I shrugged.

"We're planning for a long engagement, since we've been

dating for such a short time," I lied.

"That's pragmatic. Good for you, Hayley," he said, crinkling around his eyes. "And your mother? How does she feel about her firstborn getting married?"

"She's over the moon." I continued to bend the truth. After all, whatever had happened between them seemed to have fizzled out, and if this was the only way Alex Dietrich learned about my mother, I didn't see the point in telling the truth. The man deserved none of my compassion for fooling around with my mom while she was still married to my dad.

Millie came by at one point to congratulate me, too, which was unusual. But the worst response was from Brandon, who tucked me under his arm and said, "I thought you were waiting for me to propose, Hayley!"

"This isn't the show," I said stiffly, extricating myself from his armpit.

"Do you think that Amy and Thomas are going to get married?" he asked, genuinely curious.

"I have no idea what the writers are planning for us," I said, deadpan. I squinted, scrutinizing his face. "Shouldn't you be moisturizing?"

He turned away from me abruptly. I knew that his aging was a sore spot and I'd touched a raw nerve.

I couldn't film with the ring on my finger, so I put it on a chain and hid it under my clothes. I didn't trust anyone not to nick it if I left it in my trailer, or even in a safe somewhere on set. I was smart enough to know that ten million dollars is a lot of money, but mostly, I didn't want to lose anything that

Anthony had given me.

There was an underlying reason I was so eager to get married: I badly, achingly, wanted to have his kids. I knew the field day that would erupt in the tabloids if I got pregnant out of wedlock, but if I were married . . .

I surreptitiously stopped taking my birth control pills for the first time in half a decade.

We continued to plan our Turks and Caicos wedding, but a wrench was suddenly thrown into the mix: Paul accidentally told my mother what we were planning.

"I told you I *did not want them there*," I hissed, when I learned of Paul's betrayal. Ever since my parents told me they disapproved of my engagement, I knew they would be naysayers at the wedding, and I didn't need that kind of energy. I was proud of myself for this: putting up boundaries, getting on with what *I* wanted.

"I'm so sorry, Hales, I thought she knew!" he wailed. I crossed Paul off my Christmas list.

The Turks and Caicos wedding was suddenly dashed; the plane tickets were nonrefundable, but that was fine—I'd flash them around, make my mother think that we were still going there. But we had to come up with a different plan, and fast.

"How do you feel about Vegas?" Anthony asked spontaneously, and I laughed into his neck, because it was perfect. My parents would think we were on a speck of land to the east and instead we'd be traveling by car to a little Elvis chapel.

All up until the day before the wedding, my mother continued to touch base with me, double checking with me about her mother-of-the-bride dress, an aquamarine blue sheath that she thought would match the color of the water, or confirming hotel reservations for her and Dad and Ashley. And until the day of travel, I let her believe that the Turks and Caicos nuptials were still a go. I told her over the phone that I'd see her on the beach in twenty-four hours. She believed me. My entire family got on a flight and disappeared into the Caribbean. What awaited them there, I wasn't sure. We had continued our ruse, paying for the resort to fulfill our wedding plans, but we would never show up.

Anthony and Olive and Frankie and I piled into a sedan and drove the four and a half hours together, cracking jokes and drinking Coke ICEEs from a gas station convenience store. When we got to a chapel—any one would do—and confirmed that they were open for business, I changed into a white crop top and white pants. April and Paul were both excluded from this new plan, so Olive fixed my hair and I did my own makeup, drawing on my brown eyeliner thickly with a shaking hand. Anthony slipped a carnation in his suit buttonhole and Frankie, no longer needed as an officiant, signed the marriage license as witness for us.

It was perfect.

It was the start of my downfall.

CHAPTER 28

My parents were livid about the stunt we had pulled, and my voice mail was full of anger when I finally deigned to check it, two days after Anthony and I had returned from our whirlwind honeymoon. I was surprised by their vitriol; after all, I had done a lot of things without their knowledge or interference—this was nothing new. But my mother had choice words about the matter. "It's not even that we disapprove of Anthony—I'm sure he's a nice guy if he'd actually taken the time to meet us before you got married," she spoke into my voice mail. "But Hayley! You didn't even invite us to your wedding! What the heck? Not only that, you *baited us* to go to a different *country* to attend your nonwedding! This is unacceptable."

My father used epithets in his message to me. It's not worth repeating, girls, it's just a gibberish of anger.

The only way to get back into their good graces was to let them know, before anyone else, before Olive or Frankie even, that I was pregnant. That sure changed their tune. Before, Anthony was just "that husband." Suddenly, he was "father of your babies!" and "the daddy-to-be!"

Getting pregnant had been easy, lucky for me. I had gone off my birth control pills for a couple of months, and after a few cycles, there it was, or *wasn't*: a skipped period, a strange feeling that I was somehow not alone, even when I was all by myself in our bedroom. The two pink lines on the pregnancy test proved it, and I told Anthony, then my parents, then his parents, in that order, then hoped that I could keep this secret for a little while before the tabloids announced it.

But somehow, and I'm not sure how, someone leaked. Maybe it was a paparazzo digging through my trash and finding the pregnancy test, I don't know. Once a tabloid got wind of it, the others followed, and the paparazzi grew even thicker in swarm outside of my door every time I walked outside.

I was still filming *Third Time Around* and when the rumors were flying, Alex Dietrich took me into his office and asked if they were true. I admitted that I was pregnant. I was worried he would say something terrible about it, but all he said was, "Okay. Now we need to figure out if we're going to write it into the show."

"More sex scenes with Brandon?" I was horrified. "No, let's hide it."

"You hate Brandon that much?"

"I hate sex scenes with him," I said diplomatically.

So the fourteenth season of *TTA* had me hiding my burgeoning bump with an assortment of tote bags and purses, stepping behind furniture, and even allowing me to exit the season early for maternity leave. I was due in the summer, and by then I knew I was having twins, but I refused to learn what sex they were going to be, preferring to be surprised when the due date came. Each twin had its own personality, one jiggling mercilessly on my bladder and the other quietly sleeping most of the time. I told myself that if they were boys, I'd name the quiet one Ted.

I had a relatively easy pregnancy, as well. I know I should be thanking my lucky stars. I was still able to exercise, but I offset my Pilates with excessive amounts of pickles, dark chocolate ice cream, and raspberry jam (all together). My mother was in my life again, keeping watch on me and living in one of my spare bedrooms—I wasn't sure if she was doing that to be near me or to be separated from my father, with whom she had another estrangement after my nonwedding.

Olive, my roommate, butted heads with both my mother and Anthony. You'd think that the house would be big enough that they wouldn't get in one another's way, but they congregated in the same spaces. My mother insisted that she and Anthony and I eat together at the same time, and had my cook serve us at six o'clock on the dot. Inevitably Olive would show up as well, tabbing her gum on one finger and eating hummus out of a jar, rather than sit with us.

"Can you go somewhere else, instead of standing there?" Anthony would say to Olive. "You make me nervous just standing there."

Olive would huff and roll her eyes, and not move.

Anthony and my mother would share a glance, but they didn't push it. It killed me a little that my best friend and my husband, and my mother, didn't get along.

After dinner, Olive would go out and live her socialite life and Anthony would go "meet with the guys," while my mother would sit me down in the living room. We'd talk about our days and it was a cozy time, albeit a little boring. I wanted to be out with Olive or Anthony, dancing in a bar, sipping a cool drink that would slide down my throat and warm my stomach. But I was obsessed with making sure my babies were healthy, and that meant eating macrobiotic meals and drinking only water, no coffee. It was a huge change from my previous diets that were usually one or two ingredients or nothing at all. I gained weight, but it wasn't horrifying; somehow, I was content to let my body *be* and to grow my babies healthily.

The paparazzi were ruthless during this time. You'd think that they'd be more careful around a pregnant woman, but they shut me in on all sides when I got into my car for doctor's appointments, and flashed through the windshield as I pulled out of the garage to get on the road. The tabloids were gleeful about my changing body, stating that I was *SHOWING OFF* my belly or putting my body *ON DISPLAY.*

There was one day when Anthony and I were trying to get to the doctor because of some scary bleeding and the paps wouldn't let me out of my gated community. I started to cry, even though that's exactly what they want you to do—show emotion—and Anthony cursed as we inched forward through the throng. The photos were on the front page of every tabloid the next day, all citing that Anthony had been cruel to me and I was crying out of devastation that our relationship was on the rocks. The paparazzi are awful.

I will always remember July 20, the day our twins were born. I woke up around one in the morning to use the bathroom and my water broke. I knew I was ready to meet you two. I woke my mother and we trekked out to the hospital, trailed, of course, by a dozen hounds who had stayed up all night camped around our house, waiting for this moment as well.

I didn't know where Anthony was. He hadn't been in the house, and truth be told, I hadn't seen him at all that week. It was as if he had disappeared into the ether. He might have been out partying; he could've been hanging out with friends. Whatever it was, my mother called him every five minutes when we got to the hospital, hoping that he would be present for the birth of his children.

My contractions were growing more insistent as we eluded the photographers hanging out of their cars for a shot of me on the way to the hospital. Luckily, once we were at Cedars-Sinai, the security took over and we were surrounded no more. I was put up in a private maternity suite with the rest of the floor emptied as a precaution, and there I paced, waiting for the next step.

I knew I wanted an epidural; I had no preconceived notions that I was strong enough to give birth to two babies without medical help. I was wheeled into an OR and set there to rest. I won't bore you girls with the long story of what I listened to on my labor playlist, though Christina Aguilera featured prominently on it. Around eight in the morning, I felt an intense need to push. The nurses checked on me and saw that I was fully dilated and ready. At that moment, Anthony ducked into the OR, masked up and in the nick of time. I clenched his gloved hand while I pushed.

Jessica came out first, at 8:36, head down and ready to meet the world. Jane popped out a few minutes later, at 8:42. I held my two perfect babies and wept. I couldn't imagine a more perfect moment; Anthony on one side of me, gazing tenderly at our baby girls, and my parents at the foot of my bed, my father taking a photo of our expanded family with a new digital camera.

Series finale of *Third Time Around*—script

Natasha: I miss him.
Amy: We all do.
Erica: Yeah.

(The three women hug. Then they look down at the toddler sitting at the kitchen table, drinking juice quietly.)

Amy: But look at the beautiful child you have. Jonathan looks just like him.
Natasha: I'll always remember Zac. My forever love. My baby's daddy.

(The doorbell rings.)

Erica: I'll get it.

(She disappears from the kitchen.)

Natasha: And how are you, Amy? Are you ready to join the work-force and live on your own?
Amy: I'm not sure. About the living alone part. I'm definitely ready to be done with school. I can't wait for the graduation ceremony

tomorrow.

Erica (reentering): Amy, there's someone here for you.

Thomas: Hi.

Amy: Hi.

(Thomas walks up to Amy. He looks at her for a moment, then gives her a hug.)

Thomas: I missed you, Amy.

Amy: It's good to see you, Thomas.

Erica (cheerfully): Enough of this mushy talk! Let's go celebrate Amy's graduation! (She calls up the stairs.) Are you coming, Mom? Dad?

(The parents walk down, smiling.)

Steve: Let me just grab my sweater.

Georgette: Oh, honey, look at how much you've grown. (Embraces Amy.) I'm so proud of you.

Steve: I'm proud of you too.

Amy: Thanks, Dad.

(They hug.)

Natasha: Come on, Jonathan, let's go.

(Natasha pulls Jonathan from his seat. They walk out the front door. Thomas and Amy walk out the door together, holding hands.

Then Erica. Then Steve and Georgette. Georgette takes one moment to look back at the kitchen and turns off the light before exiting the stage.)

CHAPTER 29

It would have been easy for Alex Dietrich to write me out of *Third Time Around* during my maternity leave and subsequent first few months of my babies' lives. All I know is, he asked me if I wanted to be there for the series finale, as the show ended in its fifteenth season, and I told him yes, absolutely. So he scheduled me to be there for the final three episodes of the show.

After we wrapped for the final time, and gave one another a big group hug, we dispersed to our trailers for one last time. I took down all of my posters and little twinkle lights, gathered my scrunchy pillows and patted the tweedy couch goodbye. I had my babies to go home to, but I needed to take a moment to give a mental farewell to everything on the set, including my trailer.

On my way to the parking lot, I saw Brandon's trailer lights still lit up. I considered leaving without saying goodbye, but I had some thoughts I wanted to impart to him. I wanted to tell him how much I hated working with him and that I hoped he would find someone else to terrorize in his next role, whatever that may be. I wasn't going to go to the wrap party because I was still nursing and to be away from the twins hurt me more than I expected.

But when I stepped into his trailer, he was hunched over on the couch, head in his hands. He looked defeated. "What's wrong?" I asked. "You're gonna miss the party."

He shoved a magazine at me. *BRANDON PIKE: SE-CRETLY FORTY?* the headline blared. There were a number of photos of Brandon and his aging face, his jowls and laugh lines on display.

"You can't be serious," I said, laughing. "Who cares about this shit?"

"*I* care, Hales. *I do.* When I was new on the show, I had so many opportunities to shoot other things. I turned them down. Now my career is dead in the water because I'm no longer *hot.*"

"You didn't turn them *all* down," I said, remembering how he was in *Superman* and *Persuasion*, at the very least. But he had definitely not spent every hiatus working like I had. "Why didn't you get plastic surgery like everyone else?"

"Like *you*, you mean?"

"Hey." I crossed my arms in front of my chest. But there was no bark with his bite.

"I could've done more, that's all I'm saying. And now look at me."

"Welcome to the world." I pushed the magazine back toward him and flipped a page. The story before it was about Jennifer Aniston and how she was "selfishly" childfree. The page before that, an exposé on my best friend, Olive Green, who had started dating a shipping magnate. "Just because you *look* older doesn't mean there aren't roles for you," I said helpfully, for some reason being nice to him instead of callous like I'd expected. I *wanted* to be mean, but something about me had softened since I'd had the twins. I was gentler, more maternal. And I didn't want to kick him while he was feeling down. Old Hayley would've. Mom Hayley didn't.

Brandon pulled his head out from his hands and looked at me. "What's next for you?" he asked.

"I go home to my babies," I said simply.

"No roles, no nothing?"

"Nope."

I had started my career on the show and I was willing to end it on the show.

Because—and it might sound ludicrous—all of this? It wasn't worth it to me anymore. I wanted to be with my babies. I had enough money, enough to last me a lifetime. I had had enough of fame. I'd had enough of paparazzi hounding me for my photo. All I wanted now was to let Anthony be the bread-winner and for me to stay at home with you girls and be the best mother I could be.

"Wow," Brandon said softly. "That's really amazing, Hales. Wish that could be me." He brooded. "I can't even have kids. Know how my girlfriend and I had been trying?"

How could I forget? I wanted to ask.

"Anyway . . . never mind." He seemed so low. I was almost worried about him.

"Don't take this stuff to heart, okay?" I said, shifting my pillow to my other arm and stepping toward his trailer door. "Have a good life, Brandon."

"Thanks, Hales."

For a while, my parents didn't bug me about my career. They understood I wanted to be with you two. After the show's finale—in which Amy graduates from college and it's open-ended whether or not she gets back together with Thomas—my parents suddenly had Mr. Himes, my agent, inundating me with scripts again. I turned them all down and my mother grew frustrated.

"All of this, Hayley, we sacrificed so much for you to be successful," she said sternly. We were sitting at my breakfast table as I nursed one of the babies, and her raised voice made me cringe.

"Mom, I just want to be with my babies right now, watch them grow up," I pleaded. Surely, she understood that.

"You have to strike while the iron is still hot," she continued. "Some of these scripts don't film until next year. You can get a nanny. I'll be your nanny. You can be a working mother. Why *can't* you have it all?"

She just didn't get it. I was out. Finished. Done. I'd had a good run. Half a dozen movies, a fifteen-year television show. Oodles of money and publicity and all that. It wasn't what I wanted anymore.

But I learned the hard way that my parents would not take no for an answer.

MY LIFE WAS a seesaw: whenever things with you girls were good, things with your father were bad. And vice versa. It was like a switch had been flipped, and we began to argue about the smallest things. It was all out of concern for your welfare, of course; but it started to take its toll on our marriage.

It was slowly at first, like me being upset that Anthony wasn't home to check on your crying at three A.M. I had to drag myself out of bed every hour, with no help from him, because he wasn't home. And then when it was two in the afternoon and he was home and he was checking on the babies, and *I* slept through the crying this time, it was somehow *my* fault that I was tired. We had arguments about that.

Then it gained momentum. He had a laissez-faire attitude about parenting. Let them sleep when they want to sleep, let them eat when they want to eat, he'd say. He let you girls dictate your own schedules at around four months old. The problem with that approach was, you girls didn't *have* a schedule! And I was running myself ragged trying to keep up with sleep and feeding and everything. I thought that you girls needed some sort of sleep training. No pacifiers, no rocking, no nothing—to help you become independent sleepers. If your father had helped a little more, I wouldn't have been so tired, but he still went out with his guy friends every night, unable to give up his freedom. So we had *more* arguments.

We stopped having sex. We stopped communicating in any way that wasn't sniping at each other. We were each convinced that our way of parenting was the better method, and we could not let go or compromise. Even when my mother came in to help, it wasn't enough—we still fought. In the end, we decided that we didn't love each other enough to keep the marriage going. We thought it would be healthier to break up rather than fight all the time. I was exhausted, he was exhausted. It was time.

Hayley and Anthony Call It Quits!

The lovebirds, who were married in Vegas in 2004 after a whirl-wind romance (see our coverage of how they achieved their isolated wedding <u>here</u>) are having their marriage dissolved. The two cite irreconcilable differences.

CHAPTER 30

I learned so much that first year of your lives. Things like baby nails that have to be trimmed frequently, otherwise you will scratch your little baby faces. Or that babies make messes, so if I went anywhere, I should have multiple changes of clothes, not just for you, but for me too. The year 2006 was good for us. I bonded with you girls and you soaked it right up. Even though my marriage to Anthony was falling apart right under my nose, I would look at you girls, sleeping peacefully, and think: *I would rather be doing this than be married to him.* Not trying to knock your daddy, but *you* are the best things that happened to me in my marriage. Not him. Especially not how he got mean after we divorced. It was like he tried to get on my nerves in every single way, starting with the custody battle.

I don't remember when, but I stopped taking my bipolar medication sometime during my pregnancy or breastfeeding. I know Dr. Goodman said it was fine to keep taking it, but I didn't want anything to adversely affect my babies. So I was off my meds for a while.

I started to revert back to old habits of staying up for days at a time, though I assumed it was because you girls took turns crying. Then I'd have days of downtime, when I couldn't get enough sleep, and was so tired that it hurt to even answer the phone. That's when my mother—your grandmother—would step in and take care of you. She continued to live with me for a few months, until I hired a full-time nanny, Nanny Sheard. Truthfully, I don't think my mother wanted to go back to the house with my father, who was, at the moment, carting Ashley around as she started her ill-fated starlet life.

Ashley never got as big as I did—not sure why. Maybe she lacked the It factor, or the features that made her an Aldridge just didn't jibe with what was popular at the time. Maybe the world needed only one Hayley, and Hayley 2.0 was not happening. Whatever it was, Ashley's star rose only to the point where she was in *Shine Street* in the best-friend role, and never higher, no matter how hard she busted her ass to get there.

And perhaps that fueled my parents' desperation to keep me working. I don't know. All I know is, in 2007, some things happened that changed my life forever.

The first was that Anthony asked for a divorce. We just weren't on the same track anymore. He preferred to work and party, and I barely saw him. When I did, we argued nonstop. We had tried to make it work for the first two years you girls were with us, but we agreed that it just wasn't for us anymore. We separated in early 2007 and, at first, were okay with fifty-fifty custody of you girls.

The second was that Brandon, my awful costar, died by suicide. It was entirely unexpected, but when I thought about it, it wasn't surprising. Thomas had been his biggest role by far, and at twenty-nine, he had aged out of the heartthrob status he was used to. With *Third Time Around* canceled, Brandon was washed up, a has-been. He had been a flash in the pan, and his face aged like curdled milk.

He died on a Friday; this I remember, because I was watching *Good Morning America* while chasing around my girls and I distinctly remember thinking that I'd have a break when your daddy came to pick you up that afternoon. You two were walking by then and it was hard keeping track of you. Olive was no help; she slept late every day after being out at all hours of the night partying. It was just me and you two, and suddenly there was a bulletin about Brandon, as if he'd been as big of a deal as the president or something.

There are a lot of feelings that go through one's mind when a colleague dies. With Ted, it was disbelief, like the wind had been knocked out of my chest. My eyes had involuntarily filled with tears, and I had sobbed before I knew what had happened.

But with Brandon, the news piqued my curiosity. Perhaps it was that I was distracted by my babies, who were zooming all over the floor. I perked my head to the side, wondering why he did it. I knew I should mourn him, but I had disliked Brandon, so much so that I was feeling guilty now for not feeling worse about his death.

When Olive came yawning into the living room, the TV was on mute. "Brandon died," I said by way of greeting.

"Brandon, your costar Brandon?" she asked.

"That's the one."

"Heyyyy!" She grimaced at me, or maybe it was a smile.

"How do you feel about that?"

"I don't know," I said truthfully. I held one of my babies close as she drifted off to sleep, thumb in her mouth. "Like I should celebrate? Is that bad?"

"Hell no, I'd celebrate with you! Too early for cocktails, you think?"

She perked up one finger and went up to her room. She came back with a thimbleful of vodka in two shot glasses. "Down the booby hatch," she proclaimed, and we clinked glasses before downing them.

I don't know what I was thinking. I'd been carefully cultivating my sobriety for years now, and I had never been led astray by Olive or anyone else in that time. Hell, even during my honeymoon with Anthony we had foregone champagne and drank sparkling water flavored to taste like pears. But suddenly, my frayed sobriety and weird state of mind was followed by wine, also contraband from Olive's room, and by the time Anthony came to pick up the girls, I was halfway to drunk. He smelled it on me and said, "How can you put our babies in danger by being drunk at two in the afternoon?"

"I'm not *drunk*," I insisted. I passed him one of the toddlers, who was miraculously asleep, and he grasped her firmly to his chest. I was wobbly, though, and he saw me blink furiously to clear my vision.

"What's this?" he said, looking at her right big toe. It was bloody red on the nail.

"Oh, I just painted it—to tell them apart. This one is Jessica."

He gave me a funny look.

"Don't be such a spoilsport," Olive called from the living room.

He whirled on her, still clutching Jessica to his chest. "You're a bad influence," he accused. Olive just rolled her eyes.

Had I known that Anthony wanted full custody, would I have done the same thing?

Anthony left with the girls, and soon after, as Olive and I were languishing on one of my couches discussing Brandon, my parents arrived without warning. "So this is what you've been up to," my father roared, as he took stock of Olive and me. I shouldn't have let them in. My mother glared at me with disapproval as my father yelled.

Anthony must have called them after he'd left to let them know what was going on. How else would they have known to come over?

"Calm down, Daddy," I said, my tongue thick. "The babies aren't here."

"You've blown your sobriety, and for what?" he howled.

It was a tough question to be asked, because I didn't know. Why *had* I taken those first shots with Olive, after years of being sober? Was it just that I wanted to feel something nostalgic, the way I felt when Brandon was alive? Or was it really an action to celebrate his life?

My father hauled me up by one arm and ushered me out to the car. "You're going back to rehab, *now*," he said.

"No!" I screamed. I ran back into the house. My father stalked back toward the front door and I hid in the doorway, holding it open slightly, as I watched him advance. Through the crack I yelled, "It was only a little wine! It's not like I was doing *drugs* or anything!"

I didn't care if the paparazzi heard me or not. I slammed the door shut and locked it, dragging the chain through, before he could reach me.

Through the wood, I could hear him sigh angrily. I stepped back from the door.

"Hayley," he said, and knocked. His voice was muffled. "Hayley, open up."

"No."

"Fine. You want to do this the hard way? We will."

He disappeared, and I watched him go through the giant front windows. I sighed in relief when he got back into the car, my mother in the passenger seat, and drove off.

Nanny Sheard had the day off, so it was just Olive and me in the house at the moment. "Let's go shopping!" I said brightly. "Ooh! Wait!" I ran into my bedroom and tore through my walk-in closet. I found the Wig, a little disheveled from being stuffed in a drawer, and smoothed it onto my head. Then I reunited with Olive in the living room.

I felt *good*; more like myself than I had in ages. Carefree, like a child should feel in a wondrous world. This was better than counting every sober day, being good, being neutral, when I could be chaotic and free. When I thought about all the days I had been medicated, a drone, a zombie, a robot, I wanted to laugh. *This* was living.

Olive pumped her fists in the air and we tore out of the

house, tipsily driving my new Mercedes minivan my father had bought just for the babies. We rolled through a stop sign, giggling, and ended up in a Calabasas open-air mall parking lot. Olive parked the car across two spaces and we got out.

The paparazzi had chased us there, of course, and now were snapping us in our heels and me in the Wig. "Let's get ice cream," I suggested, and Olive agreed, so we found a Dippin' Dots. The photographers surrounded us and took photos of us enjoying our space-age treats.

TMZ was there, too, recording us as we tripped over our heels, which had seemed like a good idea at the time. I tossed them off and left them in the middle of the walkway, continuing barefoot on the pavement. "Hayley! Olive!" they called. "What are you doing? Where are your children?"

"They're with their daddy," I said snidely.

Gawkers out shopping were turning to look at us, adding to the mob. They started to push against us, crowding us. "Hayley! Hayley!" they cried, wielding pocketbooks and flip-phone cameras.

"Get off of her!" Olive shouted, pushing them away.

"Get off of me!" I screamed, barreling through the onslaught of photographers and onlookers.

By the time we made a mad dash back to the car, there was a policeman writing us a ticket for parking illegally. We had evidently parked in a fire lane.

"Ma'am, are you drunk?" the policeman asked.

"No," I huffed.

"Oh, no. You're Hayley Aldridge," he said, regret tinging

his voice.

"What about it?" I asked.

"Hayley!" Olive said, and I caught a flash coming off her hands. She had tossed the keys to me. "Let's go!"

I climbed into the minivan and turned the key in the ignition. The cop stood in front of the car, as if daring me to run him over. "I will, I swear to God," I muttered under my breath. I pushed the accelerator and the minivan skipped ahead a little bit, before I rammed on the brakes. The shocked officer moved out of the way.

More flashes and arms were in front of my car now, and Olive was screaming. "Go go go!" But I didn't want to run over anyone, even if they *were* just paparazzi.

I tapped the gas pedal again with my bare foot, my shoes littered somewhere on the sidewalk behind us. The onlookers were not moving out of the way. I tapped a man with the bumper of the car and he yelped at me. "Move!" I shouted.

I can't even begin to describe to you the chaos that was happening at that moment. So many people screaming in an incoherent jumble, Olive yelling in my ear, the police officers surrounding the car tentatively with their bodies, palms out, as if to stop the minivan with the force of their will. And all the while, photographers continued to blast their shutters.

I stepped on the gas one more time, but in my drunkenness, I couldn't connect with the brake in time. A body went under the hood. I shrieked. The officers began to pull the man out from below the car by the armpits. Luckily, he had missed getting crushed by a wheel, but he and I were both shaken. I turned the key in the ignition, killing the engine. Olive was still screaming at me to go. But I couldn't. I knew I'd gone too far.

The cops escorted me to an ambulance.

What I didn't ask was what my parents were planning as I was signed into the rehab facility in Van Nuys.

Because the next thing I knew, I was no longer a legal person.

HAYLEY ALDRIDGE RUNS OVER PEDESTRIAN

Hayley Aldridge is a mess! The *Mysterious City* actress ran over a pedestrian in Hidden Hills yesterday after a showdown with four police officers. Witnesses say that Hayley was drunk and her foot slipped on the gas pedal as she tried to elude police. The pedestrian, Michael Byrnes, 43, claims he will be suing the actress for mental and physical distress.

Rumors are now swirling that Hayley is back in rehab after falling off the wagon. Let's hope it sticks this time!

CHAPTER 31

W hat do you mean, *no longer a legal person*?" Jessica asks.
"Just that," I say. "You heard what they said on TMZ.
A conservatorship of the person means that legal personhood is
gone. I couldn't do anything without the permission of someone else."

"How is that possible?" Jane wants to know.

"I'm not entirely sure," I admit. "One moment I was in the
rehab facility, the next minute I was being told that I was being
conserved. I didn't know what it meant. My father had strong-
armed a judge to grant him a temporary conservatorship after
Dr. Goodman rolled over, because my mental health was 'a
danger to myself and others.' He told the judge that I'd been
drunk around my twin toddlers and that got her attention.
The cops told the judge that I had essentially run over a man.
Then Dr. Goodman told her I was off my meds. She signed the
mental health conservatorship right away. By the time I found
out, the ink was already dry."

"So you didn't get a say, at all?" Jessica sounds alarmed.

"Nope." I think back to the shock I felt when I was told that
my decisions were no longer mine to make, that I was back to

being a child in the eyes of the law. In rehab, they try to make you understand that your choices are always in your hands; this revelation was something new entirely. "Not only that, they signed my estate over to a probate conservatorship at the same time. I couldn't spend a dime without my parents' permission."

Was I given a hearing? Yes. I remember it vaguely. I was so nervous, still only a few days into rehab, pulled out and placed in a witness box. The judge asked me if I was in rehab. I said yes. The judge asked me if this was my first time in rehab. I said no. Had I been taking my prescribed bipolar medication? I said that I didn't think I had.

What I remember most was that Millie was there—Millie, from *Third Time Around*. I don't know why or how, but she added her two cents, that I was unstable, and had always been. She cited moments when I got upset at Brandon on set, including the moment he had given me my first kiss and I had attacked him afterward.

My father added I'd been with my girlfriend Olive, who had always been a bad influence, day-drinking. He mentioned the multimillion-dollar house that I bought with Olive's intention of living with me, the designer I'd hired for the house on Olive's direction, the purses full of receipts from the nights we'd go out and drink and I'd pick up the tab for my socialite friend, my gold Bentley bought to match my sunglasses, all that.

But I think the final nail in my proverbial coffin was that my psychiatrist testified I hadn't been willing to go to rehab, and that I hadn't been taking my medication for what amounted to be years now. That I'd been found barefoot, in a wig, eating ice cream while drunk at three in the afternoon. That it took a squad of four policemen to pull me onto the stretcher, after I'd run over another human while drunk.

The judge ruled that there was enough evidence that I lacked the capacity to make my own medical decisions and signed my life over for a year.

When I was released from rehab, it was to my house—with no one in it except a security team that was put there in place by my parents. Olive had been kicked out, served with a restraining order for multiple reasons.

"I'm not crazy," I said, as I walked around my house, peeking out past the curtains and over my shoulder at my new security detail. The guy who was picked to follow me was named Adam, and he was a formidable man: over six feet, wearing all black and black combat boots, definitely ex–Special Forces of some kind.

"Nobody said you were," Adam said.

"Then why are you in my house?"

No answer.

"Where are my babies?" I demanded.

"They're with your ex-husband" was the answer.

"It's Wednesday. I want them here with me. That's the custody agreement."

"Okay, I'll make some calls and they'll be on their way here."

I was mollified.

But the biggest surprise of all was learning that I had no way of signing contracts on my own—and that my conservator, my father, could sign them for me. I learned that when I was sitting in my dining room, drinking coffee on a Friday morning, and my mother shoved a script across my empty kitchen table.

I shoved it back at her. "I don't want to look at this," I said.

"That's too bad. You're signed to make this movie in a month," she said calmly.

"What?" I couldn't believe my ears.

"Your father and I decided that it's best if you get back on the horse," she said. "You didn't have trouble with your sobriety for the last few years while you were working on a project, and we think this will be a good distraction for you. All this time, sitting at home with your children, isn't good for you. It just makes you bored and stew. And drink."

I had gotten drunk *one time* and suddenly, I was a liability. I was livid.

"What gives you the right to *sign a contract for me*?" I shouted. "I'm not twelve anymore, Mom!"

"That's just how it is now," she told me. "The conservatorship laws say so." She tapped the script. "You'll be working on *Brother, May I?* for the foreseeable future."

"And if I say no?"

She shrugged. "Then I guess you'll suffer the consequences."

What consequences? I wanted to know, but at the same time, her voice had turned on its edge, a slight menace. I'd never heard her so in charge before. It was as if this temporary conservatorship had given her a confidence boost.

I snatched the script off the table. "Fine," I snarled. "But I won't be doing any more films after this one."

"We'll see." Her eyes glittered. I felt my heart stutter in my chest. What did she mean by that?

I'D BE LYING if I said I was miserable on the set of *Brother, May I?* It was a good film to work on, at least at first, and I was friendly with the cast and crew.

But my heart was always with my babies, with whom I didn't spend time for hours at a stretch. I requested, and was granted, to have Nanny Sheard hired on, but she wasn't allowed to live in the house. She came and went, the paps following her now, as she arrived at six in the morning until nine at night. Nanny Sheard brought the twins on set so that I could see them in between takes, but if they started getting unruly or disruptive, she had to take them home. That's when I really missed them, but I couldn't show it in my performance. I was a professional, through and through.

Anthony and I were having trouble with our custody arrangement. He would keep the girls for longer than he was supposed to—I was their guardian from seven in the morning on Monday, and he often didn't bring them until the afternoon—causing me to fume and stew. Back then, I was still allowed to have a phone in the house, and I would call Anthony. I'd calmly ask for the girls back at my house, before I'd get so tired of his attitude that I'd start screaming epithets.

One such day, he scoffed and said, "Watch out what you say to me. I can bring this whole rodeo down if I want."

"What does that *mean*?" I screamed. "Stop talking in riddles and just bring the girls to the house! Now!"

"I'll be there at one."

"*Now*, Anthony!"

Things were different now that I was under the conservatorship. I was required to go to outpatient rehab every week, sort of like an AA meeting but it was closed-door to only the people invited, to lessen the chance of a blabber. I couldn't drive myself to and from the set; Adam the bodyguard had to do it for me. And worst of all—I wasn't allowed to hang out with the cast and crew after hours. Aside from the rehab, it was as if I were thirteen again.

I spent every spare second off the set with my babies, entertaining new scripts my mother sent over (with no intention of committing to any), and gossiping with Nanny Sheard, whose first name was Susie.

Susie became my confidant in those days. She was in her fifties, perhaps, and dyed her gray hair back to her original auburn. Her favorite food was pie and I made sure that a grocery-store-baked pie was always on the shopping list so she could indulge while she was at my house. We chased the girls together, sipped tea together on the couch when they were asleep, chatted about this and that. She didn't understand the conservatorship, but she seemed to understand that I had gotten the raw end of the deal, especially since Anthony was now petitioning to have sixty-forty custody of the girls.

I was on my meds, and with Olive gone, and my only company Adam and Susie, I'd been pretty tame by myself. I was sure that I would get let off the hook when the mental health conservatorship was supposed to be renewed in a year.

And it would have all gone according to plan.

If not for the accident.

CHAPTER 32

Adam was taking me to the *Brother, May I?* set on a July morning. I remember thinking it was sweltering hot for L.A. The sun was out already, burning brightly in the sky. I had my shades on and Adam drove us around all of the paparazzi that crowded my house at seven in the morning.

What was different about that day? Was it that Nanny Sheard had been in the car with us, in the back seat with the girls? Was it that the custody battle was riling up and the paps wanted a shot of me looking upset? Or was it just random? I'll never know.

We cruised through a yellow light, but the paparazzi on our tail sailed through the red, and Adam checked over his shoulder. "Come on, man," he said to himself as he drove. "Gimme some slack."

One car got perilously close to us and Adam swerved a little so we wouldn't make contact. I could see the photographer hanging out the driver's window, snapping. That couldn't be safe, I thought to myself, and the next thing I knew, we were crashing.

I was in the front passenger seat and my first thought was

Oh. That hurts. My head had smacked against something and it felt like a bone had shattered in my skull. *Oh. This is bad.* We had stopped moving. My eyes strained against their lids as I forced myself to open them. Everything was blurry and too bright, and I realized my sunglasses had flown off my face. I turned my head to call over my shoulder, but it hurt too much to do so. "Susie? Are you okay? Are the girls okay?" I felt hysterical.

"We're fine back here," Susie's voice reassured me. "Not a scratch. The girls are tight in their car seats. Everything's fine." Jessica and Jane shrieked with fear, in unison, not helping my headache any.

Adam twisted in his seat to look at me and his face betrayed concern. "Hayley, you've got a bruise the size of Montana."

I felt my hairline and there was an egg-shaped lump on my head. "Oh, fuck!" I breathed. I checked my fingers but there was no blood.

"Who's the president?" he asked, waving a finger in front of my eyes.

"Huh?" How would I know this?

"What's your middle name?"

"I . . . don't know."

"That's bad. We need to get you checked out at the hospital."

But I couldn't think. All I could fathom was the pulse-pounding pain in my head. A paparazzo was outside of my window, snapping away, and I closed my eyes, willing him to disappear. I could already hear the wail of sirens over the girls' crying.

The ambulance ride and the hospital were blurs, moments that I couldn't seem to snatch long enough to make a memory of. And when I got home—my face was in no shape to be filmed that day, and the ER doctor advised rest—all I wanted to do was sleep.

I asked Susie Sheard to stay the night, and I slept. And slept. And slept some more. Every time I woke, I would eat, and every morning I'd take my Lamictal under Adam's supervision, then I'd go right back to sleep again. I was confused, sometimes my vision was hazy, and I couldn't take care of the girls. That's when I knew something was really wrong. I had no desire to hold them, to hear them. All I wanted was the sanctuary of my bedroom, away from noise, just to sleep and rest.

I went to a doctor and got the go-ahead to work again. But I couldn't concentrate on my lines. For the first time in a long time, I was unprofessional. I wouldn't know the script. I could feel the cast and crew getting annoyed with me as I would burst into tears for no reason at all.

My antics ate up precious time, and it cost the production money.

My mother had to come and "talk some sense" into me after she heard about the issues I'd been having. "It's just a headache," she would say, her hands folded in front of her, not touching me. "Go back and do your job."

"Okay, Mom. I will," I'd say, tears slipping out from under my eyelids. Because I knew if I acted like I couldn't get it together, they would take my babies away from me somehow.

And yet they did it anyway. My father, fed up after hearing from my mother that I was a blubbering mess, exasperatedly took me to another doctor. This time, the doctor actually listened to me and made a diagnosis. I had a traumatic brain injury, or TBI, and thus I had diminished mental capacity. "It's not her fault," the doctor said to my father softly, as I sat in the waiting room willing the room to stop spinning. I could still hear him, however. "She just needs time."

And time they gave me. They used the TBI against me in a hearing that I couldn't attend because I needed to be in a blacked-out room, and my doctor testified what he thought. My father must have been over the moon, because he was given full conservatorship over me, this time in probate court. My court-appointed lawyer, Mr. Lepore, had no objection. I feebly objected to a court-appointed lawyer, thinking that I needed someone I'd vetted, but it was too big of a headache to deal with the catch-22 of being conserved: I couldn't pay for a lawyer out of the finances that my parents now controlled. I was too tired to fight. The conservatorship swept over me like a wave.

It couldn't have been planned out better if my father had tried. My mother must have prayed hard for a miracle to happen, for them to right my course.

"Rest up, baby," my mother said, when she told me the news. Ashley was there, too, stroking my arm, not that that made things any better.

I cried. This time, I had a reason. I was infirm. I could barely hold my children without feeling like the bottom was going to drop out of me. I relied on Nanny Sheard more than ever.

I hope you girls know how much I love you and how hard it was for me to not be able to care for you in those days. I was sick and troubled. Even more so than when I was using drugs or partying all the time.

It took months for me to regain clear vision, to stop crying at the drop of a hat, to be able to read my lines and remember them again. (The production of *Brother, May I?* actually halted for me; they never recast the role. I was able to go in and do my lines, fed to me bite by bite, in six painful weeks. It is one of the worst-rated movies I've been in, and I blame myself for its low rating.) I celebrated my birthday in the dark, sleeping all day and waking up to a tomato-and-cheese sandwich that the cook had set aside for me. I couldn't eat anything too fragrant, otherwise it would upset my stomach.

The conservatorship made sense at that time. I'll be the first to admit it. I couldn't stay awake, let alone balance a checkbook. But after a year, when I felt better, nothing happened. My father told me that the probate conservatorship was permanent, that I had no way out. He did not give me any options.

One day in 2008, I dropped my Motorola Razr in the toilet. I asked my parents for a replacement. My mother vaguely said, "We'll see."

"*We'll see?* What's that supposed to mean?" I demanded. "Mom, my phone is *toast.* I dried it in rice and it still won't turn on. I need a new one."

"Here," she said, slipping me a new script. "You're signed for this one already. We'll see if you actually *need* a new phone."

I flipped to the first page, curious what it was about, but my voice was flat. "What is it this time?" I muttered.

A new blockbuster with Ed Hodges. I froze. Not *Hodges*. The same director who had asked me to give him a blow job. "Mom, *no*," I said, pushing the pages away, but she sat across from me at the kitchen table and pushed it right back.

"This is the one," she said. "This is the movie that will give you an Oscar. I just know it."

The title of the movie was *The Safari* and I was slated to play Opal, a woman who took down poachers in the African savanna. My mother was determined.

"Shooting starts in eight weeks," she said, and tapped the script again. "It'll be your comeback."

"I wasn't aware I'd gone anywhere," I murmured, and took the sheaf of papers into my hands again. "And the phone?"

"We'll see," she repeated.

I was powerless. All I could do was wait.

It wasn't lost on me that my mother was pushing her disabled daughter to work, when her other able-bodied daughter was *right there*. Ashley and I got to know each other better in those strange, hazy days. She felt ignored by my parents and I felt stifled by them. We commiserated over our careers and cried at the injustice of it all. If there's one good thing about the conservatorship, it was that it brought your aunt Ashley and me closer together.

WHEN I STEPPED foot on *The Safari* set, Ed Hodges made a big show of greeting me and then surreptitiously pulled me aside.

"I heard about your personal problems," he said. "They clipped your wings, eh?" He seemed jolly about it.

I decided that I hated Hodges. Even more so than before.

Life was so different this time around on a Hodges set. I wasn't out partying after hours, and I definitely wasn't bringing anyone home. Adam made sure of that. He seemed to be under strict orders from my parents to make sure that I stayed celibate, which left me alone in my bedroom.

I was so starved for a sexual touch, even Hodges was starting to look like a good meal . . . But no. I pushed it out of my mind.

The twins were three now, and generally good sports about coming on set with Nanny Sheard to watch Mommy work. They understood that they had to stay quiet when we were filming, and they mimicked the crew's tight mouths and throwing away the key when "*rolling*" came echoing around the set. It was a lonely set, though the crew was plentiful, because it was mostly just me doing my acting, in a fake field in a green-screened room. Opal is vengeful, calculating, and dangerous. She murders poachers before they can hurt the animals she cares for so much.

It was a lot of long days with Hodges and me, and he treated me better than he had on *Tourmaline*. He never asked me for any sexual favors, and I was glad.

I was ugly-fied for the role. Like Charlize Theron in *Monster*, my eyebrows were shaved off and a fake nose with a hump was applied over my button nose. I wore a lot of makeup, but it was to make me sweaty, grimy, and tired-looking. My parents fired my longtime hair and makeup artists April and Paul, having probably been itching to do so ever since my wedding to Anthony. I was given new hair and makeup stylists, whose names I was too depressed to learn, feeling that they were spies for my parents.

Life continued like this for a while. I would wake up, get hauled off to set, work, come home, shower, tend to my girls for thirty minutes before their bedtime, and go to sleep myself. Set times were long and inconsistent, and some days went for sixteen or seventeen hours before we wrapped and were able to go home. Adam would be on set with me, like a babysitter, and drive me, exhausted, to the Hidden Hills house.

In 2010, my conservatorship hearing came up. I was feeling a lot better by then and was ready to state my case.

When the date arrived, I got dressed slowly and deliberately, pushing away all of the fancy things I had in my closet and choosing, instead, a pair of black slacks and a button-down shirt. I fixed my hair neatly in a low bun and Adam drove me to the courthouse. No one seemed to know we were coming; there wasn't a swarm of paparazzi like I expected, and for some reason that got me even more frazzled than before. When your life is chaos, and the chaos stops, the silence can be unsettling. I remember tapping my foot on the echoing floor while waiting for my case to come up, and Mr. Lepore stilling me with a look, like I was a kindergartener being naughty.

Judge Guise didn't even ask for me to come up to the stand. I sat there, the entire time waiting for my name to come up, but it was all legalese—about money, it turns out. And at the end of the day, I turned to Mr. Lepore and asked, "When are they going to ask me for *my* opinion?"

"That's not on the docket," he said, tucking papers into his suitcase.

"*When* is it on the docket?"

But he didn't answer me.

The courtroom was nearly empty. Everyone was packing up to leave. I stayed sitting, stunned. My mother slung her Birkin—she had a *Birkin?*—over her shoulder and left the room. That's when I heard someone—I think my parents' lawyer—say, "She's doing so well. This conservatorship is the best thing that has ever happened to her."

The best thing? I wanted to scream. Instead, I began to cry. Long streaks of tears flowed down my face as I stooped out of my seat and shuffled down the hallway. I didn't care if the paparazzi saw me weeping. My heart was broken and I thought for sure that this was how the rest of my life would go.

No room to make my own mistakes. No passion to drop everything and jet off to an unknown location with my best friend, Olive. No Olive, at all. The cruelty of the moment was not lost on me as I cried and cried, dragging my feet along the hallway of the courthouse.

Permanent, my father had said. This was what my life would be like for the rest of my days.

(October 14, 2010)

People magazine

POLL: Is Hayley Aldridge's conservatorship a good thing
for the wild child?

YES: 62%

NO: 23%

NO ANSWER: 15%

CHAPTER 33

I won Best Actress at the 2011 Oscars. It was a surprise, for sure, because I thought Jennifer Lawrence would win that year. I was so depressed about my situation, though, that my speech was perfunctory and I stared at the Oscar statue for a while after I got home before I put it in my closet with my sweaters. My mother would find it when she came over and display it prominently on a shelf, but I always hid it again.

The only good thing that came of the Oscar win is that my mother slowed down her insatiable need for me to work on projects incessantly. I had a break for the first time in a while and I used it to spend time with you two, now five years old.

Your father pushed for full custody after my Oscar win, claiming you two needed consistency in parenting. Who better than *me* to offer consistency, though? I had a hiatus between projects and your father was constantly at the studio, pulling the lead in a *Spartacus* remake. I was the one who was at home, alone, craving time with my children.

It got ugly enough that mediation didn't work and we went to court over the custody battle. In the end, the judge changed our fifty-fifty split to sixty-forty, with your father holding the majority. It was a dark time for me, made darker by the circumstances of my conservatorship. I could barely hold it together. On days without you with me, I would wake up, take my Lamictal, and go back to bed. Nanny Sheard wasn't around on days when you weren't there. The only person roaming my house was Adam, strolling the periphery and staying out of my locked bedroom. I had eleven vacant bedrooms and if I passed by any of them, I could feel my heart start to sag.

My parents would come visit me regularly, bringing scripts and Ashley. They were the only thing that would get me out of bed—forcefully.

"Here's a new one," my father said one day, shoving a script toward me at the breakfast table. I was still in my pajamas, hair askew, trying to drink a cup of Earl Grey tea that was too hot. *Buffalo Range* was about a cowboy in the Wild West seeking revenge on the man who killed his family. I would be the wily partner he picked up, Anna, who had his back. "It's the perfect project to complement your Oscar win," he said, buttering his own toast and taking a big bite. "You won the part already, without an audition. You start filming in January."

I sipped my tea and digested this information. What else was I going to have to do to appease my parents? How long would this go on?

"Where's Mom? Usually she's the one giving me scripts," I said.

"Oh, she's off with Alex Dietrich doing god knows what," he responded. My head snapped up with attention.

"You know about that?" I asked, surprised.

"Know about it, yes. Care about it, no. All I care about is you, honey," my father said, caressing my free hand that wasn't holding the tea mug.

"It doesn't bother you?" I continued.

"Honey, no easy way to say this, but . . . we're getting divorced. But we still love you very much. And we care about you too much to let you go."

"Dad," Ashley said quietly, "don't you think this has gone on long enough?"

I was surprised to hear Ashley speak up for me. Dad narrowed his eyes at my sister, but didn't respond. My sister didn't say another word.

"You girls are old enough that it won't change much of your day-to-day lives," my father continued, like he hadn't heard Ashley. I nodded into my mug, trying to take this news in stride.

It made sense that Ashley would be on my side, but be so meek that she couldn't express her feelings without shrinking back into herself. To be honest, I was surprised she'd said anything at all. She and I had talked and she agreed I had the raw end of the deal, but I didn't expect her to say anything out loud. And this news about my parents didn't surprise me, after all the separation they'd done when they were younger—it made sense that they'd grow apart. The thing that did surprise me was that my mother was still involved with my old show-runner, and that my father didn't *care*.

Life was passing me by. I couldn't believe that this was my life anymore. Every day was the same: no changes, no surprises. No variety. No *passion*. I was depressed and lonely and Sick. Of. It.

(If you want to think about how I felt for the last ten years, just think of how *everyone* felt in 2020. That slightly-terrified ennui.)

I had to start looking for my means to escape. You were old enough to see that something was wrong with the picture of your mother. How isolated she was. How tired she was. How the joy of her life had been sucked out of her marrow. Honestly, if it weren't for you two, I don't know what I would've done.

But I had to be careful. You weren't legal age yet, and anything I did, they could use to take you away from me.

One day, while I was getting ready to go to do my voiceover work for Teacup the pig on the show *Tinkerbell Tunes*, I dropped my eyeliner and it rolled behind my vanity. I scrounged around with my hand until I bumped up against a little block that I wasn't familiar with. I shoved the vanity aside and got on my hands and knees to investigate.

What I found chilled me to my bone. It was a little device with a tell-tale red "on" light lit on one end. It was duct taped to the back of one of the legs of my vanity. I didn't peel it off, but I did stare at it, wondering how long it had been there. I had talked to my children in this room. I had screamed and *cried* in this room. I had muttered to myself about how much I hated my *life* in this room. And on the rare occasions that Adam lent me his phone, I had talked to other people in this room—like Nanny Sheard, who had remained a close friend, even though she didn't come work for me anymore, now that you two were in your teens.

I carefully pushed the vanity back against the wall and decided not to confront my parents about this. I tore apart the rest of my private areas: the bathroom, the living room, the kitchen. I found one more device under the living room sofa and pursed my lips in a thin line. I'd let them think they'd won, but I would be scheming on how to get out of this mess. I just wouldn't talk in the "privacy" of my rooms anymore. I would hold all of my emotion deep inside of me and let it out only when I knew I wasn't being recorded.

Girls, it was hard.

Now that you're both just shy of eighteen, I feel like we're almost on solid footing. We can do what we want, with little repercussion. What can they do once you're legal adults? Conserve you too? I doubt it. So now you see why I'm telling you this.

No one is the villain here—well, I'll try not to make anyone out to be the bad guy. But I'm tired. I need to be free.

CHAPTER 34

Something serendipitous happened recently, something that gave me a huge boost.

I was sitting in my kitchen when my father brought over the mail. Fan mail occupied most of the pile, and I stopped sifting through it when I saw the hashtag #helphayley on one of the envelopes. "What's this?" I said aloud, and pulled it free.

One of my diehard fans, a girl who signed the paper with the name Ainsley, wrote, "I will always love you, Hayley! Did you see this? Support is coming." The last line was underlined twice. She had attached a page from *Teen Orion,* the title of which was "How Badly Did We Treat Our Stars of the 00s?"

We here at *Teen Orion* weren't around in the early 2000s, except as babies, but as an offshoot of *Orion Gazette* magazine we have access to archives. And we have to say, what the hell? How did we as a society screw this up so badly? We took our famous starlets of the 00s and ran them into the ground with our headlines. Yes, Lindsay Lohan was a little bit of a mess, but she didn't deserve our vitriol. Or how about Amanda Bynes—she needed help, not ridicule. Look at how badly we messed up Hayley Aldridge, who by all means, seems like a lovely person. She has been in a conservatorship ever since she was caught outside of her house while barefoot and eating ice cream, neither of which is a crime. She's been in this conservatorship for over ten years! We say Help Hayley!

Tears sprang to my eyes. I finally felt *seen*. A decade of living as a ghost, and suddenly, out of nowhere, came this gift.

It was just one letter at first, but then more started to flow in. All said #helphayley. I didn't own my social media accounts, but I imagined that it was gaining traction across the Twittersphere and on Instagram. And you girls told me that you were getting tagged too. You told me that my official Instagram account was speckled with comments, some of them to the effect of #helphayley. So change was coming.

What we needed was a *deluge*. Something that would make real waves, not this slow trickle. What could I do to speed things up? And how could I do it without my parents finding out and putting the kibosh on it before the movement could really start?

"Wow," JESSICA SAYS, her eyes wide. "What can you do?"

"Yeah," Jane adds, "this seems *really* difficult."

What I have to do, I realize, is pick at the threads that they have sewn rigidly over my life and unsnag them one by one. What did people always say? *Follow the money.* I know my parents are getting a percentage of my earnings, so the first thing I have to do is slow the funds to a trickle. It is harder than it sounds: I have to back out of a movie.

My parents are in negotiations for me to appear in *The Girls Who Burn*, a story about the Salem witch trials. Now I need to call my agent, good old Mr. Himes, and tell him I'm not available anymore.

How could I do this without getting my parents involved? And with no cell phone of my own?

I decide to use my daughter's phone, as terrible as it sounds. I have to plan it carefully.

"Daddy," I say, the next time he is over, "do you think the girls and I could go on a hike the next time they're here?"

"I don't think so, honey," he says absentmindedly, tossing the mail on the kitchen counter as he always does.

"It's just—I think exercise would do me some good. I'm getting a little pudgy." I know I have to speak to his sensibilities. He wouldn't care if I feel cooped up or if I have low energy. But he *would* worry if my less-than-perfect midsection suddenly started drooping. As suspected, his eyes go straight to my belly, which I pooch out noticeably. The cereal and all the fruit I've been eating have helped it grow rounder.

"You're right," he says, scratching at his chin. "I thought we had you doing Pilates, honey?"

"I do, but . . ."

"Extra cardio might be the ticket, you know. You've gotta burn those calories somehow."

I am nodding along, a series of yeses. "You're probably right," I say.

"Oh, hell, I'll have Adam drive you out to the park and you

can go hiking," he says amiably.

"That should do the trick," I say.

I make sure that Anthony knows that we are going on a hike and to tell the twins to wear good walking shoes. "And a phone," I say. "I don't have one and if there's an emergency out there, I want to be sure we can call for help."

Anthony sounds irritated. I always have to call him on someone else's phone. This time, it is Adam's, as Adam listens to my side of the conversation. "You're not going hiking on a fucking *mountain*," Anthony says. "It's a park in Calabasas, for Christ's sake. There will be other hikers out there."

"Just in case," I insist, and he relents.

When the girls are dropped off at the house, I am happy to see that Jessica holds a sparkly purple iPhone in her hand.

"Girls, let me put your hair up in ponytails," I say.

"Mooom," Jane says. The twins are seventeen and don't need mothering.

"Indulge me, please?" I usher them into my big master bathroom and shut the door, turn on a hairdryer, and speak low. "When we are out in the nature, I need you to let me borrow your phone and to distract Adam."

Jessica looks surprised. "What do you have planned?" she says.

"I just need you to scrape a knee or something. Nothing drastic. Just give me time to make a call."

Jane looks determined, and she pulls her hair into a ponytail on her own and leaves the bathroom. Jessica nods and lets me pull her wispy strands into a whale spout.

Adam drives us in a big SUV to the Calabasas Hills Park. I get out and stretch. I can feel the paparazzi giving us a narrow berth. They aren't as hungry as they were ten years ago, but some of the determined ones still came out, eager to make a buck. Ever since Jennifer Garner and Halle Berry got all mother-bear and sued paps for taking photos of their children, the photographers have been more respectful toward us mothers when we have our kids around. I can hear them snapping the backs of my twins' heads as we start up the hill.

There's a lovely breeze and I breathe in deeply. It is different, being outdoors away from my house. I can hear grass swishing in the wind, and the chatter of people fades away. I understand the whole feeling of being a human animal, needing to be close to nature.

The twins are crunching along in front of me for a while, talking and giggling among themselves, occasionally pointing at a bird or a rock. It feels a little *too* much like a performance, their antics theatrical, but Adam doesn't seem to see it.

They had been conferring quietly for a little while and I could see when they decided which twin would be the distraction: Jessica nods and Jane gives her a little shove, as if to encourage her. A few steps later, Jessica stumbles and skins her leg from knee to ankle on some rough gravel.

"Oh no!" I say, hurrying toward her. Adam is right behind me, and Jessica holds her leg and hisses with pain. "Are you okay, baby?"

"It hurts," she says, a little too obviously.

"Adam, do you have any bandages?"

"In the car," he says. But he doesn't move.

"Aren't you going to get them?"

"I need to stay with you and protect you. I can't just leave you."

I grow peeved. "What is the point of you having bandages in the *car* if you're not going to use them?"

"We can all walk back that way. Jessica, you can walk, can't you?"

Jessica looks at me. She stares into me. I give her a sad nod.

"Yes, I can walk."

"Good."

We all traipse back to the SUV, slowly, and the window to call Mr. Himes grows smaller with each step. When we get back to the parking area, I grab Jane desperately and say, "I'm going to wet some paper towels to wipe off the blood. Come with, Jane," and Adam unlocks the car with Jessica standing next to him.

Jane and I hustle to the outdoor bathrooms. "Here," she squeaks, and hurriedly gives me her phone.

"Thank you, baby." I dial 311, because I sure as hell don't have Mr. Himes's phone number memorized.

"Information," the operator intones.

"I'm looking for a business. Himes, Inc.? In Hollywood."

"I can connect you."

The phone rings two, three times. I can feel Adam's impatience, waiting for the wet paper towels, and wish for Mr. Himes to answer. His secretary finally does on the fourth ring.

"Hi, Andrea, it's Hayley Aldridge," I say quickly. "Can you

patch me through?"

I am a big enough name that she does it without questioning. Mr. Himes answers.

"I need to back out of *The Girls Who Burn,*" I say.

"Hayley!" he says, surprise in his voice. "Usually—I mean lately—I get this sort of information from your parents."

I don't know if I can trust Mr. Himes to keep my going rogue a secret. So instead, I say, "They're letting me take the reins on some of my work stuff nowadays. So," I add hurriedly, knowing my time is ticking to a close, and Jane is looking over her shoulder as I am balled up in a corner with the phone stuck unsuspiciously against my ear, "please tell the director I'm sorry but I have other arrangements, and to cast someone else ASAP."

"All right," he says doubtfully.

I want to add, *I'd appreciate it if you didn't tell my parents I called,* but that would raise a million red flags. I say, "Thank you for letting me feel like a professional and allowing me to call you directly. I know my parents would appreciate it too."

I hang up before he can say anything, and hand the phone back to Jane. She tucks it into her back pocket nervously and grabs my hand. Then we walk back to the SUV with her other hand full of wet paper towels.

CHAPTER 35

My parents find out about the recasting from *Deadline*. My father comes over with his fingers clutched around his phone, the article already pulled up. "What's this?" he shouts. I flinch but take his phone in my hands and read,

Patricia Parkinson joins The Girls Who Burn, *playing Darcy. Originally, Hayley Aldridge was rumored for the part but Parkinson ultimately won the role. Parkinson will be joined by Helmut Dickins, Joy Ferrera, and Tom O'Connor in the film, based on the book of the same name by Madeline Henry.*

"Hmm," I say, giving the phone back to him.

"This is ludicrous. I'm going to have to yell at Himes," he says. "He all but assured us that the role was yours. I don't know how this Patricia person just swooped in and got the role without us even knowing."

I am surprised but pleased that Mr. Himes has taken my call so seriously. He *should* have done his due diligence and called my parents for confirmation that I was out, but he didn't for some reason. I wonder if he knew what I was doing and this was his way of showing his support.

The rumbles of #helphayley are growing a little louder, and I wondered if maybe Mr. Himes doesn't want to be complicit in my situation.

The court date for the review of the conservatorship is coming up and I'm determined to let the judge know that I want to be free. Over time, I stopped attending the hearings in person, just because I didn't think anything could be done. And nothing changed.

Until now.

#Helphayley is picking up steam. The chatter has reached the Instagram account the girls created for me, and they tell me that the hashtag has even popped over on Twitter, though it's not a trending topic yet. I don't know what this means, but the more people talking about it, the better, in my opinion.

My father has forbidden the twins from bringing a camera or phones to my house now, and Adam checks when they arrive. But it doesn't matter. The girls make reels of their own faces when they're at their father's, discussing the tightening restrictions around my living situation. They wear orange shirts while doing so. It's not lost on me that my daughters are eschewing a "normal" life and are putting their faces out there, after years of being private. My heart goes out to them.

The #helphayley chatter is frenzied now, they tell me, with more than twenty thousand followers of the account, and more exponentially coming each day. It's as if the tighter the noose around me grows, the bigger the following my Instagram account brings in.

"Adam?" I say to my bodyguard.

"Yes, Hayley?"

"I want to go to the review."

Adam looks a little surprised, but he doesn't say anything in response. It's been years since the last time I stepped foot in the courthouse. "Okay, I'll drive you tomorrow," he says.

"Thank you."

I dress conservatively for the hearing. I straighten my hair. When I arrive at the courthouse, I'm surprised by the number of people milling around in front of it, holding HELP HAYLEY signs. It's not a huge group—probably a handful, no more than twenty—but seeing them with their signs and bright orange shirts bolsters me. They don't accost the SUV like the paparazzi do, either; they wave their signs in our general direction and chant, *"What do we want?"*

"Hayley to be free!"

"When do we want it?"

"Now!"

I wave at them through the tinted-glass window and maybe they see me.

When we're all seated, I look over at my parents, hidden behind their lawyers. A thought tumbles through my mind: Why did they have to do this to me? Why couldn't it have been a small family matter? Why tangle us up in the court system?

I'm hopping mad. I pester Mr. Lepore to let me address the judge. I don't even wait. "I want to end this conservatorship."

"Ms. Aldridge," Judge Guise says, "I was not aware of this. Why haven't you petitioned the court to terminate?"

I look at the judge. His hair is white, and on his bulbous nose rests a pair of Buddy Holly glasses.

"Petitioned?" I echo.

"Yes, your lawyer should have petitioned to terminate if you were unhappy with the arrangement. We can't do anything without the petition, I'm afraid."

I glare at Mr. Lepore, who shuffles papers. I see it now: all of his lawyer's fees were racking up, coming out of *my* estate, while he dawdled on getting me out of this predicament. He probably was never going to do it.

"I'd like a different lawyer," I say in response, steam coming out of my ears.

"Ms. Aldridge, that is not on the docket for today," Judge Guise says. "Now, are you taking your prescription medication regularly?"

I fold, but I'm not defeated yet. "So how do I—how do I replace my lawyer? I didn't know I could petition to end this conservatorship."

"You should have been able to hire your own lawyer since the bill passed in 2021," Judge Guise says. "Are you dissatisfied with Mr. Lepore?"

"I am," I say.

"Is there someone else in this courtroom whom you would prefer to represent you?"

I shrink a little in my seat. I don't have anyone. "No, Your Honor."

"So for the time being, Mr. Lepore will continue to be your lawyer." He clears his throat.

WHEN I GET home, I strip off my pantyhose and leave it trailing on the floor of my living room. Lawyers. I need to find a new lawyer.

But how?

My father has followed me home and he leans against the doorjamb of my bedroom, as I try not to scream. "This is foolhardy," he says.

I ignore him.

"I see what you're doing with the Instagram account," he continues. "But this is a lockdown. You're not going to get out of this. I care about you too much."

I whirl on him. "You *care* about me? You *care about me*? You care about me so much that you hold me in a cage like a little bird? Listen to my conversations? Fuck you, Dad!"

"Don't you see," he says, "I have made a comfortable and safe environment for you. You're no longer out partying. You're clean. You're fed. You got to keep your house. And you're employed. It is for the best. You can't say that this hasn't been a good thing for you."

I take a deep breath. "But for what? So that I can never make my own decisions again? I'm not *ten* anymore! I am thirty-seven years old! That's old enough to have a midlife crisis, but I *can't*, because I'm held down like a kid!"

He approaches me, smoothing down my flyaway hair. Petting me like a dog. "You'll look back on this and be grateful," he whispers. He leaves to go to the kitchen, where I hear him rummaging around for a water glass.

I slump against the bed. Lawyers. I have to find a lawyer.

CHAPTER 36

continue to pick at the seams that my parents have sewn over my life. I realize I can't *just* back out of a movie—I have to implode my *life*. But not in the way I did back when I was young, with drugs and alcohol. No, I have to destroy my career—maybe irreversibly.

It may shock some people, but hand in hand with Oscar wins is a bevy of commercial spots right after. Once someone is prominent enough to get singled out and noticed, they have the opportunity to shill products to the masses; an Oscar winner is immediately on that list, no matter what. After my 2011 win, my parents signed contracts for me to hawk a number of items, and that never stopped. The commercial coming up next is J'Amuse perfume.

The kicker? I'm going to take the twins down with me. They're signed on to do this perfume commercial too. And from what I understand, they're *excited* about it. This would be their first foray into publicly owning their faces, making money off their genealogy. What I'm asking of them is to kick that can down the road, just until my nightmare is over. Nepotism will always serve them.

I arrive with Adam at the studio and sit down in hair and makeup. The girls are already there, excitedly chatting with each other, as the makeup artists dip and bow in front of them with their brushes.

"Girls," I say, and I give them a look. They immediately freeze up. Oh, they know what I'm going to say is not going to be good.

When we get a moment to ourselves, right before the shoot begins, I say, "I need to mess this up. I need you to help me."

"But *Mom*," Jessica says, her voice pleading.

"I know. I know how much you've been looking forward to this. I'll make it up to you. But right now, I need this shoot to go *badly*. I need them to be so mad about it that they won't pay."

"Because the pocketbook is where you're going to hit them hardest," Jane says, her voice questioning.

"That's right, baby."

Jane looks at Jessica and they confer silently with their eyes. Jessica pouts, but she relents.

"*How* are you going to make it up to us?" she asks, but her voice is soft. She isn't mad.

"Once I'm free, I'll get you signed up with another brand. I swear it. You will still model if that's what you want."

"Ohhhkay," she huffs.

"What do you need us to do?" Jane asks.

"Ruin the shoot somehow. I don't know. Throw a tantrum. Make faces the entire time. I'll let you come up with something."

If it were up to me, I would just sit in the dressing room and refuse to come out. That's the diva way of doing things. But I want the girls to feel like they've made some sort of contribution to this experience, that I'm not dictating *everything* that they need to do. Maybe it'll make them feel less sore about the entire thing.

The shoot is a combination photo shoot and TV ad. We are all bronzed, like statues, wearing bronze robes. For the still shoot we'll be lying around on each other, our sapphire eyes glowing in the midst of all the metal tones. If we completed it as asked, it would be a beautiful shoot.

It's too bad we have to ruin it.

We step onto the set and the girls are whispering to each other. The commercial is first, and we are in a fake Grecian temple with tall pillars and an inch of water on the floor. We are supposed to walk slowly in the water, arms around one another, as a powerful fan blows our hair away from our faces.

"Walk slowly . . ." the director, Laurence Wood, tells us. "Slower. Not faster! Twins, why are you speed-walking?"

The twins have evidently decided to do the opposite of everything the director wants us to do.

Finally, they slow down and grin maniacally at the camera. "Ignore the camera, girls, no, stop looking directly into the lens!"

Exasperated, the director shakes his head, and tries again. "Slower. Slower . . . Good. Relax your faces. No, don't frown. No, don't grin either." He slaps his thigh. "Why is this so hard? Jessica, right? Jessica, turn your face to the left. No, your *other* left. That's to the right. I meant *your* left. Argh!"

The commercial shoot takes forever. I'm buoyed by the sense that the girls are having fun ruining the takes, however, and don't feel the hours tick by. We are taken back to hair and makeup and our washed feet are re-bronzed. It's time for the photoshoot portion of the day.

"I have to use the bathroom," Jessica says, and grabbing her purse, disappears.

"Me, too," Jane says, and follows her.

Fifteen minutes later, they still aren't back. The photographer is looking at me anxiously, and I hear whispers of concern that the girls have substance-abuse problems of their own. That won't do. "Can someone go check on them?" I ask, and my makeup artist volunteers.

But the toilets are bare.

"The twins left," she says quizzically to me when she gets back. "Someone saw them leave out the back door. I think they're gone."

The creative director of the perfume ad is livid. "This is unprofessional! This is unacceptable!"

He continues for a little while longer, and I smile sweetly at him. "We can continue without them," I say, just to make him feel slightly better. But it embitters him even more.

"How about," I say, "you just shoot photos of me and you *not* pay?"

That gives him a pause. The budget for this commercial is in the millions. "It *is* a breach of contract," he says slowly.

"I'll do it for free. Let me know what I need to sign," I say.

But the director is shaking his head. "My agreement is with Mr. Aldridge," he says. He knows full well that I can't sign any contracts of my own. My blood chills in my stomach. What if this was all for nothing? That I ruined the girls' chances of being seen as professionals in this world? The opposite game for the commercial session could just be blamed on them being green, but them actually leaving the set for the photoshoot is very flaky. Their names could be dust.

"Call him," I say. "Talk to him about compensation. I'm sure he'll appreciate hearing from you after what happened today."

I don't know what happened on the call, but the shoot continues: just me. I am done in twenty minutes—always a pro. I'm shaking with exhaustion, though, and can't wait to get out of there.

My father is angry when he talks to me next. "You put the girls up to something," he accuses.

"The twins are almost eighteen," I say. "They aren't little girls anymore. They can choose to do what they want."

He shakes his head at me as he swigs his coffee. "I had to agree to let them cut the payment in half," he says disgustedly, and my heart soars. Then he threatens me. "Mess with me again and you can kiss your daughters goodbye."

I straighten. I look him in the eye. He puts down his coffee cup and reciprocates. "You're not a custody judge," I say. "You can't threaten me."

He snorts. Fear strikes my heart. He can do *something*; this

I'm sure of.

What else do I have to do to get free?

CHAPTER 37

I t isn't lost on me that my father feels very secure in our situation right now. What I need is to upset him. Make him feel like the world is topsy-turvy.

When the twins arrive for their weekly visit, I have a new strategy for Instagram. I ask them to record a video when they get home. "If you're a probate lawyer, can you come to the Stanley Mosk Courthouse on May 23 and represent our mother?" they ask.

TheRealHayleyA Instagram account has grown—maybe eighty thousand followers, the twins tell me, but I know that's people all around the world, so I'm not expecting much. But when the SUV pulls up to the courthouse in May, I'm surprised to see that the number of #helphayley supporters has grown. The crowd has to actively shift out of the way of the car so that we can get into the parking area. And in the courtroom, there are seven people standing nervously in the middle of the rows, as if waiting to be called upon.

After the initial introductions and swearing-in, Judge Guise looks over the top of his glasses at me and Mr. Lepore. "Ms. Aldridge," he says. "There is an unusual situation happening here. All seven of these individuals here claim they are your lawyer. As far as I know, your lawyer is sitting next to you in this courtroom."

I turn to look at the seven suit-clad people. I would need to interview them, wouldn't I? But anyone would be better than Mr. Lepore, who hadn't told me anything about petitioning the court to terminate the conservatorship. "You," I say, pointing at a middle-aged woman with red-rimmed glasses.

She points to herself and approaches the front of the courtroom. "Melissa Benoit of Benoit, Interdict, and Beau," she says.

"Is this your lawyer, Ms. Aldridge?" Judge Guise asks.

I'm not overly familiar with law, but this woman *looks* like a shark. Plus, her name came first in the law office she listed, so she *has* to be vetted and good, right?

"Yes, Your Honor," I say. I nod at Ms. Benoit.

"Counsel, in terms of your firms' trust and estate practice—does your firm have that capability?"

"We do, Your Honor. It's a pretty big part of what we do."

"Thank you, Counsel. All right, there are twelve matters that are before the Court. I expect that counsels will sign a Substitution of Attorney of Ms. Aldridge's retained counsel?"

I can feel Mr. Lepore turning to stare at me, but I look straight ahead at the judge. "Yes, Your Honor," he says. His voice is flat.

"May I take a moment to confer with my client?" Melissa Benoit says.

Mr. Lepore packs up his briefcase and sits in the back of the room, not able—or not willing—to leave just yet. Ms. Benoit takes his seat. She leans in close and says, "Thank you for the opportunity. I'm mad as hell and I'm going to fight like a wild-cat to get you out of this."

Relief floods my body. "Thank *you*," I say. "Really, I appreciate this. I can't pay you now, but—"

"It's okay, I'm your lawyer now. Is there anything I should know?" she continues.

"I want to talk to the judge," I say. I have pages of what I want to say in my bag.

"You'd like to address the court?"

"Yes, that."

"Your Honor, my client would like to address the court."

"Yes, Ms. Aldridge," Judge Guise says. "Go ahead."

I feel a small amount of indulgence coming from the judge. As if this is all out of order, and wrong, and different, from his usual cases, but I'm a dumb blonde who got the short end of the stick and I don't deserve what's happening to me. Where was this soft Judge Guise when I needed him years ago?

I pull a sheaf of notes from my purse and stand to be heard more effectively. My hands are jittery and I feel the coffee I drank earlier making little gurgles in my stomach. I clear my throat once, twice, and steal a look at Judge Guise, who is patiently waiting for me to begin. I focus on my pages.

"THANK YOU, YOUR Honor. I'm here today with my new lawyer, to ask the court to end the conservatorship. I'm also requesting that my parents be removed as my conservators.

"So, like, in the past fifteen years I've been under lock and key by my parents. I'm treated like a child even though I'm in my thirties. Almost half of my life has been under this conservatorship and it has to stop. I'm not allowed to have a cell phone. Do you know how strange that is, for it to be 2022 and to not be able to call or text someone? I haven't had a cell phone since 2008. When my Motorola Razr broke, they wouldn't let me replace it and years passed. It would have been so easy to get me a new phone, but they refused. I've been isolated from friends and even my best friend has been removed from my life due to a bogus restraining order that they forced against her.

"My parents control everything in my life, from my social media to how often I go outdoors with my daughters. It's only recently that my kids have created a social media account for me to actually use when I'm with them.

"I don't understand how I can be considered in need of a conservatorship if I'm working. I won *an Oscar* while under the conservatorship. I gave that performance *while* I was conserved. My parents said if I didn't do that movie—*The Safari*—I could be sued for breach of contract because they had signed me up for it. So I did it. I didn't want to, but I'm a professional. And the work speaks for itself.

"In 2017, I was even a voiceover actress for a kid's show. I played Teacup the miniature pig on *Tinkerbell Tunes*. I didn't want to do this job but my parents had signed the contract for me, so again, I went. It was on the air for three years and the entire time I was doing the voice, I was suicidal. I hated it and wanted to die. For a miniature pig! But, again, I'm a professional so I went and did it. And that show has been formative for children and in retrospect I'm proud of what I did. But I also want people to know how miserable I was while I was acting in it. I haven't been able to drive myself anywhere, I've been isolated from my friends, the only people I've seen are my bodyguards and my family. I think my family should be sued for what they have done to me. The only person who has stood up for me in this entire mess has been my sister, Ashley, but no one listens to Ashley.

"I haven't driven myself anywhere in a decade. I'd always held onto my car keys but my dad took them away in 2019. Then the pandemic hit and their rationale was that everything was delivered to the house, and I shouldn't risk my health by leaving it, so I was a prisoner in my home until I got the vaccine in early 2022. And this entire time, my lawyer—Mr. Lepore—wasn't going to bat for me. He wasn't helping me at all.

"And yes, the vaccine came out in 2021 but my parents wouldn't let me get it until January of this year. The fact that I haven't been able to make my own medical decisions is criminal, in my opinion. I wanted the vaccine ever since I heard about it from Ashley, my sister, when it came out in March or April of 2021. But I had to wait. And wait. And wait. I have been cooped up in my house for *years* and when I bring it up to my dad, he just says that that's life, and I know he is deriving joy from my situation.

"I know I haven't been in court in person for hearings over the last few years but I didn't feel like lying to the court about how great this conservatorship has been. I know in years past I just let it all slide but now I want to say that I'm not happy. I can't sleep. I'm depressed. I cry every day.

"I was worried about saying anything publicly because I didn't think people would believe me. *Hayley Aldridge has everything she could ever want*, they would think. *How could it be so bad?* I would like to be able to share my story with the world and what they did to me instead of it being a secret. And all I want to do is to own my money and my life.

"This conservatorship is literally allowing my parents to ruin my life. I want to get my parents removed.

"Thank you, Your Honor."

I DON'T LOOK at my parents when I sit down. I can feel their hostile glares.

"All right, Ms. Aldridge. I'm certainly sensitive to everything that you said and how you're feeling. And I know that it took a lot of courage for you to say everything that you had to say today. Counsel Benoit, I anticipate that you will be filing petitions that will be before the court."

"Yes, Your Honor," my new lawyer says. "Since I've just been retained, I'll need a continuance to have time to meet with my client and file a petition before a subsequent hearing."

Ms. BENOIT AND I have to find a way to communicate. I use Adam's phone to call her and ask that before the next hearing, I get a phone for myself.

And I do. The next hearing isn't until December, so I have to wait a couple of months, but Ms. Benoit secures a cell phone for me. Not only is it an iPhone, my first, it's the newest one—

shiny, silver, and thin as a wafer. I don't trust that someone won't use the facial recognition to gain access to it while I'm asleep, so I disable that and program it to have a six-digit passcode that only I know.

I have access to my @TheRealHayleyA Instagram handle! I don't post any more frequently than my daughters already have, but I check the comments every day—they multiply on old posts, supportive words like *Hayley, you've got this* or *Hayley, I'm praying for you.* I prefer that the twins continue to administer my posts on there, taking photos of me just being me and sharing them to the account. Always in an orange shirt.

Ms. Benoit and I start discussing strategy. The end result is to terminate the conservatorship.

But as the summer wraps up, I still find myself conserved. What is going on? Nothing *really* has changed. I have a phone, yes. But my parents are still in charge of everything, and my money is still wrapped up in their greedy little hands.

I have to admit that I am losing faith in Ms. Benoit.

"Give me the benefit of the doubt," she texts when I let her know I have concerns. Texting is hard to get used to. I poke and prod the screen with one finger, while my daughters use both thumbs to type. I'm slow and would prefer to call, but I want a paper trail. Words are too ephemeral. I need reassurance that the conversation has happened.

Benoit: Be patient. I'm working on a mountain of paperwork to get you out of this. And your next hearing hasn't been scheduled until December.

Me: But it's been MONTHS. I'm tired of living like this.

Benoit: It'll happen. Keep the faith.

Faith? Faith is not something I have right now. But I have no other option but to wait.

ANTHONY MARTENS REGRETS
HAYLEY'S CONSERVATORSHIP

Heartthrob Anthony Martens, formerly Mr. Hayley Aldridge, gave a rare interview in which he announces his regret in playing a part in Hayley's conservatorship. He says, "Hayley and I brought out the worst in each other. I believed that she needed the conservatorship to live safely. Now I'm not so sure."

Aldridge's conservatorship has been ongoing since 2008. Recently, there have been calls from Hayley's supporters to terminate the conservatorship. Hayley's former lawyer, Mr. Al Lepore, had no comment on any legal procedures.

CHAPTER 38

M s. Benoit has me go to a psychiatrist. Initially, I object, but she tells me that it's important that a psychiatrist gives their sign-off on the termination of conservatorship. I purse my lips as she texts, "And it won't be Dr. Goodman. I have a feeling she was bought off."

Bought off? Was Dr. Goodman getting a kickback from my parents every time she went to court and said that I needed to stay under their lock and key? If so, I'm hopping mad.

The new psychiatrist, Dr. Gold, is a kindly old man with oversize glasses and a full shock of white hair. Ms. Benoit takes me to him, shuttling me along in her car like a nanny service, eschewing my bodyguard for the first time in probably a decade. I don't know how she managed it. I settle into the seat opposite Dr. Gold and wait for him to speak.

Dr. Gold says, "How are you today, Hayley? How are you feeling?"

"Fine," I say, though my throat is parched with nervousness.

"Let me just ask you a few questions, okay?"

"Sure."

"Have you been taking your medication? The one hundred

fifty milligrams of Lamictal daily?"

"Yes."

"And how do you feel while on it?"

"I feel . . . nothing, really. I guess it stabilizes my moods but I don't really notice a change from before."

"Hmm. Mm-hmm, okay, and you're not taking any drugs or alcohol, is that right?"

"I'm sober now, yes."

"Excellent," he says.

Ms. Benoit doesn't say anything when we walk outside of the facility and to her car. I wonder, though, if it will make a difference, and I say so.

"Don't give up," Ms. Benoit says, holding my hands. It's a surprisingly chilly day and her fingers are icy.

I nod at her. But I don't mean it. After all this time, hope is hard to hold on to.

THE COURT DATE arrives before I know it, and, heart in my throat, I dress and have Adam take me to the courthouse. This time, there are hordes of people, all wearing orange, holding banners, chanting, and sharing pictures of my face on poster boards. An involuntary smile lights up my face and I wave at them through the tinted windows of the car, amid cheers.

Security at the courthouse today is tight. There are a number of bailiffs who hold the crowd back as I'm ushered in through the rear entrance, and they've cordoned off a path for me inside the building. I sit down next to Ms. Benoit and start to fidget with my hands. My lawyer places a hand on top of mine, not to quiet or still me, but to show solidarity.

I don't understand legalese. That has never bothered me before, but as Judge Guise starts the proceedings, I realize I'm in way over my head. Ms. Benoit leans over and whispers explanations as to what is happening, but I wish I knew what was going on by myself. I fidget some more, this time with my hands under the table so that the judge can't see.

"The nature of proceedings—termination of conservatorship as filed by Hayley Aldridge on January twenty-fifth, 2023, to begin."

What will happen if I lose this case? My mind wanders. What will I do then? Will I keep fighting, or will I roll belly-up and let my parents dictate my life forever? In my darkest moments, I think about death. The sweet release from the life would be like floating away, into the unknown, finally able to take a risk at last . . .

Dr. Gold is called up to the box and I try to pay attention.

"Do you know Ms. Aldridge?" he is asked.

"I do."

"Are you her treating psychiatrist?"

"Yes, as of several weeks ago."

"Does Ms. Aldridge have a mental illness?"

"Yes."

"Do you have a diagnosis?"

"She's been diagnosed with bipolar I disorder."

"And what is your assessment of Ms. Aldridge's mental state at the present?"

"She's doing beautifully," Dr. Gold says in response. "She takes her medication, she's sober."

"Do you think she can live on her own?"

"Yes, I think, given the chance, she could live on her own and continue with her medication regimen with no problems."

Ms. Benoit squeezes my hand under the table.

My mind is splintering into a thousand thoughts. This could be it. This could be my ticket out of the confines of my parents' clutches. I tamp the excitement down, knowing that Judge Guise could just as easily ignore what Dr. Gold has to say.

"Mr. Gerald Aldridge objects to the idea that Hayley can live on her own," my father's lawyer says. My head snaps toward him. "She obviously is unwell, and we have years of proof that she cannot live independently."

"The Court has looked at the evidence that your client has supplied," Judge Guise says. "The court finds that sufficient evidence has been provided to grant the matter on the calendar this date based on the reading of the moving papers and consideration of all presented evidence. The petition to terminate conservatorship filed on January twenty-fifth, 2023, by Petitioner Hayley Aldridge is granted."

I lift my chin slightly, eyes widening, hands gripping each other.

"The Court finds and determines that a conservatorship of the person and estate of Hayley Dakota Aldridge is no longer required and is terminated effective this date."

Wait—is that it? Am I free?

Judge Guise bangs his gavel.

I hadn't said a word this entire court hearing. It hasn't even been half an hour since I sat down. It couldn't have been this easy—could it?

After fifteen long years, it's just—over?

Ms. Benoit is standing now, putting papers away in her brief-case, and I just look at her. Frozen in my seat. She gives me a shark's smile and nods at me.

I jump to my feet, knocking back my chair in my rush to hug her. She pats me on the back lightly. "Congrats, kiddo," she says. "I knew it would happen."

I turn to look at my father, standing at the table across the aisle. I flick him off. I'm cutting off this whole damn family. I can live without talking to my parents ever again. It feels great.

Who cares what I do now? I'm *free*!

Someone who had been in the courtroom must have an-nounced the decision to the mob outside, because I can hear them screaming even through the cement walls. "I want to go out there," I say to no one in particular. "I need to be with them."

"Hayley, that's not the best idea," Adam tells me.

I look him straight in the eye. "You're still here? You're *fired*."

He takes a step back and coughs. Ms. Benoit touches me lightly on the upper arm and says to him, "It's fine, I'll drive her home."

The bailiffs who had kept the mob off me when I walked, hunched, into the courthouse forty minutes ago are summoned now to create a bubble for me to walk out onto the front steps.

The mob, surprisingly, keeps a respectful distance and no one tries to trample me. But there's a swell of noise when they spot me, and I raise my arms in greeting. They scream.

CHAPTER 39

And just like that, I am free.

I'm a little pissed, to be honest. It was so *simple*, in the end. One good lawyer and one understanding judge—and a *whole lot* of supporters that swayed the public opinion—made this happen.

Life is like coming out of a cave. I dimly remember Olive's phone number and dial.

"Xochitl Hernandez," answers a familiar voice.

". . . Olive?"

"No one calls me that anymore, but yes," she says.

"It's Hayley."

"*Hayley?* Girl, I heard you were free. How does it feel? Am I the first person you called? I better be, bitch." She laughs. It's like the restraining order never happened. She sounds joyful. I realize I haven't kept up with her for so long that I don't know anything about her life anymore.

"You *are*! Um, how's Stavros?"

"Stavros? The shipping billionaire? Man, a name I haven't heard in a while. I'm done with all that socialite bullshit. I own a nonprofit now. Turns out I know a lot of wealthy people who want to donate money to help save the manatees."

"Are you joking?" I ask. This sounds like a wildly different Olive—Xochitl—than I know.

"Nope! I've been clean, too, ever since your parents kicked me to the curb. I used my *October Adventure* money to take my ass to rehab."

"That's amazing, Olive. I'm so proud of you."

"And I'm proud of *you*. Getting out of that mess. I want to hear the whole story one day."

"So you're not mad?"

"Why, should I be? It wasn't *your* idea to get rid of me, was it? I know if you'd had your way we would've been back together by the next day."

It's comforting to talk to Olive. We make plans to see each other as soon as possible—once we get the restraining order lifted. It'll be a piece of cake, my lawyer tells me.

I'M GETTING READY to go out with my daughters—the freedom of it! To leave the house when I want, to drive when I want!—when I get a phone call; I don't recognize the number. I pick up anyway. "Hello?"

"Hayley? It's Millie."

Millie. My old costar. The one who fed me to the wolves.

"How did you get this number?"

She doesn't answer me. Instead, she says, "I just wanted to say I'm sorry. For . . . everything. I thought I was helping."

I could be angry, but I let out of a long breath, one that she can hear as a hiss on the line. I debate what I should say. "It's okay," I answer finally. "I would've done the same to you."

She laughs. It's the well-worn laugh of someone who smokes too many cigarettes. She's, what? Forty-one now? Forty-two? I don't remember the last thing she was in. Was it *Third Time Around*? Has she worked on anything since? "Touché," she says.

"Is that all . . . ?"

"I want to add that you're so strong, Hayley. I doubted whether you would get out of this and you did. I know I have no right to be, but I'm proud of you." She pauses. "That's it. That's why I called."

I feel a touch of warmth in my chest for Millie. She *had* been like a big sister to me—moody, yes, but she helped me in the bathroom at the Tween Choice Awards, hadn't she?

"Do you maybe want to get a coffee sometime?" I ask. "We can catch up."

"Wow. That'd be great," she says.

When we hang up, I look at my kitchen counter and swipe my car keys close to my body. I dangle them in the air and watch the silver on them dazzle. I smile to myself.

What should I do next with my life? The whole world is open. I can do whatever I like. I can sell this house, this prison, and buy something new. Something fresh.

Something the *real* Hayley A. would like.

But first, lunch with my daughters.

After all, there's nothing much wrong with me.

About the author

About the book

Insights,
Interviews
& More . . .

Meet Elissa R. Sloan

Caitlin McWeeney

ELISSA R. SLOAN grew up in Houston, Texas. Born to a Japanese immigrant mother and Jewish American father, Elissa understands the importance of representation in stories and media, and cites Claudia Kishi as one of her young heroines.

Elissa attended the University of Texas at Austin, concentrating on WWII history and English. When she's not writing, Elissa is also an artist and professional photographer, spending the last decade shooting weddings for a living.

Though she's not a gossip in real life, she loves to keep up with celebrity dirt; her debut novel, *The Unraveling of Cassidy Holmes*, was born from that interest. She currently lives in Austin with her husband and two cats in a house with a rolling library ladder. ∿

Behind the Book Essay

Second books are hard; that's what everyone told me. I didn't disagree with them. The entire time I was writing my first book, *The Unraveling of Cassidy Holmes,* I assumed I'd be a one-and-done author. That was the book of my heart and the only one I could consider myself writing at the time. I even told my agent I wanted a single book deal, not the multi-book deal that is coveted by many debut writers. I didn't want to be on the hook to deliver something I didn't know I could write.

After the publication of *Cassidy,* I suddenly wanted to write everything! As the pandemic raged, my world shrank to just my computer and myself. But then I started a project that ended up getting shelved. And another. And another. I began to wonder if perhaps *Cassidy* was the only project I could finish. Maybe my renewed vigor for life, given to me by antidepressants and anti-anxiety medication, sapped me of my creativity.

Maybe I had to be depressed to write.

But creativity comes in ebbs and flows, not a steady stream. I went to bed one night and suddenly had the title of the next book in my head: *The Unshackling of Hayley Aldridge.* (The title did change during the publication process.) The Britney

Spears conservatorship had been in the news a lot in those days as #freebritney began to pick up steam, and I wondered what it would be like to be a starlet whose life was no longer her own. How could it come about, and what would she do to get out of it?

There were so many themes in *Cassidy* that I had wished I could explore further and deeper: toxic stage parents, hostile coworkers, stan culture, and more. I knew we'd hear everything from Hayley's point of view, and so I stuck with her voice for the entire book. I'd heard from readers that they were dissatisfied with Cassidy's robotic response to everything that happened to her, but at the time, I couldn't help it. I'd been steeped in depression for so long, I didn't know there were other emotions to describe anything anymore; everything had been dulled. *Hayley* was the first book where I was able to recall and put to page a character's emotional process as she felt it, and I thank my medication for helping me get there.

I was also inspired by Soleil Moon-Frye's *Kid90*. This documentary was pieced together with video clips taken by the actress while she was growing up, amidst all of the Hollywood kids who were cast alongside her in shows and movies. The character of Ted was the amalgamation of several high-profile celebrity boys that succumbed to ▶

addiction or depression or both. I always knew I was going to have to kill Ted, but it hurt to do it. I even considered saving him and wanted to have him pop up at the end, but I realized the story just wouldn't work that way.

When I started writing *Hayley*, I knew I was out of my depth. I was going to follow Hayley from 1991 to 2023, through puberty and pregnancy and motherhood, and deal with laws that I didn't understand at all. I am not a mother; I'm the youngest in my family and I have never even babysat before. I had to learn a lot of specific little things, very quickly. (Thanks go to my friends with children who were able to answer my questions swiftly while I was drafting.) I've never done drugs and had to ask health professionals to describe cocaine, addiction, and overdosing. I was even an extra in two movies, so I knew what it felt like behind the scenes on a set. I also began following #freebritney champions of the Britney Army on social media, listening to their podcasts and reading court transcripts, to better understand what was going on in Britney's world. I didn't want *Hayley* to be a Britney book; rather, Hayley is a fictional character who just happens to live in the same Hollywood that would allow this situation to happen to another young woman. Finally, I interviewed and had my work checked by California conservatorship lawyers so that I didn't make a huge fool out of myself. Luckily, they steered me in the right direction.

And while this book isn't all sunshine and rainbows, and it deals with some heavy topics, I think it's more optimistic than *Cassidy Holmes*. Hayley gets her freedom. She has her happy ending, which is just the beginning of the next chapter of her life.

Like with *Cassidy*, my years of reading gossip blogs came in handy when writing about Hayley's life. Underage grooming, the perception of virginity and chastity, and 2000s fashion and culture and tech all make appearances in this book. I also think *Hayley* is more *book*-like, in that it follows a formula for a story rather than the vibes and slow arc I wrote in *Cassidy*. Hopefully you readers will enjoy it! ∿

IMDb page: Hayley Aldridge (1984–)

Tinkerbell Tunes (2017–2019)—
  Teacup (43 episodes)
Lost in Orbit (2014)—Flannery
Buffalo Range (2012)—Anna
The Safari (2010)—Opal

Brother, May I? (2008)—Theresa
Third Time Around (1991–2005)—
  Amy (319 episodes)
Mysterious City (2003)—Denise
Tourmaline (2002)—Linda
Only Human (1999)—Charlotte
A Poem for Jeanie (1997)—Jeanie
Portrait of a Year (1996)—Elsie
The Sky Below (1994)—Whitney

Reading Group Guide

1. Do you think Hayley was always destined to "go off the rails" or do you think there was a specific thing that caused her to go down the wrong path?

2. Despite the fact that there was such a big age gap between Hayley and Trey, the media never mentioned it and seemed to encourage their relationship. What did you think of this?

3. Why do you think Hayley never confided in anyone—Olive, her mother, her father, Tom—about the inappropriate and abusive behavior she experienced?

4. Ted began drinking alcohol at a very young age and progressed into heavier drugs as he got older. Do you think this is a common issue for child stars, and why?

5. Hayley's parents separated Olive and Hayley. Was this the right decision? Or were they completely misguided? ▸

Reading Group Guide *(continued)*

6. What do you think life is like for Hayley's twin daughters, Jessica and Jane? Do you think they only recently understood their mother's situation or do you think they've always understood the unfairness?

7. Can you spot any real celebrity or tabloid stories from the 90s and 2000s in the book? Which ones?

8. How pervasive do you think conservatorships, for both famous people and average citizens, really are in America?

9. Do you think a conservatorship is truly beneficial to a person, or do you think it only works against them?

10. At the end of the novel, Hayley says "there's nothing much wrong with me." Do you think that's true? Can someone who has experienced everything she has gone through truly be fine? ⌒

Discover great authors, exclusive offers, and more at hc.com.